D0983097

HEARTLESS

LEAH RHYNE

The following is a work of fiction. Names, characters, places, events and incidents are either the product of the author's imagination or used in an entirely fictitious manner. Any resemblance to actual persons, living or dead, is entirely coincidental.

Cover and jacket design by Magie Serpica
Interior designed and formatted by E.M. Tippetts Book Designs

ISBN 978-1-940610-87-0
eISBN 978-1-943818-10-5
Library of Congress Control Number: 2015960646

First hardcover publication April 2016 by Polis Books, LLC
1201 Hudson Street, #211S
Hoboken, NJ 07030
www.PolisBooks.com

This book is for Jonathan and Charles, who love Jo…and me.

And for Zoe. Because it's always for Zoe.

PART 1:

PRESERVATION

PROLOGUE

I'M DEAD.

Sort of.

I thought you should know that right away, because this story won't end well for me. I don't have much longer. The battery that's powering my brain is shutting down.

I'm sitting in my dorm room in the middle of the night. My mother's asleep on the bed, and she's snoring. It's not a loud snore, not by any means, but it's soft and it's nasal and it's there. I hear it. It transports me back in time, back to the days before things went sour and I had all the time in the world. Back then, sometimes, when I was very small, my mother and I had sleepovers in my bedroom, pretending we were girlfriends. We'd paint our nails and eat ice cream and giggle for hours.

Then my mother would fall asleep on the bottom bunk, and she'd snore like she's snoring right now. So soft, so gentle. I'd lie in the top bunk and listen to her for hours. I loved feeling so close, so intimate, like I was the only one in the world who got to be with her like that. I felt so safe, those nights in my room so far away from here.

Right now, I wish I felt safe. I wish I could fall asleep to the sound of my mother's snores, like when I was a little girl. I'm so tired. But I won't let myself sleep yet. Because if I do, I won't wake up, and I haven't told you my story. I want you to hear it. I *need* you to hear it. Are you ready?

First, and most important, I'm not almost-dead by choice. I didn't *choose* to be this way. I didn't *choose* to become a monster.

That choice was made for me.

And second. Second is this: the smallest decisions, the smallest choices in your life, can sometimes have the biggest impact. You never know where you're going to end up, and who you're going to hurt in the process of living your life carelessly.

Me? I made a series of choices that tangled me up with some of the ugliest sort of people I could have imagined. I got my best friend, my boyfriend, even my parents involved. It's been a disaster, and though the end has come for me, it hasn't for everyone else. These bad guys won't stop. No. They have big plans, regardless of the outcome of my little story.

So that's why I need to share it with you. Maybe if you listen, if you hear, you can help stop them.

CHAPTER 1

A BLIZZARD RAGED OUTSIDE Eli Peterson's apartment, and I ran back to his bed and pulled his tattered, stained comforter tighter around my shoulders, shivering against the idea of the snow outside. He, in turn, pulled me in closer to his bare chest, the warmth of his body soothing and comfortable. Slowly I stopped shivering.

"Why'd you get up?" he asked, his voice thick and sleepy.

"I had to pee."

He laughed and wrapped his body around me, turning me to my side, sliding his legs through mine until we were as tangled as a pretzel.

I couldn't get used to sleeping that way. I always waited for him to fall asleep, and then I'd wriggle out from his grasp and over to the far side of the bed, where sometimes, if I was lucky, I'd manage to catch a few hours of rest before the next morning's classes.

Wind howled outside, slamming a tree branch into Eli's window. I jumped. "Stupid storm," I said. "I'll never fall asleep with all that noise. I'll be late for Price's class, and he'll dock my grade, and when my father sees my report card he'll kill me." I groaned and pulled away.

Eli wasn't bothered. Still half-asleep, his voice was a mumble. "Maybe it'll be so bad they'll shut down campus tomorrow. Maybe we'll have the day off."

I laughed, and it was sharp and somewhat rude. "Yeah, right," I said, poking at his hand as it tried to slide back around my waist. "Are you crazy? This is Smytheville. Smytheville *never* closes for snow. *Ever.*"

Eli quit grabbing me, quit trying to pull me back to him, and rolled on his back, fully awake. He sighed. "Aren't you just Little Miss Sunshine tonight."

"I'm just tired," I whined. "And you were snoring, and the storm is so loud, and I can't *sleep*!"

He sighed again and sat up, swinging his legs out from under the covers.

"Where are you going?" I asked.

"To get a drink."

Eli stood, his boxers hanging loose on his hips. When he opened the door to his room strains of Pink Floyd filtered in from one of his roommates' ancient stereo systems. I flopped back on the bed, pulling his pillow over my head. "Why does everything have to be so loud?"

By the time Eli shuffled back to bed, my frustration at not being able to sleep had me raring for a fight. He slid in beside me and tried again to pull me to him, but I pulled away.

"What now," he said, and I could tell from his voice that he was getting irritated.

I smiled my sweetest, most innocent smile, one I knew he could see in the dim light from the streetlight barely visible through the raging storm outside. "I was just wondering," I said, "what you've decided about med school, and what we'll do when you graduate in May."

Eli groaned. "Really? You want to talk about this now? It's two a.m. and you have class in the morning."

"Whatever," I said. "It'll be canceled, you're right. And I'm just curious."

"Why are you curious *now*, Jo?"

I ran a finger down his side, satisfied when I felt goose bumps rise to the surface of his skin. I kissed his shoulder. "Well, it's just…" I paused, giving him some time to think. "It's just that the guy I told you about last week—the big German soccer player in my bio lab—well, he asked me out to a show this weekend."

Now it was Eli's turn to pull away. He gave me a hard look. "And you're telling me this why?"

"Well, I told him I'd think about it. I wanted to see if it would bother you if I went?"

"Bother me? Would it bother me? Are you serious? Would it bother me if my girlfriend went out with another guy?"

I sat up straight in the bed, pulled my bare legs out from beneath the covers, and slung them over the side. "Oh, so *now* I'm your girlfriend? Now that someone else wants to take me out? Why aren't I your girlfriend when I ask about med school? Or when your friends want you to go hang out with them instead of me? I'm not your girlfriend then, am I?"

"Oh, come on, Jo," he said, and his hands balled into fists. He took a deep breath and counted silently to ten before he spoke again. "Knock it off. You're tired, and when you're tired, you get crazy. You know you're my…"

"Now I'm crazy, huh?" I felt my cheeks turn pink, and my hands trembled. Tears burned in my eyes—I always cried when angry, and the presence of tears never failed to increase my fury. "Crazy. Wow. It's nice to know what you really think of me, Eli. Now I know why you won't talk about May with me. A doctor doesn't need a crazy wife!"

"Jesus, who's talking about getting married! You're nineteen. Jolene Hall, would you *please* calm down and go to sleep. We'll talk about this in the morning."

I stared at him. His cheeks were flushed, his body tensed for a tussle. We stood on opposite sides of his rumpled bed. Outside, the winds howled, but inside we were electric, charged, ready to explode. I turned my back on Eli and walked over to my pile of clothes in the corner of his room. I dug out my jeans and pulled them on.

"Come on," Eli said, walking over to me and taking my arm. "What are you doing?"

"Going home," I said, tears finally spilling out of my eyes. "I don't want to burden you with my craziness anymore."

He tried to pull me to him, but I yanked my arm away from his grip. "Leave me alone," I said. "It's nice to finally know what you really think."

"Jo," he said. "You know I don't think you're crazy. I misspoke. You're not going home in the middle of this storm and we both know it. Now take off your jeans and come back to bed."

Part of me wanted to. Part of me wanted to let him comfort me, let him hold me and kiss me and apologize for calling me crazy.

But a bigger part of me was led by a need to get out, to run away, and so I made a choice. *The* choice. The choice that would change everything.

I slapped his hand away. "I'll be fine," I said. I pulled on my boots and heavy winter coat. "I'm not afraid of the snow. And I don't want to stay here with you another minute, you stubborn, stupid asshole."

Eli had a slow fuse. It was hard to get him angry. "Fine," he said, his voice shaking. His shoulders rose and fell with deep breaths. "Go then. Go be the spoiled little brat I always knew you were. Go out with your Russian guy…"

"He's *German*!"

"I don't care! Go out with whoever you want, and get the hell out of my life."

It only took me a minute to finish getting dressed. I slung my bag over my shoulder, pulled out my cell phone, and stomped down the stairs. When I opened the door, the force of the wind outside was almost enough to make me turn around and wait out the storm in the living room, but then I saw Eli coming down after me. I gave him one last, defiant look, and I stepped out into the blinding, pelting, violent snow.

The next thing I knew, I woke up inside a morgue.

Of course, it took me a few minutes to figure that out. All I knew at first was that I was cold. So cold, in fact, I couldn't feel my hands or feet. And I know people say that all the time, that they can't feel their hands or feet, but what they *really* mean is that their hands and feet hurt in that bizarre way we all equate with "not feeling them."

But me? Right then? I *really* couldn't feel my hands and feet. There was an absence there that my brain couldn't explain, an inability to move my fingers or wiggle my toes. I shivered in the cold, and I could feel my body shake, but not at all my hands or feet. They were gone.

My eyes were shut tight, the lids glued together like a kid with crusted-over pinkeye. I would have reached up a hand to pry them open, had I been able to feel even one of my hands. Since I couldn't, I lay on my back, blind, as cold seeped upward from whatever hard, freezing surface was beneath me. I definitely wasn't in my dorm, nor was I on the creaky mattress at Eli's. Like Dorothy and Toto, I wasn't in Kansas anymore. In fact, I had no idea where I was.

I tried to open my eyes. I tried so hard the muscles in my neck spasmed with the effort. But my eyes remained closed, and my hands and feet remained numb.

So then I moaned.

Really, I tried to cry out, to shout for help. But all I managed was a moan, and even that came out all wrong. It was an inhuman sound, unlike any I'd ever uttered. It became another lopsided piece to the bizarro puzzle my brain couldn't fit together in those first few seconds. Because that's all it was. Just a few seconds.

I moaned again, that creepy, guttural sound. I tried to roll to my side. I couldn't. Groaning, I leveraged the little movement I'd managed to roll to the other side.

I was perhaps a bit too successful. I rolled over the edge of the rock-hard bed (or at least, in some terrified, panicked part of my brain, I *thought* it was a bed) and fell with a crash to the rock-hard floor. My head hit the ground with a jolt that sent something like electricity crackling through my body.

And then I was on again. Zap. Just like that. The bang to my head was all I needed. My eyes flew open, crusties be damned, and my hands and feet sprang back to life. Sitting up, I rubbed my head with a hand that felt new and exciting. I was no longer cold, filled suddenly with a burning energy that flowed through my muscles with a twitching intensity. I blinked a few times to clear my eyes—they felt dust-bowl dry—and ran my hands through my hair, catching them in a few thick tangles. As my vision came into focus, I was able to begin to process my surroundings.

The ground on which I sat was as hard as the bed from which I fell. *But no,* I realized. *Not a bed. It's a table.* It was tall and made from stainless steel, with long legs ending in dusty black wheels. The floor was white tile, flecked with gray, and it was spotless but for some splatters of green goo that surrounded my immediate location. I wrinkled my nose at the goo, afraid to look beyond it to see whatever else there was to see. From that first impression, I wondered if I was in a hospital…or a warehouse.

A warehouse? That doesn't feel right, I thought. *But a hospital. Yes. That makes sense. Something must have happened. I'm a patient somewhere. But where is everyone? Why am I alone? Why am I on the floor?*

I...began to freak out. Just a little. The weird thing was, even though I was terrified, even though I should have felt my heart racing and my stomach flip-flopping and my face sweating, I felt nothing. I wasn't even panting.

Or breathing.

Not even the tiniest bit. I took a deep breath to see what would happen, and the *mechanics* of breathing worked. The air came in, the air went out. But as soon as I stopped thinking about it, I stopped breathing again. And I didn't feel like I needed to breathe, which was *really weird.*

So then I panicked.

A lot.

I yanked myself to my feet (it was a little more difficult than normal, but really, what with waking up alone in some crazy, unidentified space, I hardly had time to notice), and finally saw the room around me without table legs and shelves blocking my view.

Definitely not a warehouse.

Fluorescent lights in stainless steel hoods swung from chains below a high gray ceiling. Perfectly square cabinets covered with white Formica filled three of the four walls. They looked vaguely familiar, like maybe I'd seen cabinets like them in some '80s detective rerun. *Matlock. Murder, She Wrote.* A flash of light flickered against a silver table, and I turned to it.

Beside me stood three other tables, identical to the one from which I'd fallen, and on each of the three tables lay a dead body. Three dead girls, just like me.

Dead. I'm in a morgue.

I opened my mouth to scream. All that came out was another moan.

From the OoA files, dated December 12:
Design Doc 32-A
Iteration 3

Vocal cords are problematic. They are delicate and rupture easily. Care must be taken to preserve the integrity of a subject's voice in order to achieve full integration. This can be accomplished via a swab of oil (vegetable or olive; peanut has caused reactions in those with allergies) along the back of the throat every two hours during procedures.

How is this happening? Why am I dead? How am I still standing here?

I stood in the morgue, my hand resting on the table from which I'd just fallen, the room wavering this way and that. I was crying.

Well, I *thought* I was crying. I thought tears and snot ran down my chin, but when my hand flew to my mouth to stifle another of those awful, bestial moans, it found nothing. Dry nothing. No tears, no snot. Nothing.

I touched my nose, my cheek. They felt surprisingly solid, all things considered. I passed my hand before my eyes, and I couldn't see through it. It was as solid as the table, as opaque as the floor.

I'm not a ghost. At least, I'm pretty sure I'm not.

I tried to speak again, but it still didn't work. I moaned, because it was all I *could* do, and I had to do *something.* Something felt a lot better than nothing, and when I realized that, I decided to do something else. I bolted for the door on the far side of the morgue. I had to get out of there. A wet, sick ripping sound exploded behind me. I wondered what had caused it, but not enough to turn around or stop running.

I made it across the room in five drunken, lumbering steps. I reached out for the knob. The heavy metal door gave way easily, and it opened with a slippery silence that made me pause. It wasn't chained, or locked, or barred in any way. I'd expected to be trapped, locked in, and the fact that I wasn't was, simply put, terrifying.

I'm dead. Dead people don't escape the morgue because they're dead.

It was absurd, but I was afraid to laugh, afraid another terrible moan might escape. Instead I took a deep breath, pulling air into lungs that didn't need it, and stepped over the threshold. The door slammed shut behind me.

Once again, what I faced was nothing like what I expected, with as much of a passing thought as I devoted to any one thing in those first moments. I expected to find myself in a hospital basement. I expected to find stairs leading to a waiting room, or a nurses' station, or somewhere, anywhere, that I could find help.

Instead, I stood in a snowdrift on a blinding, sunny winter's day. I was outside, somewhat sheltered by an overhanging roof, but not at all in a sterile hospital wing. There were stairs in front of me, leading down to more than a foot of snow. I stopped in my tracks and spun around.

Behind me, framing the door I'd just exited, stood a small, innocent-looking mountain cabin. I happened to be standing on its quaint, downright *picturesque* front porch, in a snowdrift that had blown in from a storm. The wooden banisters were well-covered with white, and there was evidence of a welcome mat beneath my toes. A cozy-looking wooden swing hung on my right, rocking slowly back and forth in the gentle breeze.

That was when I realized I was really in trouble. Waking up inside a normal morgue was bad enough; waking up in a morgue in a quaint little mountain cabin was something else entirely. I swallowed a mouthful of nothing, not even saliva, and I reopened the front door to make sure I hadn't dreamed up the whole thing. But there it was, the morgue, complete with cadaver cabinets and dead girls on tables. *Naked* dead girls on tables, I noted. Whatever had happened to me, and to them, hadn't just been your average snowy-mountain accident. Because that was no average, snowy-mountain morgue.

I shuddered, and reached up my arms to hold myself together. I realized, then, that I was naked too, just like the girls on the tables, which led to my next realization: even though the breeze blew frozen snow particles through the air around me, I wasn't cold. At all. I wasn't shivering, I didn't quite feel the breeze's bite, and I couldn't see my breath. Probably because I wasn't breathing. Again.

I wanted to throw up, but my body didn't seem able to cooperate so instead I just opened my mouth and made a pathetic attempt at gagging. Nothing happened. So I decided it was probably time to go, since leaving felt more productive than standing there, waiting for something to happen. Inside the morgue, I'd noticed a giant snow parka hanging on a hook beside the door, less than three feet away. I walked inside one last time, grabbed it, and yanked it over my arms. It was a reflex gesture, a reaction to being naked and exposed and not wanting to run without something covering me up. The coat was long, reaching almost to my feet. Outside again I zipped it up with a yank. Terror bubbled up again as I stared at my feet, bare beneath the parka, toes touching the icy snow. They weren't cold either. They were fine, cozy, even as I stood barefoot in a snow bank.

This is wrong. Bad. All that money I've spent on shoes…

I ran. I didn't know what else to do.

I ran through the snow, through the forest, down the face of one mountain and up the face of another. I ran blindly, not paying any attention to where I came from or where I was going. It was a panicked run. There was no sense of reason or rationale left anywhere in me. I ran from the morgue, from the devastating absence of feeling I remembered in my fingers and toes. I ran from the grim sense that I was in the worst danger of my life.

As I ran, and as roots and rocks hidden in the knee-deep snow tripped me up and sent me tumbling, and as branches grabbed at my face and coat, I tried figure out what could be going on.

I leaped over an icy stream, sliding my bare feet across its frozen, pebbled edges. I felt nothing.

Maybe I really am dead.

I tripped over a rock and tumbled head-over-heels down a hill.

That didn't hurt. I must be dead.

I pulled myself to my feet and pulled the parka tighter around my body, more out of habit than need.

Am I crazy? Drugged?

I'd heard of drugs that stopped pain or caused hallucinations; I'd seen friends strung out on some of them. But I'd never heard of a drug that allowed you to live without breathing. And though I ran, and ran fast, in the dry, icy air, never once did a pant or even a shallow, panicked breath escape my frantic lips.

Time passed while I ran, but I wasn't aware of how much until the sun began to set behind the mountains. When it was so dark that the only light came from a bright, waxing moon, I found a spot under some overhanging rock. It was mostly free of snow, a reasonable shelter in which to pass the night, so I sat down and pulled my knees to my chest. *At least I won't be cold,* I thought, and I came close to smiling. Whatever was going on, it had at least one benefit. I'd always hated being cold.

The night passed slowly. I tried to sleep, but whenever I closed my eyes, my brain swirled and twirled in a dance of terror. The more I tried to shut it down, the harder it worked. By sunrise, all I had were more questions.

Like, why *wasn't* I cold? And why *wasn't* I even the least bit tired? And what *was* that green gunk on the snow beside me? It looked just like the goo from the morgue, and it made me want to hurl.

With the first crystal glimmers of sunrise came more bits of rational thought. I needed to find help. I needed to walk instead of run so that I wouldn't break my neck on top of everything else. And I needed to figure out where I was and what to do next.

In a flash, I knew. I needed Lucy. My roommate. Lucy had a way of solving everything. She was just that kind of a girl.

And thus a second choice was made, small though it seemed at the time. I pulled Lucy into the dangerous web surrounding me, and changed her life forever.

Once I realized what I needed, it was easy enough to accomplish. Initial waves of panic finally abated, I took a deep, unnecessary breath and crossed my fingers, hoping for a little bit of luck in the soft dawn light. I eased my way out of the rocky overhang, and turned to look up. The rock under which I'd passed the night was at the base of Mount Schnoz, aptly named by Smytheville students because of its resemblance to a giant nose, sniffing the hills around it. There were two caves on the southeastern side of the mountain that looked like nostrils and doubled as make-out spots for students in the warmer months.

I'd been sitting, cowering, in the left nostril.

My first break of the day. Mount Schnoz was less than five miles from campus. I started to jog.

I reached campus quickly, making use of my newfound ability to run flat-out without ever getting out of breath, or, you know, needing *any* breath. The gates of campus were welcoming, if snow-covered, offering a promise of security beyond their awe-inspiring arches.

I crossed the threshold onto campus and immediately relaxed. Comparatively speaking, of course, since I still couldn't feel my heartbeat. But at least I was home. I pulled the parka's hood over my head, shielding myself from the lone runner heading toward the track for his morning workout. It was early, based on what little I knew of the sun's path through the New England winter sky, but it felt strange for my typically bustling campus to be so stark and empty. Especially on what I thought was a Thursday morning (because hadn't I left Eli's on a Wednesday night? Wasn't it a Thursday? Suddenly I wasn't sure), when classes started early and winter sports started even before that.

Is it a snow day? I wondered. *Did they finally close campus?* I looked down to my feet, buried in the snow, and almost laughed at the thought. The snow was only knee-deep. Smytheville *never* shut down, not even when it was over my head. Instead, they kept snowplows on duty for the entire winter, ready to keep our streets free from snow and our sidewalks safe for student pedestrians.

The buildings around me looked sleepy in their thick winter blankets, the gothic towers standing straight against the wind, blurred and softened with white. Drifts collected on the faces of gargoyles high overhead, hats and scarves hiding the ugly faces that had kept watch over college co-eds for centuries, or so the school's administration wanted potential students to believe. Me? I just thought they were creepy. I shuddered as I passed them on my path toward home. My dorm.

Smytheville College, my father's alma mater and the only school to which my parents allowed me to apply even though it was far from our Colorado home, was created in the image of the classic Ivy League schools. In warm months, buildings crawled with ivy. It blanketed them, made everything look lush and verdant and like it belonged here in the mountains. It was stunning, really. Once I'd arrived on the busy Smytheville campus, with its hiking parties and skiing excursions, I rarely missed the west. Smytheville quickly became home. Comfortable. Cozy, even on those frequent snowy nights.

But suddenly I was disconcerted by the absence of people on the usually crowded campus, where students often built snowmen like small children celebrating a snow day. It was creepy, and empty, and the soothing, homey feeling wore off quickly.

Where is everybody?

I cut behind Shepherd Hall, home of our English Department, past the athletic center. My dorm, Calvin Hall, stood behind them in all its nonconformist glory. Calvin was a recent addition to the campus; it was covered with cheap yellow stucco, and it stood out like a dandelion among the ivy. Still, it was home, and I wanted to go inside. The only problem? The front desk, where a student attendant would be waiting to check my ID card and make sure I was allowed inside. Too bad a naked girl who couldn't speak, oozing greenish goo from *somewhere*, would likely cause a stir. I had to hope not to draw any attention to myself if I had any hope of reaching Lucy inside.

I walked past the front doors of the building, peeking in. A girl sat, dozing, at the front desk, her face cushioned in an open palm. Her head bobbed and nodded while she tried and failed to stay awake.

I knew her, sort of. She was an RA on a different floor from mine, a mousy little thing with thick glasses and curly hair. She sat at the front desk most mornings, and probably knew my face well enough to raise an alarm if I looked as bad as I suspected I looked. Since she was half awake, I didn't trust my battered body's ability to sneak past her. I wiggled my toes in the snow and thought for a second.

What I needed, really and truly needed, was the perfect thing to say to shut her up if she saw me. Only problem was I hadn't said a word since the morgue the day before. I'd only moaned. I'd need to practice first.

Staying outside, I slipped past the dormitory's doors, cringing when they auto-opened, and sneaked around the corner of the building to the bench where students often gathered to smoke. Even in the snow, the ground was littered with cigarette butts.

But the area was blessedly empty; even the ever-present smokers were missing, and I shuddered at the oddness of it all. I brushed the snow off the bench, sat down on gems like "LC & JB 4EVER" and "FU PROF PRICE," and I tried to talk.

My first attempt at the not-so-creative "Can I talk?" came out like a gravelly *"Cra gaaa tass?"* I was a six-pack-a-day-smoking, broken old lounge singer.

I cringed. *That's not gonna cut it.*

I tried again. "How about now?" Another moan. Throaty, dry. Way too raspy to formulate proper vocal sounds. I took a handful of snow and forced myself to swallow it, focusing hard on engaging my throat muscles in a downward thrust. It took a minute, but finally the snow went down. I tried to speak again.

Lubrication worked like a dream. On my attempt at "Maybe third time's the charm," I managed "time" and "charm" without too much difficulty. From there, it was only a few more minutes before I was able to say s's and th's. I still sounded scratchy and weird, but I didn't care. It was progress, and progress was good, no matter how small. I headed back to the front doors of Calvin Hall.

They opened before me, wide and welcoming. A lusty breeze flew through the open doorway and scattered papers on the front desk. The mousy RA startled awake, shoving her glasses up on her nose. Her eyes widened and her mouth formed an O when she saw me.

I pulled the hood tighter around my face and stared into her eyes for a second.

I smiled, as best as I could manage. My face crackled and creaked. I spoke.

"Rough night."

I barely croaked it out. I sounded like a frog with a hangover.

But she nodded, her mouth hanging open. As I walked past, she rubbed her temples and shook her head in confusion or disbelief. There was really no way to tell.

It didn't matter to me, though. I was inside. It was time to wake Lucy.

LUCY AND I MET ON the first day of freshman orientation.

One of the benefits of attending a pricey and prestigious liberal arts school in the mountains of New Hampshire was that parents could pay extra to get their precious children into single rooms. As in, dorm rooms that weren't shared with random roommates from random other parts of the country. Lucy was the daughter of the United States ambassador to a small, newly formed country in the Middle East that was presenting itself to the world as modern, secular, and safe. With her mother in such an important role, trying to preserve peace and help a fledgling nation, Lucy's parents, like mine, had seen fit to get her a private room.

Even the private rooms shared bathrooms, though, and we shared a tiny one, sandwiched between our two generously sized bedrooms. It had a toilet, a standup shower made of what looked like cement, and two small sinks. But at least we didn't share it, and a set of communal showers, with the dozens of other girls on our floor.

And that was our meeting place. The bathroom. I'd just walked in to set up my toiletries on a small metal shelf, moments after my mother's dramatic exit from my room, and was taking my first breaths of freedom. I'll admit now, too, that I was also a little sad, and maybe even a little sniffly from our goodbye. Suddenly Lucy bounced in, all six feet of her, gawky and energetic and redheaded and freckled and gorgeous.

"HI I'M LUCY YOU MUST BE JOLENE!" she said, opening her arms to hug me, her voice super-sized and enthusiastic. "ARE YOU LIKE THE

WHITE STRIPES VERSION OR THE DOLLY PARTON VERSION OF THE SONG?"

"I DON'T KNOW BUT YOU CAN CALL ME JO!" I answered back, shocked to find myself returning her hug, and her excitement, enveloped by her height and wingspan. Something about her enthusiasm was infectious. Around Lucy, I would learn in the coming months, nothing could ever be wrong for long.

LUCY WAS EXACTLY WHO I needed to see after my long trek through the snowy mountains. Besides, I didn't have my room key, and since I was naked and purse-less beneath the parka, going through her room was the only way I could get into mine.

I trudged up the two flights of stairs to our floor, not sure what I'd say to Lucy when she opened her door. It was as quiet in the dorm as it had been outside, which was unexpected on a Thursday morning. Normally, people were running out for class, or at least breakfast. But the hallway and stairwell were empty. The only signs of life were the quiet echoes of girls giggling filtering out from the one communal bathroom on my floor.

In the dull metal elevator doors I caught the first glimpse I'd had of myself. Even in the hazy stainless steel, I could see: I looked like I'd lost a fight with a mountain lion, but somehow lived to tell the tale. Pale, messy, completely disheveled. *Lucy's not going to let me past her. I've got some explaining to do for sure.*

My steps slowed as I approached her door. I stumbled, my legs unsteady all of a sudden, crashing into another girl's door. It cracked open, and the room's occupant peeked out. I saw an eye, and the eye saw me. It widened, and I curled my lip into a sneer, hoping to scare her into staying inside. It worked. The girl gasped, and the door clicked shut again. I stumbled on down the hall.

On her dry-erase board, Lucy had scrawled a typical Lucy-ish message. "Studying. Please disturb." I stifled a grin, then paused, taking a deep breath to gather the confidence to face what I figured was going to be a stressful situation. Then I remembered the whole "I don't have to breathe" thing was one of the major reasons I was having a crisis in the first place. So I didn't bother with a second deep breath. It wasn't doing anything for me anyway.

I knocked.

Nothing.

I knocked harder.

This time I heard some movement, some shuffling within the room, so I knew she was in there. I knocked even harder.

From behind the door, Lucy groaned. "Come *on*," she said, in a voice so muffled I could practically see her head buried under her fluffy, ragged comforter. "It's too early. Leave me alone. Please." Always polite, in her own, special way. That was Lucy.

I banged on the door, still afraid to trust my voice.

"Please please *please* go away, I said." She was grumbling, whining, but at least she sounded more conscious.

I moaned. I couldn't help it. It slipped out. But then I tried out my voice again. "Luce!" I said. "Lucy! It's me!" I didn't sound like me, that was for sure, but it was enough.

The door jerked open. "Jo? Is that you? Jo, what the *hell*! Where have you been? We've been worried *sick* about you! Come in, come *in*! What are you doing? Whose coat is that? Eli's been by seventeen times looking for you, he's so worried. I didn't call your mom, but I almost did. Where the *hell* have you been?" A mile a minute, that was Lucy. Finally she stepped aside to give me room to pass. "Ugh, you smell like *ass*!"

I looked at my friend as I stepped into her room. She was still muffled, wrapped up in her favorite blanket, with big, fuzzy pajama pants peeking out the bottom. From the way she squinted, it was obvious she didn't have her contacts in. She was blind as a bat without them.

No wonder she let me in. I didn't think it would be this easy to get inside.

"Get your glasses," I said. "Please."

"What's wrong with your voice?" she said as she shuffled back toward her nightstand, where her black-rimmed glasses sat on top of a philosophy textbook.

"Put them on."

She did.

"Now look at me."

She did. Her eyes flew open, her mouth dropped wide, and she stared. *Stared.* "Jo? What's going on? What's wrong with you?" Her voice rattled like tree branches in a wind storm. She stepped back, closer to the wall.

"Luce," I said, my voice gravelly and *wrong*. "Luce, I think I'm dead. Can you help me?" I reached for her. I wanted to be held, to be told everything would be okay. I stepped closer, arms still outstretched.

Lucy's mouth opened wider as if to scream, but no sound came out. She stumbled away until the backs of her knees struck her bed frame. Her legs gave out and she wobbled dangerously. I reached a hand out to catch her and the parka slipped from my shoulders, revealing all of me.

Lucy fainted. Naked again, I caught her and lowered her gently to the bed.

I should have expected that, I thought as I headed to the bathroom. After catching a glimpse of myself in the mirror, I realized I'd faint too, if faced with a walking corpse.

From the OoA files, dated February 8:

Memorandum re: sequence of events during the escape of Subject 632G-J

1400 h: Agent DG leaves laboratory. Four (4) subjects accounted for on main floor. All comatose. Brain waves minimal. All hooked up and charging.
1500 h: Agent DG returns to lab from scouting mission with two (2) new subjects in van. Three (3) subjects remain accounted for. All comatose. Brain waves minimal. All hooked up and charging. However, Subject 632G-J missing. Pieces of electrical cording remain attached to socket. Internal fluids puddled on table and on ground. Front door closed. No other sign of struggle.
15:03 h: Agent DG raises alarm. All agents report to lab. Search begins, agents fan out in the mountains. However, cold temperatures and sustained winds render tracking near impossible. All tracks hidden by additional snow drifts.
15:45: HQ notified of missing subject.
16:30: Search called off in mountains on account of darkness. To recommence at 0700 the following morning.
18:00: Agents notified. Failure to return Subject 632G-J is not an option. Project security is of utmost priority. All agents must report to HQ for further instruction and/or punishment no later than 19:30.
19:45: Agent DG eliminated.

MY IMAGE IN the bathroom mirror stopped me cold.

Dead, I thought. *I'm definitely dead.*

I certainly looked it. My skin was pale and chalky, eyes hollow and dark. White lips curled downward beneath a bloodless gash on my cheek, which hung open to reveal dry, dehydrated flesh. My hair was filthy, tangled with leaves and branches and hanging down in thick, matted ropes.

But that stuff? That was a piece of cake compared to the lower majority of me.

Below my neck, I was a science experiment gone wrong. Terribly, horribly wrong. So wrong, in fact, I closed my eyes and reopened them five times, hoping against hope that maybe I'd see something different the next time I checked. Something better.

It didn't get better.

From my neck to my pelvis stretched a long, ragged incision, held together by rusted silver staples. The skin puckered and tore around each staple, so some holes gaped wide. Tiny metal bumps poked out at regular intervals on either side of the incision, as if the Tin Man's nipples had been transplanted onto my tattered body.

The skin on my legs and feet was scratched and torn, no doubt from my trek through the forest. Like the cut on my face, though, all the lacerations were bloodless. Empty.

I stood at the full-length mirror for a long time, forcing myself to take it all in. My body shook, but my heart neither raced nor even beat.

Maybe I'd never appreciated my body enough in my lifetime. Maybe my tummy always bulged too much over the top of bathing suit bottoms. Maybe my breasts had never been big enough, my abs never tight enough. But it had never, not ever in my lifetime, been painful to look at myself in a mirror. Until that moment. Suddenly the sight of my body in the full-length mirror burned. It hurt. I could have been stabbed a thousand times in those moments, it hurt so bad. I stood frozen in a state of voyeuristic horror; I couldn't look away, could only stare in paralyzed, shocked silence.

Moments passed. Breathless, silent moments. Finally, I shook my head in an attempt to force myself away, but something else caught my eye. A black something danced behind me as I moved. I reached around to find it. In the center of the small of my back, my hand touched cold, brittle plastic and thick, sticky goo. I jerked it away. My hand came forward covered in a green and viscous substance. *Gross.*

I wanted to throw up. I wanted to scream, to cry, to wail, to have some kind of normal physical reaction to the sight of something so terrible as my own mutilated body, but nothing came.

I turned from the mirror and stared at the toilet. *Come on*, I told myself. *Puke! Do it. You know you should! This is disgusting.* But my stomach didn't spasm. Didn't roil. Didn't clench or spin or do any of the things I wanted it to do. *Screw you, stomach.*

I pulled myself back to the mirror, stepping so close to it my nose touched the glass. *Come on,* I thought. *Cry! Just a single tear. You can do it!*

No tears appeared. Just a whole lot more nothing.

All I could do, it seemed, was shake my head, letting it hang heavy on my neck. My shoulders slumped. My knees buckled. But those were the things I could control, and they only did it because I could move them. My auto-responses, any sort of fight-or-flight adrenaline reaction, were shut down. I'd never in my life been so entirely, utterly empty.

I left the bathroom and sat on the shaggy rug in the center of my bedroom floor.

What's my next step? Should I run some more? Away from here? Away from that terrible reflection that can't possibly be me, but somehow is?

That didn't feel right. Neither did hauling myself to a hospital. I couldn't bear the idea of an ER doctor, fresh out of med school, probably not all that much older than Eli, pulling a drab blue curtain closed behind him, and then running back out through it at the first sight of my battered incision. No. I wouldn't come out of a hospital alive.

Should I wake up Lucy? Go to Eli's?

Eli and I were still in a fight. I didn't want to scare Lucy further.

Maybe I'll try to patch myself up. At least I can do that much alone.

First things first, I thought as I wandered around my room. *Cover myself up. Then fix my face.*

Covering up was easy. I grabbed a thick, fluffy robe, a remnant of life back home, from its hook in the closet. Green goo smeared the back of it as I slipped it around my shoulders, and fibers from the fabric tangled in the little nodes on my abdomen. I cringed, but pulled the robe tight around me, hiding the evidence of destruction.

My face wasn't hidden so easily.

Although it didn't hurt—really, nothing on my body hurt, not even that long, gaping incision across my entire torso—the flap of skin hanging from my cheek looked awful, all white and tattered. When I looked closer, cheekbone was obvious and visible, killing a long-standing family theory that my face, in fact, lacked cheekbones entirely. *Mom would be proud,* I thought, and I almost smiled for a millisecond. Almost. The sight of the skin flap curbed it fast. I couldn't let my skin hang like that. I had to fix it.

Thus began a search for supplies. My desk yielded some basic office materials—Scotch tape and staples—but neither seemed a good candidate for a permanent fix for my cheek. Staples would be shiny and obvious against my pale skin, and I shuddered at the memory of the nasty, rusty ones on my abdomen. Scotch tape would be better, transparent at the very least, but was far from permanent. It would peel as soon as I got into the shower, something I needed to consider doing soon. The dirt beneath my finger- and toenails was enough to set my OCD on fire, not to mention the sticks in my hair.

I left my desk behind, heading for the closet. *Maybe some hanger wire or something?* I slid open the closet door. There, in the corner, exactly where my mother left it on the day we arrived in Smytheville, sat a small red sewing kit. "Just in case," she'd said.

"In case I decide to make my own clothes?" I'd answered with a laugh, and she'd shoved my shoulder and rolled her eyes.

This probably wasn't what she had in mind either, I thought. I pulled the kit from the closet and unzipped it for the first time. It was sparse, just some needles and thread and a measuring tape, but somehow I knew it was the best solution to my problem.

I pulled out a needle, and stared at my thread choices. After a few moments of careful consideration I vetoed a sassy shade of pink in favor of basic white. *Subtlety,* I thought. *Subtlety will be best here.*

Once the needle was threaded and the knot set, I sat down at my small vanity. I had an expensive magnifying mirror which was suddenly much more helpful than it had ever been for lining my eyes or applying mascara. Turning on the light as bright as it could go, I glared at my cheek.

The skin flap was triangular, and the way it hung left an ugly hole in my face. I reached up and slid it back into place. It was a little tacky, and it stayed put for a second when I let go of it, but then it quickly fell back open.

That won't do, I thought. I wanted to start sewing at the bottom, but I needed a third hand to hold the skin up while my other two were busy fumbling with the needle and thread. I looked back to my kit and saw a few straight pins sticking out of the tomato-shaped pincushion. *Those'll work.*

A few test pricks of my fingertips confirmed I didn't feel any pain, but the thought of jabbing a pin through my cheek wasn't exactly pleasant. It reminded me too much of Pinhead, a bad guy from an almost-forgotten horror movie from my childhood. Yet I had no choice. I held the flap in place with one hand while I readied the pin with the other. Biting down on my lip, I wanted so badly to close my eyes while I stuck myself, but I was afraid I'd wind up stabbing through my eyelid. I'd always been a bit of a klutz. I bit down a little harder, tried not to move, and slowly slid the pin through my skin.

I…felt nothing. I exhaled some stale air from my useless lungs, holding fast to the habits of the living, and began sewing in earnest, turning my face this way and that to ensure the best light for the smallest, most accurate stitches. The sensation of having no sensation as I pushed a needle through my own skin should have turned my stomach, but didn't, and after a few minutes of careful stitching I found I could ignore the facts of the situation and simply sew.

In and out, up and down, I sewed, until at last the skin flap stayed attached to my cheek with no noticeable gaps when I pulled my hand away. I squinted at my face in the mirror, turning my cheek, tilting my chin to ensure my sewing was as good as I could get it. Once I was convinced, I leaned in closer and snipped the end of the string off with a tiny pair of sewing scissors.

"So I wasn't dreaming then, was I?"

I jumped. Lucy stood in the doorway, her hand against the frame, propping herself up. Her eyes were still full of sleep, but her glasses were on, and she stared at me so hard I could feel it.

"You're awake."

"Yes. What are you doing?" Her voice was flat, absent all emotion.

"Sewing my face back together. Why aren't you fainting anymore?"

"Once I realized I hadn't dreamed it, and since I just watched you sew your face back together, I figured panic was no longer an option." She sat down by my feet, crossing her long legs and pulling them up to her chest. "So, how do we fix this?"

"Thank you," I said, relief flowing through me. "I love you. I knew I could count on you for help."

Lucy sighed. "I love you too. You're my best friend. But do you really think you're dead? I mean, couldn't this be some kind of freaky drug thing?"

I looked away, back at my face in the mirror. At the white skin and dull eyes. At the white thread that held my cheek skin in place. "No. Not drugs. I think I really am dead. Sort of, anyway. Mostly, maybe. I can just…still think, I guess. And move. And, I don't know. I know I don't have to breathe."

"Jo, what the hell happened?" Lucy started to cry, and I wanted to cry with her but couldn't. So I handed her a tissue from my nightstand.

"Here. And…I don't know. Honestly, I don't even know what day it is. Last thing I remember was leaving Eli's Wednesday night."

She sniffled. "It's Sunday. You've been missing for three days."

I nodded. That explained the stark, empty campus that morning.

Lucy continued, wiping at her eyes. "Eli came by Friday and said he couldn't get in touch with you, but that you and he had a fight. I guess I just assumed you were staying somewhere else while that blew over. Maybe you'd found a new guy or something. Not that you've ever done anything like that before, but it seemed like something I'd do, just to have a little fun, right? I thought you deserved some fun." She took a shaky, watery breath. "Anyway, I didn't worry until yesterday, when I realized you hadn't returned a single one of my texts. And your Facebook page had all these messages from people asking where the hell you were. But still. I figured you were somewhere safe, you know? Not turning into some creepy dead zombie girl." Lucy dissolved into the choking kind of sobs, but managed to say in between them, "This is my fault! I should have called someone! With my mom's contacts…."

Three days. Three *days*! How could I have been gone three days? It was hard to believe, but so was everything else. I shrugged, my shoulders creaking.

"It's better you didn't call anyone," I said. "Can you imagine the headlines? Especially if I'd turned up fine? *Ambassador's Daughter Sets Off World War Three When Roommate Finds New Man,* news at eleven…Anyway, I'm not a zombie, and this is *not* your fault. This is someone else's fault entirely. Have you even *seen* the stuff on my stomach?"

Lucy nodded, her tears slowed, and the corners of her mouth turned upward. Slightly. "Yeah. I saw you *naked* before. In my room."

As if I could have forgotten.

I would have blushed if I was able. "Sorry about that. The parka was loose."

Her smile broadened, and her voice was soft but amused. "I never saw you naked before, not in all this time together. We've shared this bathroom for months. And yet it takes you dying or something like it to have the ultimate roommate experience."

I giggled a little, happy to see a little spark of life, of normalcy, from her. "I'm sorry," I said. "I didn't realize all this time you *wanted* to see me naked. I'd have taken my clothes off for you ages ago, Luce."

But then Lucy darkened again. "It was the scariest thing I've ever seen."

I frowned, nodded. "Yeah."

"What *is* all that stuff under there, anyway?" She gestured vaguely in my direction.

I kept the robe pulled tight, but I felt the pieces of metal through the thick cloth when I ran my hand over my stomach. "I don't know," I said. "There are staples holding me together, and the metal things kind of remind me of the tips of batteries. And there's something on my back, but I haven't quite been able to see it. I'm a little stiff, and I can't turn all the way."

"Well, then, let's see it. We need to know what we're dealing with here." Lucy wiped her eyes, stood up, and squared her shoulders, although I noticed she still kept a hand on the doorframe.

I stood, too. "Are you sure?"

She nodded. "Bring it on."

I dropped my robe and turned, watching her face in the mirror.

Poor Lucy. She staggered backwards, crashing into the door and knocking it into the wall. Her hand flew to her nose as her mouth clamped shut and her face paled. I thought she might pass out again, but as soon as I thought that she pulled herself back together and stepped forward again.

"Oh God," she said, gagging even through her pinched nose. "You smell terrible." But she took another step forward, her hand outstretched.

I was almost aware of her touching my back, in the way that you can almost feel someone looking at you. She gasped. "Jo. It's a wire, like a jack in a wall, with a wire sticking out! Almost like an electrical plug.

But it's all messed up and hanging off."

"What? A plug?" I tried to turn, to see my own back or at least its reflection in the mirror, but the placement was such that I couldn't get there. "I don't understand."

"Wait," she said. "Hang on." She ran through the bathroom and came back with her cell phone. "Turn around and show me your stuff!" The phone made a little electronic click as she snapped a photo.

She handed me the phone and I stared at the picture. There was a piece of plastic hanging loosely from my back, held on by several wires. Inside the plastic was a torn electrical cord. I was wired for electricity. The phone fell to the floor with a crash.

"Hey," she said. "I just got that for Christmas. Don't break it."

"Sorry," I said, leaning against the sink with my head in my hands. "But do you think you could not fuss at me for a second? Seeing as how, oh, I'm suddenly *electric*?"

"Oh. Right. Sorry." She reached out and patted my shoulder, then started to pull me into a hug, but she gagged again, a little stronger this time. "Girl, we gotta get you into the shower quick, before I puke."

I nodded, and Lucy walked to the shower. Seconds later the bathroom was filled with steam. I stood there, letting the fog hide my nakedness for a moment, but then I realized: nudity no longer mattered. I was dead.

So I hauled myself toward the shower and pulled back the curtain. Lucy stood there, leaning against the sink. I paused. "Get out," I said.

"Why? I want to be here for you."

"But I'm electric. I don't know what's going to happen when I touch the water. I don't want to electrocute you."

"You won't…will you?" She sounded frightened.

I stuck my tongue out and crossed my eyes. "Not on purpose, of course," I said.

"Don't make that face. It might get stuck that way. For real, now, since you're dead and all."

I stifled a laugh. "Would you please just step back? I really don't know what's going to happen here."

She nodded, and then retreated behind the heavy bathroom door. Once again, I took one of those unnecessary deep breaths. Then I reached my hand out to touch the water.

Nothing. I saw the water touch my hand, saw it cascade over my fingers and my arm, but I could feel nothing, even though I knew it was scalding hot. I bit my lip to stave off any tears that couldn't have escaped my eyes anyway, but this discovery stung. I always relied on the comfort of a hot shower to clear my head, and it seemed like whatever was going on, suddenly that one comfort was stolen from me as well. It shouldn't have surprised me, I knew, but it did.

I glanced back at Lucy, peeking around the door, and then stepped into the full force of the shower.

Suddenly sparks flew everywhere, and the lights in the bathroom surged. A bulb over the sink popped.

"Crap!" I shouted. "Stay back!"

Lucy shrieked from the bedroom, and I screamed as well while I reached through the flying sparks to turn off the water. Since nothing hurt, I was able to do it pretty easily. I stood, dripping, in the cement shower in the middle of a steamy, smoke-filled room.

"Well," Lucy said in the ensuing silence as she pulled back the thin shower curtain. "That didn't go well."

"No. Not so much."

"And you've probably woken up the whole building by now."

"Yep."

Sure enough, there was a knock at the door. "It's okay, we're fine!" Lucy called over her shoulder.

A masculine voice answered. "You sure? Are you girls on fire?"

"No, we're *fine*, thanks. I promise. Don't…um, don't worry?"

There was a husky laugh. "Then shut up in there! People are trying to sleep."

Lucy rolled her eyes. "Oh-*kay*. Sorry." She turned back to me, waving smoke away from her face. "Urgh, I didn't know you could, but now you smell even worse. Jo! What are we going to do?"

"Damn if I know." Water dripped out of my hair, over my body. Every so often a droplet attempted to settle on one of my new metal nipples, and it sparked and then sizzled into the air. "At least now I know what *not* to do," I laughed weakly.

"Don't laugh. This is very serious," Lucy said, but her hand covered her mouth and her eyes smiled a little.

"I was just saying a couple weeks ago that maybe Eli and I didn't have any spark."

"Now he would find you truly electrifying."

There's something about two girls together in a terrible situation. I stood in a puddle of possibly-charged water, naked, dripping, eviscerated from chin to chest. Lucy, my best friend, gazed at me in utter terror and confusion. And all we could do was laugh.

So we did. Lucy sat down on the lid of the toilet, pulled her knees to her chest, and laid her head down on her legs. Her body shook with the force of her laughter. I leaned against the concrete shower wall and slid down to the ground, where I rocked back and forth.

After a few minutes, Lucy's laughter turned to tears. I wasn't surprised; I wanted to cry, too, even while I laughed. I crawled out of the stall to kneel in front of her and laid my wet head against her leg. She reached down and stroked my hair, her face still hidden from view.

"It's going to be okay," I said, even though I knew it was a lie.

"How?" Her breath sounded ragged, thick with tears and saliva.

"I don't know. I just need to figure some things out."

"Like what?"

I shrugged. "First and foremost, who did this to me, and why. After that, I guess I'll figure out the next step."

"But you're dead."

"I know."

"Murdered."

"Lucy, I *know*!"

Her head popped up and she jumped to her feet, knocking me back against the wall. Her face was flushed, her eyes red-rimmed, but she was suddenly determined, too. I'd seen that look on her face before, usually before telling off some frat boy at a party. Something bad was about to happen. "What? What are you thinking?" I asked, nervous.

"You're *murdered.* Someone *did this to you.* This is bad! I have to call my mother! She'll know what to do!"

She reached for her cell phone, which sat atop her dresser, right outside the bathroom door, and she started dialing. I struggled to my feet, wincing when I heard something tear behind me, grimacing as my feet slipped on the slick tile floor.

For the second time that morning, I knocked the phone to the floor. "No!"

She jumped back, startled. "What?"

"Don't you see?" I said. When she shook her head I continued. "I'm dead, but I'm alive. I'm still talking to you. I can still think. If you call your mother, the cops'll come! They'll be here in, like, less than thirty seconds! And they'll take me away! To a hospital or a laboratory! They'll have to! And the doctors? What if they can't fix this! They might make it worse! And then I…I might…" I couldn't say it.

"You might die," Lucy finished for me, staring at the electrodes on my stomach. "All the way this time."

"Exactly. So please don't call the cops. At least not yet. Please, will you just help me?" I sighed, a weighty sound I felt compelled to make even without breath in my lungs. "We can do this together. We can find out what happened. Find whoever did this. Maybe they can fix me. I can be persuasive, right?"

"I don't know. What about your parents? Don't they deserve to know what happened? Can't they do something?"

I took Lucy's hand, trying to ignore the squeamish look in her eye when her arm brushed my breast. This was all new to me, too. I wasn't used to being a monster. "I don't want to scare them," I said. "Or bring them into it if I don't need to. I think I can fix this on my own. I really do."

"But how?"

"First, I need to rejoin the land of the living," I said. "If I've been missing three days, people are going to start to worry. My mom's probably already worried."

"You're probably right," Lucy said. "About that, at least. So you better go boot up your computer. If people are looking for you, someone's gonna call out the cavalry soon. Even if I don't."

Another choice. A joint one this time. One that would lead us further into disaster. Of course, we didn't know that at the time.

Instead of contemplating the decision to go it alone, not to seek the normal authorities, I nodded, and stood up to head to my room. Lucy reached out a hand to stop me. I thought we were about to have another moment when she said, "But…can you please put your robe back on first? You're grossing me out."

BEFORE I COULD SIT DOWN at the computer to "rejoin the land of the living," we had a bit of work to do. First I had to scrub the green spot from the interior of my robe so I could stomach the idea of putting it on again. (Not that my stomach seemed to mind anything at that point, mind you. Not that I was even sure I *had* a stomach anymore.) As I scrubbed, Lucy tried unsuccessfully not to stare at me.

"You know," she said, leaning over my shoulder and pointing. "It's just going to get all goopy again if you don't do something about your back." Then she backed away, gasping. "Ew, sorry. Just got another whiff of you. Can we speed up the cleaning-up process? So you can be destinkified?"

I gave her a look. "Yes, if you help me. I can't do anything about my back on my own, and since that's the part of me that's open and oozing, I'm guessing that's where the stink is coming from."

"I can help, but I can't get close to you," Lucy said, frowning. She leaned against the wall on the opposite side of the room, looking greenish and disgusted. Then her face lit up, and her eyes danced like a little kid with a big idea. She grinned. "I've got it," she said. "I need a mask!"

She trotted over to my closet and began to rummage through my scarf collection. She selected a bright red one and began to tie it around her face.

"No, come on," I said. "That one came from India. My mother brought it back from her first trip there. Use a different one."

It was Lucy's turn to give the dirty look. She pulled out another, and I shook my head. "No, that's my favorite."

After three more failed attempts, Lucy threw up her hands in frustration. "Jolene. I cannot help you if I cannot get close to you without vomiting. The only way to make that happen is to wrap something around my face. Find me something. Please."

I pulled myself up from my desk chair, and Lucy cringed. "You moving makes it worse," she said, holding my blue silk scarf in front of her nose. I ignored her and marched to the door. Beneath my ski jacket was a ski mask, last worn on a trip to Snowy Lodge before Christmas. I tossed the mask to Lucy.

"Here," I said. "It's thick, and it's wool. All you'll smell is sheep."

She put it on before stretching her arms out before her, cracking her knuckles like a doctor prepping for surgery. "Okay. I'm ready. Lie down."

I lay on the carpet, stretching out on my stomach to give her a better view of my mangled back. She knelt over me. I couldn't see her face, but she pressed down in a few spots on my back with something akin to clinical probing.

"Ew, the wires are sticking out," she said, and then she ran for the bathroom. I thought she'd gone to throw up, but in a second she was back, holding Q-tips and hydrogen peroxide. Her voice was muffled by scratchy wool, but she'd turned matter-of-fact. Definitely clinical. "There's green goo inside you, Jo. Why is there green goo inside you?"

I tilted my head to the side. "I'm sure *some* of the goo inside *you* is green, don't you think? And anyway, I'm guessing it's some kind of formaldehyde mixture. Isn't that green? Maybe it's some embalming fluid? I have no idea."

"Stop it," Lucy said, gagging again behind the mask. "You're gonna make me hurl. But yeah, that's what it smells like. Formaldehyde. That, and rotten eggs."

"Sorry about that." I spoke into the crook of my arm, ashamed of my own stench. In real life—because this was very quickly starting to feel like an alternate reality—I was always clean and good-smelling. I loved fancy soaps and body sprays. This stinking thing was humiliating.

There was pressure on my back as she pressed down. "Ooh, if only I…could just…I need to…snap it…something needs to snap into place!" But instead of a healthy snap, we heard a crack.

"Um, was that a bone?" I asked. "Or some plastic?"

"Did it hurt?"

"No, not really."

She sighed. "Then does it matter?"

"*Yes*, it matters!" I pushed up on my hands and craned my neck to get a look. "Just because I can't feel it doesn't mean you get to be all careless and break my bones!"

"Well, whatever it was, you're as repaired as I know how to get you. We really need to get you to a professional at some point."

I groaned. "A professional what? Doctor? Electrician? What *kind* of professional exactly do you envision knowing how to help me?"

She shrugged, and then pulled me to my feet. "No need to be a bitch about it. Come on, let's bandage you up. Lucky for you, I have gauze!"

I rolled my eyes. "Lucky for me you're accident prone."

She grinned, then held a piece of gauze up to my back and began wrapping it around my waist. "A couple more wraps and, there you go, good as new."

I shot her a look. I was definitely *not* as good as new. But then I turned to look in the mirror. I still couldn't quite see the back, but the bandage was smooth, and I didn't see any green ooze dripping down my legs. "Hey, nice job. You should be a doctor."

"Maybe I will." She tossed me my robe. "Someday. *Now* will you please get dressed? Maybe even, imagine this, put on some underwear?"

"Let me just wipe myself down a little more. You said I stink right?"

Lucy rolled her eyes, a strange-looking thing behind the ski mask. "I hardly even notice it anymore."

"Still, though." I grabbed a washcloth from the sink and began carefully wiping down my arms and legs. Before I could finish, though, there came a knock at Lucy's door.

It was forceful, purposeful, and before we could blink, a male voice called from the other side.

"Police. Open up."

"OH CRAP-A-DOO," LUCY spoke in a forced whisper as she hopped to her feet and pulled off the ski mask. Her hair was a tangle of tumbled red curls. "What do we do?"

I looked around, frantic. "Why do you have a cop at your door?"

"I don't know! I shouldn't have a cop at my door! I'm an ambassador's daughter! My mother will kill me!"

"What are we going to do?"

Lucy smiled. "Wait. I'm an *ambassador's daughter*. That means I'm great at diplomacy, just by association. I can handle this. Right?"

"I don't know!"

We paced the room in tight, frantic circles. I don't think either of us was particularly confident in Lucy's diplomatic skills, but we had little else upon which to rely.

He knocked again, a more forceful sound. "Open up please."

"At least he's polite," Lucy said. She shrugged. "Maybe someone finally reported you missing, and he's here to investigate? I swear I haven't done anything wrong this week. But he's going to wake the whole dorm if he keeps banging like that."

It was 9 o'clock. We'd woken up a few of our hall mates with our bathroom shenanigans, but for the moment, they'd been leaving us alone. A cop, on the other hand, banging on our door would bring the whole Smytheville student body a-runnin'. I wasn't ready for that.

"Okay, I have a plan," I said after what felt like a millennium. I darted to the bathroom, as best as a mostly-dead girl could dart. As I closed the door I said, "Give me three minutes. Just stall him. I'll come out in a sec."

"Stall?" she hissed. "How?"

"I don't know," I whispered back. "You're Lucy. Do your Lucy thing. Trust me."

Through the crack in the door I watched Lucy wrap herself back up in the bulky, tattered comforter. She set her glasses crooked on her nose as she walked toward the banging.

She opened the door, a crack. "Hello? Can I help you?" Her voice was little, shaky, but not at all unsexy. She had a husky thing going.

I grinned. Lucy was a pro. She knew *exactly* what to do.

While she had the door handled, for better or for worse, I turned back to the bathroom. In the medicine cabinet I found exactly what I needed: a goopy, green, exfoliating mud mask. Not that I cared so much about exfoliation in that moment; what I liked was the "mask." I squeezed a glob of green goo onto my hand and smeared it across my face, taking care to cover as much of my pasty, dead-looking skin as possible. Soon I looked like a whole new girl—a Frankenstein-girl, perhaps, but no less new. I wrapped an orange bath towel around my hair and pulled my robe on, tying it tight to cover me up to the neck. Though I'd have killed to find a pair of leggings to cover my legs, I didn't think I could pull them on by myself without breaking something, so I had to hope the long robe covered enough. I shoved my feet into a pair of fuzzy pink slippers left over from an old Halloween costume, and, for better or worse, I considered myself ready. I took a glance at myself in the full-length mirror.

I looked ridiculous.

But at least I looked alive. Ish. Enough, anyway, to keep the cop from calling an ambulance, because I had a vague idea of what would happen if an EMT tried to find my heartbeat and failed. It wouldn't be pretty.

I went back to the bathroom door and pressed my ear to it, listening.

"What do you mean, missing?" Lucy said. "She just in her room over there. She was with me all night."

"Then why do I have her boyfriend calling our station, saying she's gone?"

I'd heard enough. I opened the door. "Gone?" I said, trying to play up my voice's new rasp. *I can play husky and sexy, too.* "Who's gone?"

The officer stood, leaning against the closed hallway door, blocking any escape that might have been rendered necessary if the meeting went downhill. He was tall and blond and quite handsome, and I thought I caught a bit of swoon in Lucy's eyes. He jumped when I walked into Lucy's room, and I was pretty sure I saw a silent giggle cross Lucy's lips. I had to keep a poker-face on, though, despite the fact that I looked like a clown. I stepped nearer to the shadowy room corners.

"Jolene Hall?" the officer said.

"Yes, sir. Well, it's Jo. Only my parents call me Jolene." I tried to smile. "And you are?"

"Officer Adam Strong, Smytheville Police Department. I'm here investigating your disappearance. Do you have any identification?" He was suppressing a smile.

"Sure," I said, a picture of innocence. "What's so funny?"

Next to Officer Strong, Lucy's giggle was becoming less silent, more manic, and I shot her a look. She covered her face with her blanket, but her shoulders still shook. I understood—I was fighting hard to keep hysteria at bay, too.

"What's with the getup?" the officer said, pointing to my face.

I shrugged. "Sunday morning spa time. Normally Lucy's in on this, too, but someone overslept today. It's how we get ready for church." I tried to grin, but the mask cracked and crumbled. My bone-dry skin had sucked all the moisture out of it already. "I'll go get my ID."

I tried to walk bouncily from the room, like a typical college girl, while behind me Lucy gave up and burst out laughing, her face buried in the comforter. "I swear I don't look like that, ever," she said, choking. If Officer Strong responded, I didn't hear him.

In my own room, I looked around frantically. I didn't see my purse, and I tossed a few pillows around, looking for it, before realizing I'd probably lost my purse at the same time I was kidnapped and turned into a monster. "Craptastic," I whispered. But I had to do something, so I walked back through the bathroom. In the mirror, I saw the tail of white thread starting to poke out of the green goo on my face, and with one finger I wiggled it back into place.

When I reentered Lucy's room, I stayed as far from Officer Strong as I could. I tried to look sheepish. "Sorry, Officer. It's still early and I forgot. I lost my purse last week and haven't found it yet."

"Did you report it stolen?"

"No, because it's not stolen. It's lost. I lose stuff all the time, right Luce?"

"Yes, sir, she does. Once she lost my favorite hat for a month before she found it under her pillow. True story." Lucy's freckles had darkened as blood rushed to her face. She was flushed and gorgeous.

I gave her a dirty look, but smiled at the cop. "Yeah, so I can't say it was stolen, right? I was hoping it would turn up this weekend, around the dorm, but I plan to start getting stuff replaced first thing tomorrow morning. Girl Scouts' honor." I tried to make the salute, but was frustrated by knuckles that didn't bend the right way. I slid my hand back down to my side and laughed weakly. "I was never *actually* a Girl Scout."

The officer ignored Lucy and narrowed his eyes at me. I felt him stare. I watched him take in every inch of green goop on my face, every thread of my robe, every centimeter of pasty skin that managed to show through all my attempts to cover it. He was onto something, I just didn't know what.

"Why am I getting reports that you're missing?"

"I don't know."

"A fellow named Eli Peterson says he hasn't been able to reach you since Wednesday night. Calls to your dorm and your cell have gone unanswered. Emails ignored. Where have you been?"

"Eli *Peterson*?" Lucy snorted. "Officer Strong, that's because she broke *up* with Eli Peterson Tuesday night. He's been practically stalking her. I *told* her not to take his calls. If he's calling the police, you should be picking him up for, like, obstruction of justice or something! For placing phony reports. He knows she doesn't want to talk to him!"

I wanted to kiss Lucy. She was perfect. I bobbed my head up and down. "Yep, that's pretty much exactly right."

"In fact," Lucy said, yanking on Officer Strong's brawny arm. "In fact, if he keeps on bugging her, do you think she should file one of those, oh, those restraining order deals?" For a redhead, she played dumb blonde very well.

Officer Strong never showed a crack in his smooth, official demeanor. His mouth was set in a grim line. "Phony reports, eh? I can go have a talk with Mr. Peterson, ladies, as long as you're sure you're not missing, Miss Hall. Reporting people missing who aren't is definitely an offense worthy of a strongly worded talk." Office Strong stared at me as he spoke, as if he had x-ray vision and was trying to see what was going on beneath the mask. Then he sniffed, and blanched ever so slightly. "What's that smell? It's terrible."

"The bathroom," I said. "The shower has a funk sometimes. I think the pipes are old."

He looked around, craning his neck toward our bathroom. "Really? It's, um, pretty potent. I'm surprised they let that go on in the rich kids' dorm." His words were dagger-sharp all of a sudden, and accusing.

Lucy ignored them. "Yeah, it happens all the time. Crazy, right? We call the RA, and she calls someone, and they say they fix it, but yuck. Still stinks. Hard to live with. I plan to live somewhere else next year."

"You should call again," said Officer Strong. He looked annoyed.

Behind him I heard the sound of life beginning in the hallway as people started moving around, calling out to each other through closed doors. The dorm was waking up, and in my opinion it was time for Officer Strong to leave.

"It's fine, Officer. You can go. Get out of the stink. I'm not missing at all," I said. "I'm right here, see? Been lying low all weekend, actually. Lucy and I watched chick flicks. *Breakfast at Tiffany's. Pretty in Pink. Sixteen Candles.* We have a couple more to watch before class starts again tomorrow. Want to stay and watch with us?"

He shook his head, but then half-smiled, as if we'd broken through his exterior wall. He really was good looking, all pale skin and chiseled jawline. Lucy's eyes hadn't left his face through most of our exchange, and he finally turned to her, eyeing her body that could be seen through the thin, ragged T-shirt and fuzzy pants. "What are you ladies watching next?"

Lucy reached behind her to pull a movie off her bookshelf. "Here. *The Notebook.* You're welcome to stay." She batted her eyes at him.

He laughed, but it was forced. The rough exterior had been rebuilt. "*The Notebook?* Yeah, I'll pass. I can't stomach that tearjerker stuff. You girls enjoy your spa and movie time. I'm, uh, glad to hear you're not missing."

Officer Strong left the room, closing the door firmly behind him.

As soon as it clicked, Lucy grabbed my arm. "Oh my God, did you *see* that guy? Officer Strong? Hell yes, Officer Strong, you can strong-arm me anytime you want!"

"Lucy."

"He was *gorgeous*, Jo! How can you just stand there calmly when I just met my future husband? Did you *see* his eyes? Green! My favorite. It's fate!"

"Lucy!"

"I'm so going to start breaking laws and stuff just so he comes back to visit me again."

"Lucy!"

"What?"

I pointed to the gap under the door. The hallway light was blocked in two spots by two large feet. "He's standing right outside the door."

Lucy squealed and dove for her bed. I threw *The Notebook* at her and stalked off to my own room. That had been a close call, and I wasn't sure we were really going to get off that easily. He'd stared at me too intently. He's noticed too much. I wasn't out of the woods yet.

I sat back down at my desk, ignoring my grotesque reflection in the mirror. I flipped open my laptop and powered it on. While it booted, I picked at a loose thread on my robe. It wasn't unlike the loose thread I'd tucked back into place on my face not five minutes before.

A minute later Lucy reappeared in the doorway, her face set back into a serious mask, hiding whatever emotion she was feeling. She handed me a damp towel. "Here," she said. "Wipe your face." Then she stared for a moment at a picture of the two of us, arms wrapped around each other, hanging on the tackboard above my desk. She frowned. "We're going to fix this, Jo. You and me. Together. You're going to be fine."

I'm not sure if either of us believed her.

I nodded, and pulled up a web browser on my computer. It was time to be alive again.

Jolene,

Hi sweet girl. I miss you.

What happened the other night? Are you okay? You were telling me about the fight with that Eli boy, and then you hung up. Did I say something wrong, sweetie? If so, I didn't mean to.

Next time you call me in the middle of the night, though, please don't hang up so abruptly. And then definitely don't stop answering my calls the next day. It makes me worry. It made Daddy worry, too. I actually had to stop him from calling the cops out there, just to check up on you. You know how he gets, hahaha.

I've given you some space now, but I am *starting to worry, so please do call when you can. I love you, sweetheart. Daddy and I both want you to know that if things with Eli can't be patched up, we have a nice boy in mind. Daddy's ex-roommate's son goes to Smytheville, and I bet you two kids would hit it off. He's pre-law.*

Give sweet Lucy our love and please, call me soon.

Love, Mom

Hey Mom,

Relax. I haven't been mad. I'm sorry I made you worry. I lost my phone the other night, still haven't gotten it replaced. I'll go to the store tomorrow. I spent most of the weekend in Lucy's room. We watched a bunch of movies and had girl time. I'm not too worried about Eli. I'm only 19 I'm sure I'll find the right guy someday, and I guess I never really *thought Eli was it anyway. I mean, who marries their freshman-year boyfriend, right? And it's not like I'm even THINKING about marriage to ANYONE yet. That's all you and Daddy.*

I'm sorry I hung up on you the other night. I...didn't feel well, I guess.

I'm going to be busy again this week, what with mid-terms coming up soon. Lots to study for. Maybe one day I'll pick a major. Ha ha.

Thanks for not letting Daddy call the cops—that would have made me the talk of the dorms for the next three months! Ugh! How embarrassing!

Anyway, I'll call when I get a new phone. Until then, x's and o's to you and Daddy.

Love, Jo

Oh, I'm SO glad you're not upset with me. Daddy and I are on our way to the spa for a couple's massage, hee hee. He actually has the day off, can you believe it? Have a great Sunday, honey.

Love, Mom

Eli,

We need to talk. Something happened after I left the other night. Are you at your place today?

Jo

P.S. I'm not missing! Quit calling the cops on me. Freak!

Jo!

Jesus Christ, girl, where have you been? Why didn't you call me back? Sorry about the cops, one of 'em came by and read me the riot act. He was a total dick. I was glad to hear you're alive, though. I really was worried. We should talk about the other night.

I'm at the apartment. Be here working on a paper all day, at least until tonight when the bars open, hahaha. Come on by.

E

Jo1995: Long weekend. Lost phone. Bunked down with @LucyGoosie. Will catch up on emails soon. #crazyday

LucyGoosie: @Jo1995, you can bunk down with me any day…except for right now. You smell.

Jo1995: @LucyGoosie, hush.

EliPete21: @Jo1995, good to have you back among the living. Sorry about the other night. See you soon.

Chapter 5

I snapped my computer shut, suddenly aware of the weight of the prior twenty-four hours. Even though I'd been unable to close my eyes the night before, like a girl strung out on caffeine or cocaine, as I sat at my desk my eyes grew heavy and my thoughts grew thick.

I tried to stand but couldn't, trapped by the weight of muscles that no longer listened to my instructions. My arms moved as though through water, and then molasses. I shook my head to clear it of the storm of cobwebs that had gathered in an instant.

"Luce?" I called, my thick tongue moving through a cotton mouth. "*Luth?*"

She poked her head into the room. I tried again to rise from my chair, but once I reached my feet my knees gave way beneath me and I tumbled forward, crashing into the desk and then falling to the floor.

"Oh my God, Jo! What's wrong?"

I hit the ground on my hands and knees, crawling like a baby to my friend. "Something's not right." My words came out slow and slurred. I crept toward her, crashing into my desk chair and rolling to the side. "I think I'm shutting down."

Lucy dropped to the ground and pulled my upper body into her lap. The towel fell from my head and she brushed my hair back from the cracking green mask. "What should we do?"

In her lap, I shrugged, my shoulders a thousand pounds each. "Maybe I'm dying," I said. The thought came slowly. "Maybe my battery's running out."

Only it sounded more like, "Maybe my batryth runnin ow…"

"Battery?" Lucy looked down at me, her upside-down face looming over mine. "Oh my gosh, we need to charge you!"

"What?"

"When you woke up, you said you were attached to something from the back, right? That's a plug. You were plugged in! We need to plug you in and charge you!"

The light bulb in my brain flickered, but it was dim at best. "Can you plug me in?"

Her face fell. "I can't. The wire was torn off, remember?"

"Can't you hook it up somehow?" *Can oo hoo ugh thumhow?*

"Do I look like an electrician all of a sudden? I don't even own a soldering gun!"

"You can splice it!" *Thplithe it.*

"What?"

I was really starting to slow down. I wanted to talk fast, but instead I drawled, "I don't know, tie it together."

"I don't know what you're saying." Her voice rose an octave. "I'm losing you, I can feel it!"

I stared at her. Even slower, I said, this time clear as day, "I don't want to be lost." I leaned forward out of her lap then pulled myself across the floor, tortoise-like. I felt the synapses in my brain, each one, firing slower and slower until they barely sputtered. My goal was only inches away, though. I was almost close enough.

One more tug and I was there, at the wall. I yanked out the computer charger that took up the whole electrical socket, then reached my hand out and closed my eyes. I touched the socket; a current flowed out, into my finger. I pushed harder against the holes. As though it was made of clay, my finger squished in on itself, sliding deeper to press harder into the warm electric wave.

Lucy screamed, and the lights surged in the room. I felt the first true sensation I'd felt since waking up on that cold metal table. I felt warmth.

Electricity flowed through my finger, up my arm, then through my entire body. My brain came back to life, synapses shooting off fireworks of color and light behind my eyelids. My toes tingled and the remaining hairs on my arms and legs stood upright.

I stayed attached to the wall socket for five minutes, until I finally felt like I'd be steady on my feet. I pulled away, ignoring the singed and smoldering skin left behind on the plastic, ignoring the blackened bits remaining on my hand, and turned to Lucy. She'd stopped screaming after the first power surge, but looked pale and nauseated, so I smoothed the hair on my head back down and tried to smile. "I feel better now," I said. The mask on my face crumbled to dust around my mouth.

"I'm glad," she said, panting. She leaned back against the wall, her knees and hands shaking, and she nodded her head.

"Thanks."

"I thought I'd lost you."

"Me, too. Maybe we should fix my cord? I think I messed up my fingers doing it the digital way." I tried another green smile.

"Digital?"

"Yeah, digital." I wagged my fingers. "Digits. Get it?"

"I got it. It's just not funny."

"I know." I changed the subject. "I heard from my mom. She

emailed, panicking. But I calmed her down."

"Good." She patted my head. The crackle of static electricity was loud in the thin, dry air.

"I heard from Eli, too."

Lucy sat up straight, popping back to life. "Eli. Right. We need to go see him. Come on, get up. Let's get you cleaned up!"

"ARE YOU SURE?" I SAID to Lucy. I was nervous.

She looked at my face, her mouth in a tight line, considering. After a minute she said, "Well, I don't think I can get you to look much better, honestly. Your skin looks less pasty, and most of the stitches are under your sunglasses. Everything else is covered up. You still don't look right, but I just don't know what else to do for you. I'm not exactly a makeup artist."

I nodded. She was right; Lucy barely wore any makeup. Ever. She was gorgeous enough without it.

We stood in my room in front of the long mirror. It had taken me the better part of two hours to scrub my body clean so Lucy could no longer smell me from across the room. I'd have to be careful when washing moving forward, though. My skin was starting to slough off in some spots, especially near my hands and feet, leaving dry, crusty-looking sores. They were just more flaws I'd have to keep hidden, since I didn't have much hope of healing on my own. The fewer spots with missing skin, the longer I could pass for normal. Based on the speed with which I was falling apart, I probably wouldn't have a lot of time.

"But am I doing the right thing?"

"I think earlier today you had two choices." Lucy held my hand, tucked into an old glove. "You could have gone to a hospital or the police, and they would have helped you in one way, right?" I wasn't sure, but I thought her voice sounded thick, choked up. Like she was trying not to cry. "Instead you came home to me. You're my best friend, and someone did this to you, and we're going to find out who, and why, and how to fix it. And whoever did this to you did it after you left Eli's on Wednesday night. So we start at Eli's. Together this time. You and me. We'll get you fixed, even if it kills us. Right?"

For the hundredth time since waking up the day before, I wanted to cry. When the tears still wouldn't come, when I couldn't even summon a deep enough breath to sound convincing, I threw my arms around Lucy's neck. Something crackled in my shoulder as I did it, but it didn't hurt. I felt the pressure of her arms going around my waist. "I love you, Luce," I whispered in her ear.

"You smell," she said. "Still. But I love you too." She pulled away. "Let's do this."

It was cold outside. Bitingly, disarmingly cold, from the way Lucy's head jerked back as if slapped when we walked out the front door of Calvin Hall. The girl at the front desk had gone, leaving a cute upper-class guy who lived a few floors above us. He nodded as we passed, as if nothing was out of the ordinary, so I congratulated myself and Lucy, silently, on cleaning me up so well.

But I couldn't feel the cold outside. I felt nothing. Lucy's cheeks, exposed between her sunglasses and scarf, turned an immediate and alarming shade of pink. "I think my nose is going to get frostbitten on the way over," she gasped, covering it with a mittened hand.

"If it does, we can fix it," I said. "As soon as we fix me, first. Your nose should be a piece of cake after that."

"Hilarious. Really." She groaned. "It's a long walk to Clove." I saw her resolve freezing with the rest of her. "I might not make it."

The Clove Street off-campus apartments were about a mile away, which was nothing on warmer days, but certainly significant in sub-zero temperatures. We'd only gone two steps.

"If you want to go back upstairs, I won't be mad," I said. "I get it, it's cold. I can do this on my own."

"It's just that I'm not lucky enough to be a walking corpse like you," she said, and then she paused and looked at me. I didn't have to say anything. Her cheeks, already raw and chapped from the harsh wind, turned even redder. "Sorry. You know I hate the cold. It makes me say stupid things. Let's go."

It was pushing lunchtime and the campus was fully alive and teeming with students as we trudged through the snow toward Clove. Winter track team members braved the elements to get in their daily workout. People walked to the library, burdened with overstuffed backpacks and unwieldy jackets. Intrepid shoppers carried grocery bags filled with Ramen noodles and Kraft Macaroni and Cheese.

"Oooh, macaroni," whispered Lucy. "Can we stop at the dining hall real quick? I haven't eaten. You should probably eat…never mind." She looked down at her hands. "We don't have to stop."

But I nodded and tried to look encouraging, though inside I was feeling restless, like we were wasting time. Still, I knew from experience that if cold made Lucy grumpy, hunger turned her into a raging bitch. "You should eat, for sure. I'll wait for you."

We changed course and headed to the nearest dining area, a little pizza joint called the Rat in the basement of the student center. Their food was greasy and kind of gross, but also kind of amazing, and I knew how much Lucy loved their macaroni and cheese. Plus, being in the basement, it was dimly lit, so I could sit back in a corner and blend in with the exposed-brick walls. I hoped.

Lucy took the steps down two at a time, but I followed more carefully. I noticed the popping and crackling noises of my joints grew louder with each step. They crunched. They snapped. *How long is this body going to keep working?* I wondered.

Lucy bounded straight for the pizza counter, where the macaroni bubbled under a plastic-looking sheen within the circle of the heat lamp; I turned and headed for a table in the darkest corner. I slumped down in a chair, my legs stretched straight underneath the table so as to not strain my joints. The less I moved, the better, I figured. I pulled my sunglasses off for a second, but when I remembered the stitches in my face I put them back on again.

The dining hall filled rapidly with students coming in for lunch. Two girls sat at the table beside me, carrying binders and textbooks and wearing lots of makeup. A few days earlier, I'd have fit right in with them. Now, I was a pariah. They sniffed at the air like little puppies, then made faces and left, each giving me a nervous glance as they walked away. I stared at them and smiled.

Minutes passed. Most people in the area had similar reactions to my scent—what I dubbed the gag-face-run-away—and I was starting to garner some unwanted attention. By the time Lucy walked over with her plate of mac and cheese, I felt like the whole room was staring at me.

She sat down. "Ugh. I can smell you again. The break from you brought it back. I thought I was over it, but I don't know if I can eat around you."

"Yeah," I said, gazing around at staring faces. "That seems to be the general consensus. I'm turning the stomachs of diners everywhere. Or at least, diners here in the Rat. I'll wait outside so you can eat."

"Probably a good idea. Do you want me to grab you a slice of pizza to take with you? You've got to be getting hungry."

I wondered what would happen if I tried to eat.

I wondered if I had a stomach.

I shrugged. "No thanks, I'm good. I'll be outside on the bench."

Outside was better in some ways. No one seemed to notice the smell that stuck to me like drying rubber cement. I couldn't smell it, of course, but I could imagine what it smelled like. A cross between the chemically smell I remembered from dissecting fetal pigs in A.P. Biology two years before, when my lab partner and I had named ours Hamlet, and also straight-up decay. I'd smelled dead animals before. I knew the deal. Had the weather been warmer, my stench would likely have drawn crowds of vultures circling overhead. Luckily the cold kept them at bay.

But outside was also worse. The blinding sunshine refracted off the thick, ubiquitous blanket of snow, shedding a spotlight on me, sitting alone on a bench with my flaky, dry skin and huge sunglasses. Everyone hustled by, I imagined, to avoid my stench. But then I realized: they raced by simply to get from one warm spot to another. I was just scenery along the way.

I sat silently on the bench, immobile, statue-like, un-shivering. I had no foggy breaths around me. Even though I tried harder to breathe real, warm breaths, the air that came out of me was as cold as the air outside. And so I sat, as obvious as fire in the snow. *One of these things is not like the others…one of these things just doesn't belong…* I hummed to myself, hoping no one took too much interest in me. It didn't work, though, and people stared.

Luckily, though, my giant shades kept me well-disguised. Dozens of students filtered by, people I recognized from classes and complete strangers, but no one showed a spark of recognition. Still I squirmed, sitting there, not belonging. After what felt like a year but was maybe only five minutes, Lucy appeared through the dining hall door.

"Are you doing okay?" she asked. "You look concerned."

I tried to smile. "I'm fine. I just like it better when we're on the move. I feel less conspicuous."

Lucy pulled me to my feet, holding my gloved hands in her mittened ones for a moment before letting go. Then she linked her arm through mine and carried me along with her bounding steps. "Well, then let's go!"

The rest of the walk to Clove was uneventful, a complete and utter relief. But when we approached the apartments from the bottom of their hilly parking lot, and the buildings loomed ahead looking sparkly and innocent with their blanket of clean snow, I grew nervous. Terrified, even. So I stopped walking as Lucy continued forward.

Suddenly, standing there, alone, I remembered what happened that night after I left Eli's apartment.

Tears froze against my face and I shook with anger, fear, and cold as I left Eli's place that Wednesday night. I knew the walk back to my dorm would be long and dangerous in the howling winds and blinding snow. *How could he do this to me?* I thought as I stomped down the stairs leading to the parking lot. *I'm never gonna speak to him again.*

It was late, close to two a.m., but my mother would probably still be up. She always stayed up late, and besides, it was three hours earlier there. I dialed her cell phone number, holding my phone in a bare hand that grew colder with each step I took. As I stomped, I jerked my head from side to side, watching around me, a bundle of nervous energy, looking for anyone who could give me a ride. But everyone, it seemed, had taken shelter from the storm. I was alone.

The phone rang four times before I heard my mother's voice on the other end of the line. "Hey, Sweets, what's up?"

I sniffled dramatically, then started bawling, sobbing uncontrollably.

"Baby, what's wrong? Honey? Sweetheart? Mommy's here! Talk to me, darling!"

My only answer was more crying. I took shelter beneath a massive pine tree, where I leaned against the trunk and tried to catch my breath, slightly protected from the fury of the snow. I crouched, hugging my knees with my free arm, while I breathed several shaky, watery breaths.

My mother was silent, waiting. Finally, she said, "Honey, I'm terribly worried. Please. Tell me what's wrong."

Finally I managed to speak. "Eli and I had a fight and he made me leave."

She snorted with laughter, and it struck me as cruel that she could laugh at a time like this. "Is that it? Here you had me thinking the world was coming to an end out on the East Coast. Baby, relax. It's not like you were going to marry him."

"But I really, really like him, and now I have to walk home in the snow! I'm going to freeze to death and you're laughing at me!"

"Honey," she sighed. "It's okay. I bet you kids'll patch things up first thing in the morning. And you won't freeze. You'll be moving."

"But the snow!"

"Can't you call one of those campus security guards? Won't they pick you up? There, honey, hang up with me, call security, and then call me back. See? There's a solution to every problem."

That was typical of my mother. *A solution to every problem.* She and Lucy were the optimist twins. But that silly phrase, heard hundreds of times throughout my childhood, was the last thing I heard before pain ripped through my head, starting at the back and catapulting forward until I felt it with my whole body. I jerked forward from the force of an unseen blow, my phone flew from my hand, and I collapsed into the snow. The darkness, which had felt so complete a moment earlier, became something entirely different as the world closed in on me.

From there my memories grew spotty, but they were there. Memories of the days following.

There was motion: bumpy, jerky motion. I lay on a hard, ridged surface, and with each bump my head crashed into the side of what sounded like a van. Each crash sent more pain throughout my body than I'd ever felt before. The metal beneath and beside me was cold, but on the other side of me, I felt something warm. I heard another girl moan.

I remembered being carried, my feet getting jammed up as I was pushed and shoved through a doorway. But it was dark, or my eyes were held shut, and I cried out in fear and in pain.

I remembered cold. Being so cold I couldn't stand it. I remembered shaking and trembling and crying as ice filled my veins, and all other feeling left my body.

I remembered voices. The cries of other girls. I remembered knowing I wasn't alone, but wishing that I was.

I remembered knowing something felt terribly wrong.

And then I'd known only darkness.

I'd known nothing more until waking up in the morgue on the side of the mountain.

Design Doc 32-D
Iteration 1

We continue to perfect the formula for the fluid that allows us to sustain controlled life.

Requirements include:

1. *Conductive—subjects cannot remain animated without a consistent flow of electricity; however, wires may be threaded through key veins and arteries to aid in ebb and flow*
2. *Viscous—it must be thick enough to keep veins and arteries from collapsing in on themselves*
3. *Low freeze point—subjects must be able to endure the coldest of winters*
4. *High boil point—subjects may not shut down in warmer climes*

Substances under consideration:

1. *Formaldehyde*
2. *Arsenic*
3. *Methanol*
4. *Alcohol*
5. *Barium sulfate*

Chapter 6

Standing in the parking lot in the midday sun, I cried out as the darkness of memories flooded into my brain. Lucy jumped, spinning around to face me.

"What happened? Are you all right?"

I wasn't.

In a shaking voice I described what I remembered. The darkness, the banging, the other girls, the terror. Lucy listened, nodding, patting my arm when I faltered. My brain was racing but my body felt flat, and I wondered if I'd ever get used to living without physical reactions to emotional distress. I doubted it.

That said, in my past life, the stress of something like, well, dying and coming back as a monster-girl would've caused a crippling migraine by that point. I was relieved to still be on my feet…sort of. In a weird, dead sort of way.

"Well, that settles it," Lucy said as soon as I stopped talking.

"What does it settle?"

She gestured around us. "We came to the right place. This is where your adventure started, so this is where we'll start getting to the bottom of it. Do you remember how far you'd gotten before you were knocked out?"

"My adventure?"

"Yes. I'm silver-lining this for you. It's an adventure. Adventures have happy endings." She paused and looked away for a second. Then she turned back, her face once again set in a grim mask of calm. "So. Where were you knocked out?"

"I was over there." I pointed to the pine tree at the edge of the lot in the direction from where we'd just come.

"Well, let's go look around for some clues. I feel like Sherlock Holmes all of a sudden."

"Are you sure you're up for it?" I asked. "You *have* to be freezing."

"Elementary, my dear Watson. I am, but that's okay. We're gonna find something good, fast. I know it." She shivered. "I'm a little jealous that you can't feel the cold, though, I have to admit."

I wrinkled my nose as best I could, which wasn't great. It felt stiff and leathery when I tried to move it. "Want to trade?"

"No. Come on, let's go."

Lucy trotted and I trudged across the parking lot, following our own footsteps to make walking through the thick snow banks easier. When we reached the tree to which I'd pointed, we spread out and started looking around. "What exactly are we looking for, Miss Holmes?" I said to fill empty airtime.

"Clues! Anything that might tell us about the bad guy."

"Like this?" I said. I noticed something small and black sticking up out of the snow, leaning against a rock. I bent at the waist and picked it up, eyeing it with suspicion. "My phone."

"No way!" Lucy ran to me. "That's lucky. At least now you don't need to buy a new one!"

"Battery's dead, or it's completely shot." I shook it, and then held it up to my ear. As if *that* would fix it.

"Yes, but also now we know for sure you were here. It means your memory holds up!" She looked excited, but I didn't see the big deal. I *knew* my memory was right, phone or no phone.

We searched through the trees and snow for ten more minutes, until Lucy's nose was so red I was afraid it was going to fall off. After the phone, we hadn't found anything more interesting than some gum wrappers, cigarette butts, and beer cans. "DNA check?" Lucy said, holding up an empty can of Bud Light.

"No. Nobody who could do this would have such terrible taste in beer."

We laughed together, a low, comfortable sound. We both tried to make light of the situation, even though we both knew how serious it was. There was a fine line between laughter and tears, and we skirted it constantly. Or, well, Lucy did. I couldn't cry, so laughter was my *only* option. That said, there was little to do but keep on moving, so we headed up to see Eli. It was time to get Lucy in out of the cold and to find out what, if anything, Eli knew.

I knocked on the door to his apartment, and his roommate Kyle answered. "Eli's upstairs, Miss Houdini," he said, less than friendly. To Lucy he at least smiled.

"Houdini?" I asked.

"Yeah. You know, you disappear and reappear at will." He looked annoyed. "Thanks for the visit from the cops this morning, by the way. Had to flush some stuff down the toilet. You owe me for that." His eyes were red and bloodshot, though. No way did he flush *all* his stash.

"Oh, shut up," I said, pushing him aside. "Don't be a dick. I'm in no mood."

He stalked back to the couch, pushing aside the empty beer cans and open pizza box, half-full of partially chewed crusts and open tubs of marinara. Kyle picked up a video game controller and un-paused a monster-slaying game. As Lucy and I walked up the stairs we heard swords crashing and creatures moaning and groaning behind us.

The moans and groans made me shudder. Those game designers were on to something…maybe they knew something I didn't. I moved more quickly.

Eli's bedroom door was open, and he stood when he saw us coming. He'd been reading, stretched out on his bed among papers and textbooks. The rest of his room was spotless, though. Always spotless. Perfectly neat, perfectly studious, that was Eli. He never liked when I came in and left my stuff haphazard in the corner of his room. It drove him nuts, but I did it anyway, just because I could. I remembered the night of the fight, how my bag had lay in a heap with my clothes piled willy-nilly. I wondered where those clothes and that bag were now, and I realized they could be back at the morgue, where I never wanted to go again.

Eli's voice pulled me back from my reminiscing. "Ladies," he said. "I didn't know to expect you as well, Luce. Come in, have a seat."

Always well-mannered, too. Except for when he kicked me out of his apartment in the middle of a nighttime blizzard. But who was counting?

Lucy stared at Eli and looked around his room with narrowed eyes, and I was amused to realize he was Suspect Number One in her mind. I knew better; Eli couldn't hurt a fly, and wouldn't even if he could. He wasn't always exciting or passionate, but he was sweet. I wished I'd never mentioned that stupid German boy to him. I wished I'd settled down and stayed with him forever. Then I wouldn't be in the predicament in which I found myself. Then I'd be alive.

He reached out to give me a hug, but I sidestepped him and walked to the desk chair in the corner, sitting down. "We need to talk," I said. "About the other night."

"I know," he said, eyeing Lucy's suspicious face. "I'm sorry I let you walk home so late. So sorry. That was dangerous, and I should never have let you leave in the middle of a snowstorm. You have every right to be angry."

"Something happened," Lucy said, still glaring. "You should be more than sorry."

Eli's face paled. "What? What happened? Are you okay?" He rushed to me and knelt down. His face changed as his eyes scanned my glasses, my hat. My pasty white skin. I watched panic set in. "What's that smell? Jo, what's going on? Why are you still wearing your coat and glasses? Take off your glasses. I want to see your face."

I looked at Lucy, who hovered over his shoulder, and she nodded. "Close the door?" I said to her, and she did.

I leaned closer to Eli. "Are you ready?"

He nodded. I took off my glasses.

Eli staggered back. "What the hell, Jo? Is this some kind of a sick joke?"

"It's not a joke," I said. "I'm sorry to be the one to tell you, but we think I'm dead."

I don't think he heard me. He was too busy learning for himself what Lucy and I already knew.

From the safety of a few feet away, he leaned closer, staring. His eyes traced each curve of my face, at first with a clinical precision. He saw skin, still milky-white beneath our amateur makeup job. He saw my eyes, once blue but now leeched gray, the irises having bled out their color hours earlier. He saw the flap of skin I sewed back in place with careful little stitches that no amount of foundation or blush would hide.

Eli's clinical precision melted. He stood, backing away, his face a mix of terror and disgust. His hand flew to cover his mouth, and he ran. Seconds later the sound of him retching in the bathroom echoed down the hall.

"Poor guy," I said to Lucy. "He's always had a sensitive stomach."

"Yeah, and you're starting to get more grotesque again," Lucy said. "Maybe you should have prepared him better?"

"I'll know for next time."

"Are you planning many more of these reveals, Jo? Because if so, I want to start recording them with my phone. I'm sure we can make a great montage sequence of you making random people hurl."

"You can show it at my funeral."

Lucy looked away and closed her eyes. "Shut up," she said.

For lack of anything better to do, I kicked the ground and pushed the desk chair in a circle, relishing the slight change in equilibrium as a chance to feel something physical. At least my brain still registered movement, if not heat or cold or touch. The room swam before my eyes while I spun and spun and spun.

From her seat on the floor, Lucy frowned. "Don't talk like that. It doesn't have to be like that."

"Yes, it does," I said. "Expect the worst and you'll never be disappointed." I spun again, and again, eyes wide open, watching the room fly past. When Eli appeared in the doorway as it whirled by, I tried to stop, but only succeeded in launching myself from the spinning chair. As I tumbled to the ground in a heap of arms and legs, I heard a snap.

"Jo!" said Lucy. "Are you okay?"

"Yeah, of course," I said, though honestly I wasn't sure. Lucy and Eli appeared on the floor beside me, pulling me up, disentangling me from myself. When all was said and done and I was once again on my feet, my right forearm dangled limp inside my thick black pea coat. It didn't hurt, but it also didn't seem right, the way it wiggled.

"Can one of you help me take this off?" I asked.

Eli peeled the coat carefully off my shoulders and set it on his bed. When he turned around and saw the crazy way my arm wriggled and dangled, his face turned green again.

"Really?" Lucy said to me. "You had to break your arm on top of everything else?"

I shrugged. "Sorry," I said. "Does it matter?"

"Yes, it matters!"

"I don't think it does."

I couldn't meet Lucy's eye.

"Jolene Hall, you're starting to sound like a defeatist! I thought we came here to get some answers, and now I think you're giving up." Lucy took my cheeks in her hands and forced me to look up from the floor. "I'm not going to give up on you this easily, Jo, and I think it's time you reevaluate how you're looking at things."

"Girls." Eli's voice was timid, quiet. Not at all like his usual self.

I ignored him. "It's not like I have much to hope for at this point. Look at me! I'm falling apart! Do you really think they'll be able to put me back together?"

"Yes! I have to believe that because I'm not about to start writing my best friend's eulogy today!"

"Girls!"

This time Eli was louder. He stepped in between us, arms extended as though to keep us from attacking each other.

"What?" We spoke together, turning on him. His skin had turned from green to gray, but he was much more steady on his feet.

"I'm sorry to break this up," he said, his voice growing stronger. "But would you two please knock this crap off and tell me what in God's name is going on? Because really, Jo, you're standing here, smelling like shit, looking like shit, with a broken arm, and telling me you're dead. And to be honest, it's starting to scare me. A *lot*. So would you fill me in? Please? I think I have a right to know."

His eyes were wide and filled with tears that shocked me. I honestly hadn't known he cared enough to cry. I'd certainly never seen it happen. My arms fell to my sides, and I opened my mouth to speak, but nothing came out. A tear escaped his left eye and trailed down his cheek.

We faced each other, and I wanted to let him hold me, but he made no move to do so. From the corner of my eye I saw Lucy walk to his bookshelf and pick up a tattered paperback. She approached. "Here," she said, holding it out. It was Mary Shelley's *Frankenstein*. "I think this will explain it best."

I knocked the book to the ground, where it lay, cover-side-up, a promise of terrible things to come. Eli sank to the floor beside it.

"That's not funny, Luce," I said, my voice shaking with rage.

"I'm not trying to be funny."

"I know." My head hung low on my shoulders, barely held up by muscles that atrophied while we argued.

Eli looked at me, pleading. "Please," he whispered. "Please tell me what's going on."

So we did, taking turns telling pieces of the story, from me getting hit on the head after leaving his apartment, to waking up in the morgue, to trying to trick Officer Strong into believing we were having a normal girl weekend in the dorms.

"Crap," he said when we were done. His eyes were red and his hands shook, but he was still upright, just like Lucy had been. I was glad I had come, glad he hadn't given up on me either. At least not yet. "But one thing I don't understand is why didn't you let him help you? Why'd you sic him back on me?"

Lucy sighed a sigh of someone so far put out that she couldn't believe a person's stupidity. I thought about reminding her that she'd asked a version of the same question earlier in the day, but I held my tongue for once. "Come *on*, think a sec," she said, when I didn't answer. "It's obvious."

"What's obvious?"

"Look at her. She's dea…I mean…sorry, Jo. You're not dead. I didn't mean it."

"No problem, I'm getting used to it," I said.

"Anyway, we want to find out who did this and get them to fix her. Whatever's going on, it's our first priority to make her well again. But she's our only clue. And the cops would take her and use her and send her to the hospital, and we think that would kill her."

Eli pulled himself to his feet and walked to his window to crack it open. "Sorry, I need fresh air. I need to think." Lucy put her coat back on as a breeze blew in, knocking the papers around on Eli's bed. He stared at the book that still lay beside me. "*Frankenstein.* Yeah, I guess that makes sense. And I think you did the right thing, coming here. I think you're right about what they'd do to you."

His eyes filled again as he stared at me. "You're still beautiful, you know? Still Jo. But so different now. So much whiter, more pale. Like porcelain. Or something. I don't know, I'm sorry. My head's all messed up right now." Eli shook himself like a puppy after a bath, shaking out his troubling thoughts like so many droplets of water. He knelt beside me and pressed his forehead into his bed. "I'm so sorry, Jo. This is my fault."

Eli cried for a few minutes, and I let him. There was really nothing I could do or say to make it easier on him. While it wasn't Eli's fault, not really, there was no way to convince him it wasn't. He didn't bash me on the head or cut me up or stitch me back together. But he did let me go out into the night to the person or people who did.

Lucy stood and left the room. Her eyes, too, were red with tears.

I rubbed his back with a hand thick and clumsy. "I'm sorry," I whispered. "I know this is hard."

He finally lifted his head. "You're sorry? *You're* sorry? No." He paused a moment. "I'm the one who's going to be sorry the rest of my life. I made you leave the other night. Over a stupid, childish fight."

"You didn't make me," I said. "I chose to go."

"But still. I let you. This is all on me, kid. But I'll do my best to fix things. To fix *you*. So tell me. What can I do to help?"

I smiled, and let him pull me to my feet. "Thanks, Eli," I said. "I hoped you'd be willing to help. Lucy and I, well, we hope if we find the people who did this, that they can fix me. But we need time to find them. So maybe cover for me? As best you can? If people ask where I am or what I'm doing, you know, just say normal stuff. I'm studying, I'm at the dorm, you and I are hanging out later. You know?"

"Lie for you."

"Yeah."

"That's fine. What else?"

I walked to the door and opened it. "Lucy, come back in!" I called.

She emerged from the bathroom, calm once again, a brave smile plastered across her face. "What's up?" she said.

"Come in. Sit down. Eli's on board to help us, and I think I have a plan to save me."

Eli and Lucy took seats on the bed and I paced the floor before them as I laid out my plan.

Our first goal, in my mind, was to locate the place where I'd awoken. That seemed the logical primary step in finding the people who dismantled me and who could, in a logical progression of assumptions, put me back together. I thought we could start by running searches on mountain properties that could possibly house all that equipment and space. "I'm just sorry I ran," I said. "I should've stayed and looked around. Why'd I run?"

"Oh, come *on*. What *else* were you supposed to do?" Lucy said, encouraging me. "Don't beat yourself up. You woke up in the middle of a nightmare and you ran. It's what I'd have done."

"Right," said Eli. "Me, too. So let's not waste time second guessing right now, okay? Right now what we need is your plan. Like you said, we do a search. We know the area pretty well, right? Most places I know within walking distance are pretty small. Not many sprawling estates big enough for a secret lair." He cracked up, and his laughter sounded nice. The mood was lightening, and I liked it. It made me feel less despondent. "I sound like I'm in a comic book, don't I? Anyway, we can probably narrow down an area to search pretty quickly. Just look for the big houses."

"Exactly," I said, grateful. "And while we search, I need to lay low. Luce, we're going to need smell-controllers for our rooms. Candles, sprays, whatever. We need to control the funk. You guys are turning green just sitting here with me, and I don't want the cops turning up again looking for a dead body. I don't think I can fool them again."

Lucy grinned. "I'll handle Officer Strong if he comes back around."

"That guy!" Eli groaned. "He was such a dick!"

"Was he?" I said. "Lucy liked him."

She threw a pillow at me. It hit me in the face, and a cloud of dust flew up around me. "Ew," she said. "Jo-dust."

I tried to roll my eyes, but they wouldn't move that way. So I ignored her, talking instead to Eli. "I'm sure Strong was only doing his job. That said, I don't think Lucy or I really fooled him. Lucy was doing her giggling thing, and I looked like a circus freak when he showed up. He was definitely onto something."

"Jesus, it sounds like we're in a movie," Lucy said, groaning. *"He's onto us! Oh no! Somebody get my gun!"*

"Luce," I said. "Stop! This is serious."

She shot me a crooked grin. "I know, but it's also kind of absurd. We want to find the house, to find the guy, while avoiding the cops and anyone else who might want to find *you*. Because I bet they're looking. And we're doing all this to get you back to normal. Which we don't even know is possible."

Eli stood up and looked out his window. "Don't forget revenge," he said softly. "Someone did this to you. They're going to pay."

His voice was chilling. I wasn't sure what to say, so I nudged Lucy with my foot. She looked up at me, shrugged, and then said, "Right, okay, well, there's *that* too. But for now, let's focus on finding them. Maybe when we find them, we can let Officer Strong handle the revenge part. He'll get to call it justice, and you won't go to jail."

All at once, my head thickened again, like it had earlier in the day. My thoughts slowed down, my arms and legs grew heavy. I looked up at Lucy. "It's happening again," I said, only I slurred so much it sounded more like, "Itsh hoppen gen."

"Oh no," she said, and she immediately slid an arm under my shoulders and hauled me to my feet.

"What's happening?" Eli asked, terrified. "Is she dying?"

"No," said Lucy. "It's just…her battery's running low. She needs to recharge."

"How's she do that?"

Lucy and I fumbled our way toward the nearest wall socket. She set me down next to it, then said, "Mind if I don't stick around to watch this time?"

I nodded. "Yeth," I said. "Takim wif you."

She turned and pulled on Eli's arm. "Come on. You don't want to see this." She dragged him, protesting loudly, out of the room and closed the door.

As I plugged myself into the wall socket, using a different finger this time, the lights surged in the room. Judging by the shouts and cries I heard from the rest of the apartment, they did so in the whole building. When the warmth stopped flowing and I knew I was charged enough to last for a while, I pulled my hand away from the socket.

It took about eight minutes this time, much more than the two or three minutes it took me to charge the first time.

But this time, most of my left index finger stayed behind.

"Oh, *crap*!" I said.

Lucy burst back into the room, Eli on her heels. "What happened?" he said. "Why'd the lights go crazy? What were you doing in here for so long? Lucy wouldn't let me in."

"Ew," said Lucy, seeing the problem immediately. She wrinkled her nose and covered her mouth with her hand, but she recovered quickly. "Okay, I think it's time to get you home and patch you up again. Should we…take that with us?"

"Oh, dear God," said Eli, staring at my finger in the socket. "Is that what I think it is?"

I nodded, and Eli left the room again. The sound of his retching filtered down the hall.

In the end, after an endless debate over what to do with my detached finger, Eli drove Lucy and me back to our dorm. With all the windows down, it was a chilly ride for both of them, but I was focused on my broken arm and on my detached finger, which made the trip home jammed into its correct location inside my glove. We stopped at the pharmacy, where Lucy bought bandages, more sewing supplies, and a bunch of air fresheners and candles.

Eli dropped us off, and we agreed to meet later that afternoon. He looked pale and tired, so I told him to go home and rest. As Lucy and I walked into the dorm, I saw Officer Strong milling about outside, wearing a black knee-length parka that made him look like a storm trooper from 1940s Germany.

Lucy smiled and waved when she saw him, as if she didn't have a care in the world. Still smiling, and through clenched teeth, she whispered, "What's he still doing here?"

I shook my head and pulled her away. "No idea," I hissed. "But don't draw attention to us, okay? I didn't think we'd get off that easily, and I don't want him nosing around here until we get this figured out."

She squeezed my hand. "I know, I know. Let's get you inside."

Dear Ms. Hall,

I was sorry to see you miss class Thursday and our lab on Friday. Please be aware that one more unexcused absence from class will result in the lowering of your final grade.

Dr. Stanton
Biology Head

Dear Jo,

I was sorry you missed class Friday. Were you getting a jump on the weekend with some skiing? Class wasn't the same without you to lead the discussion. Please let me know if you're sick and are going to miss additional classes so I can have someone take notes from my lecture for you. Otherwise, I'll see you Monday, prepared to discuss Romeo and Juliet, k?

Sondra Lewis
English Dept.

Dear Dr. Stanton and Prof. Lewis,

Thank you both for your emails to check up on me. I've been down for the count with some flu, but am finally on the mend, I think. I hope to see you both in class this week. (Dr. Stanton, I will try to get a doctor's note so you can see I'm not faking, but I forgot to get one when I went

to the school clinic on Friday. Hopefully they'll write one out for me, though. I'd hate to accidentally lower my final grade.)
Thanks again,
Jo Hall

Jo1995: One thing I've never been is a good liar. Hear that friends? You will always know if I am lying to you.

EliPete21: @Jo1995 I have to say I admire your honesty. But I'm with @LucyGoosie. You smell.

LucyGoosie: @EliPete21 @Jo1995 Hey, be nice to Jo! She's had a rough weekend.

Jo1995: @EliPete21 @LucyGoosie That's putting it a little lightly.

Hey Mom,

I just wanted to let you know—the next few days are going to be a little busy for me, but I did find my cell phone. Sadly, it was beat up by the snow so it's completely busted. Still, I may not have a chance to get a new one, what with midterms coming up, so if you don't hear from me for a couple days, don't worry. I love you and Dad and I'm just a bit tied up at the moment.
Love,
Jo

LUCY NAPPED MOST of the afternoon, claiming exhaustion from the unexpected amount of drama in the morning. In reality, I think she needed a break from my stench, which was starting to peel paint around the borders of my room.

I spent the time by myself, responding to more emails, researching real estate, and occasionally zoning out with a game of Solitaire.

All I could think about, though, was that time was slipping away while I continued to deteriorate. I knew Lucy needed sleep, and Eli needed to figure out what the hell was going on, but I was getting scared. No matter how many times I turned the facts around in my head, I couldn't come up with a resolution in which I'd come away from this experience alive, at least not without finding the people who did this to me and somehow convincing them to undo what was already done. But that felt so unlikely. When I mentioned it to Lucy she threw a pillow at me, told me to get out, and buried her face in her comforter, groaning. "You're going to be fine," she said. "Unless you don't let me get some *sleep*!"

I wasn't so sure. *What if they won't fix me? What if they can't fix me?* Those questions plagued me as I switched from staring at my computer screen to staring at my hands, never without a manicure in my normal life, but now without half my fingers or fingernails. I couldn't bear to look at my face anymore, and covered my makeup mirror with a scarf.

Nor could I look at the pictures on my tackboard from earlier in the year. Lucy and me, smiling and hugging. Eli and me, arms around each other. Blissfully happy. Blissfully beautiful. Blissfully ignorant of any trouble greater than a C on a calculus test.

That was the old me.

Finally, I hung a scarf over the tackboard, too, so the old me would stop tormenting the new one.

At seven that evening, Lucy wandered back in and lay across my bed, her nose twitching as she readjusted to my scent. "More rotten," she said, sniffing the air like it was a fine wine. "Less chemical." I sat at my desk, running searches on local real estate listings. The knock on the door made us both jump. I almost fell from my chair, but caught myself at the last minute. The banging of my wrist against the desk corner sent a few chunks of skin sloughing to the floor.

"Ew," said Lucy, looking slightly gray. "Be careful!"

The knock sounded again, and Lucy cocked her head like a puppy. "Shave and a haircut?" She hopped to her feet. "Are you expecting someone?"

"Don't know. I guess it could be Eli. Look through the peephole!"

She crept to the door. "Yep, it's Eli." Lucy pulled the door open and I grinned when I saw him. Eli stood with his arms out, holding a pizza box in one hand and flowers in the other.

"Sustenance for Lucy and me," he said, sheepish. "And prettiness for you. Because don't guys bring flowers when they're sorry?" He slid his backpack from his shoulders to the ground, and held out his offerings.

"Didn't we go over this already?" I said. "What's done is done, no need to be sorry. You're here and you're helping, that's what matters." I stood up slowly from my seat at the desk. My whole body was stiff; it was getting harder to move. I ignored Eli and Lucy when they both cringed at the popping and rattling sounds from my joints, and walked toward Eli, arms outstretched to thank him with a hug.

He ducked away, looking sorry as he did it.

I dropped my arms and walked to the window. "Well, thanks anyway." Though no tears came to my eyes, I stared out the window, regretting their absence.

Lucy went into damage-control mode. "They're pretty, Eli! What can I put them in? Oooh, I know, I think there's a vase in my room. And thanks for the pizza, I'm *starving.*" She smiled at each of us in turn, and then bounced over to her room in search of the vase. I was relieved she was being nice to Eli again. That would help, whatever our near future held.

Eli set the pizza and flowers on my desk. "It smells pretty good in here," he said, surprised.

"I had the windows open all afternoon, and clearly Lysol does wonders. I've even Lysoled myself a few times." I didn't point out the candles that burned in every corner and on each raised surface, lending the room an eerie, coven-like feel, and covering up the stench I emitted. I knew he saw them. I tried another thin smile. "So, I smell okay now. But how do I look?"

"Jo…"

"I know. It's okay."

My skin was gray by then, without any lingering hint of healthy flesh color. The hair from my eyebrows and eyelashes fell out in frequent, delicate clumps. A splint held my arm in place, but it was crude at best, my forearm still bending in a suspicious way. I was quite literally falling apart before my own eyes, and his. It was hard enough for me to handle; I couldn't imagine being a third-party observer.

Eli appeared beside me and patted me awkwardly on the shoulder. Like a scratch on an old, decrepit dog's chin, though, the contact was over far too soon as Eli let his hand drop. He shrugged. "How are you feeling?"

"Me? Oh, I'm fine. Really fine." It came out sharper, more sarcastic than I intended.

"I know. I'm sorry." He patted me again. Once, not long before that day, Eli liked to sleep with his whole body pressed against mine. Suddenly he was afraid to touch me with more than his fingertips.

Still no tears came. I pressed my forehead to the glass, wishing I could feel its sharp coldness against my skin. I felt nothing.

Eli exhaled, a low, sad sound, but quickly brightened again. "I almost forgot. I have two other things for you." He walked to his backpack and pulled out some papers and a small plastic bag.

"What's in the bag?" I asked.

Eli opened it and pulled out a long electrical cord, with a plug at one end. "I cut it off one of the lamps in the apartment. It was Kyle's. Consider it his payment for being such a dick to you earlier today. I thought I could try to hook you up for a while with a real plug."

The thought of Eli "hooking me up" would have been nauseating, had I had a stomach with which to feel nauseous, but anything was better than burning off another finger every time I needed a recharge. "Great, thanks! And what's in the papers?"

"Real estate listings! Tons of them. Rentals, mostly, but lists of other properties too. Neighborhood descriptions, things like that. I thought we could go through them together and see if you recognized any of the cabins."

"You're awesome," I said. "Really, Eli. Thank you." Still, I felt sadder in his presence than I had alone. I turned back to the window and stared at the smokers' bench below. It was covered in fresh snow from a minor squall earlier in the day and looked more like a hump than a bench, but the ground around it was trampled with footsteps, and the snow on the ground was dirty and brown instead of pristine white. People were smoking, just not sitting. Moonlight reflected across the whole area, lighting it almost as brightly as a cloudy day.

"Come on, let's work on your plug first," he said. Then he laughed, a tentative, quiet laugh. "Mark that down for things I never thought I'd say to a girl."

When Lucy returned minutes later, I was face-down on my bed, my shirt pulled up and the crusty, green bandage that had been around my waist discarded on the floor. Eli sat on my butt, his knees supporting most of his weight on either side of me, with Vicks VapoRub smeared beneath his nose.

"I'm sorry," Lucy choked, almost dropping the heavy glass vase she carried. "Am I interrupting something? Should I come back another time?"

"Quiet," Eli said from his perch. "I'm concentrating." I couldn't see, but could almost hear the scowl on his face; his voice always changed when he was irritated.

As I lay, immobile, and Lucy watched, Eli used wire strippers and electrical tape to splice the two cords together. He had me sit up, and he rewrapped my waist with a new, clean bandage, wrapping it carefully around the cord. Just as he was about to plug me in for a test drive, there was another knock on the door.

"Now who?" Lucy said. "Do you know if anyone else is coming by?"

I shrugged. "Go check," I whispered.

Lucy peeked through the peephole as Eli brushed the wires and bandages under the bed. "It's a lady," she whispered. "I don't recognize her."

"Help me get to the door," I said to Eli. I was stiff, and it was hard to get up. He pulled me up, taking care to touch only my sleeves. "It's my professor. Professor Lewis. What's she doing here?" I knew we went to a small, fancy college, but still, house calls from English professors weren't the norm.

She called out. "Jo? Are you in there? I hear people talking. Are you all right? I came to check on you."

"Shit!" I squeaked.

"Quick," said Eli. "Into your bed."

"Toss me my sunglasses," I said. "I told her I have the flu."

"Why would the flu make you wear shades?"

"I don't know! Just give them here!" Eli did.

Lucy waited a few seconds for me to get settled in, and then she opened the door. The sounds of Sunday evening dorm life filled the room. "Can I help you?" she asked.

Without waiting to be invited in, Professor Lewis breezed into the room, like a tropical storm into port, windblown and dangerous. Her presence made me nervous, an outsider in our little dead girl club. "Yes, hi, I'm looking for Jo Hall. Do I have the right…oh, Jo, *there* you are! I'm sorry to barge in like this, dear, but when I got your email this afternoon I just had to come check on you for myself." In her arms she carried a plastic shopping bag, which she set on the desk next to the pizza box. "I brought you some soup, and some other supplies, to try to help you get over your flu. I know how hard it is when you're sick so far from home."

I pretended to try to sit up, but collapsed back on the pillow. I coughed, a terrible sound that was much more like a goose honking than anything human. It was the best I had. "Professor Lewis. Thank you so much!" I played up my voice's rasp to my advantage. "I'm so sorry to have missed class last week. I just couldn't get out of bed. My friends have been taking care of me. This is Lucy and this is Eli." Eli eased himself down beside me on the bed, acting as a barrier between the professor and me, but taking care not to actually touch me.

She nodded at each of them. "What a lucky girl, to have such lovely friends to care for you. You must be a deserving girl indeed." She stepped closer to the bed. "But Jo, how are you feeling? Are you any better? Fever? Chills?" Professor Lewis reached out a hand as if to feel my forehead.

Lucy spoke up. "She's had the chills for days now. We try to keep her covered up." She stepped in between Professor Lewis and me, knocking my teacher's hand away before she could reach my face.

But the professor wouldn't be held at bay. She reached around Lucy, nudging her aside, and then placed her hand on my forehead. The pressure forced my head to sink deep into my pillow. "That's strange. You don't feel like you have fever. You feel cold to me."

"See?" I said, as weakly as possible. "Chills."

"Excuse me," she said to Eli, almost knocking him to the floor as she sat beside me on the bed. It made me uncomfortable, to have a teacher so physically close to me, but in a way it was nice to have someone being motherly. She looked down at my face. "Gray. Your skin looks gray. How terrible to be so sick. But, dear, why do you have sunglasses on?" Then, as though she *were* my mother, she brushed my hair back from my forehead, allowing it to slip through her fingers for a moment before she pulled away, still eyeing the rough, jagged split ends.

"Migraine," I said, too quickly. "The light hurts my eyes. But Lucy and Eli are being so sweet, staying with me, I couldn't ask them to sit in the dark."

"I see. My dear, you really look terrible. Can I make you some soup? I brought Campbell's and Cup-o-Noodle." She stared at me, her eyes lingering on every detail I tried to hide.

"No!" we all said simultaneously. I could barely swallow, let alone choke down Cup-o-Noodle soup. I raised my head. "I mean, I've been struggling to keep food down. They've each had to clean up after me a couple times."

"Jo!" Professor Lewis sounded alarmed. "Dear, we need to get you to the clinic. Right away."

"We did," Eli said quickly. "They gave her Tamiflu. Lucy and I are on it as well, so we haven't gotten sick. But that's what's causing Jo's migraine and nausea. The Tamiflu. But we can make her the soup when she's feeling up to it."

Eli, you genius. I smiled at him. Professor Lewis noticed. So did Lucy.

"Yes, and you shouldn't be here anyway," said Lucy. "You definitely don't want to catch this, and Jo's still very contagious, Professor Lewis. Thank you for stopping by, of course, but..."

"Yes," she said. "I've seen enough. Jo, dear, please consider yourself excused for last week's absence and, from the looks of things, tomorrow's as well. I can come by again if you need anything. Just drop me a line and let me know. You have my email."

"Thank you, Professor," I said, and I meant it. "It was sweet of you to come by to check on me."

Professor Lewis nodded. "Yes, I've surely seen enough," she said, her voice quiet. She stood and headed to the door, Lucy and Eli on her heels to usher her out more quickly. She turned one last time and narrowed her eyes at me. "Dear, if you do get worse, please call me. I can help." And with that, she handed Lucy a card, then headed out the door.

I sat up in the bed as Eli closed the door. Lucy looked confused. "Since when do teachers make house calls?" she asked. "And leave business cards with their cell phone numbers?"

"I was wondering the same thing," I said. "But I'm one of her better students, I think. Sometimes when she asks a question, and no one knows how the hell to answer, I make something up to get a discussion going. I bet with me being out last week, she was listening to crickets the whole time."

"What class of hers do you take?" asked Eli.

"English Lit of the Sixteenth Century."

"Gah," said Lucy. "No wonder nobody talks. I didn't even know there *was* literature in England in the sixteenth century."

I laughed, while simultaneously attempting to extract myself from my bed. It wasn't easy, since my knee decided at that exact moment to lock completely. "Oh, shut up," I said, sharper than I'd meant. "I know you've heard of Shakespeare. Please tell me you've heard of Shakespeare."

Eli leaned over to give me a hand, wincing as he did. With his help, reluctant though it was, I was on my feet again a moment later, which was better than being stuck in the bed.

"Okay," he said. "Enough about English Lit and teachers who make house calls. Let's get back to work. Jo, mind if I test my handiwork on your cord?"

I shook my head and shrugged.

"Come on over to the wall then. Have a seat."

Once I sat in my desk chair, Eli leaned over to plug me in. As I watched him near the outlet, a thought occurred to me. I held out a hand to stop him. "You better let me. Just in case."

He stepped back, but his eyes never left me. "You sure? I don't mind."

Nodding, I took the cord from his hand. I leaned over and gently pushed my cord into the wall socket. The lights flickered, but barely, not at all like when I'd reached directly into the sockets. I felt the warm buzz of electricity surge through me.

"It's working!"

Eli grinned. "Great! And now you won't mess up your fingers." His face was smug. "I don't know the first thing about electronics, to tell you the truth. I'm glad I was able to help."

Lucy clapped her hands together and did a happy Lucy dance. "Good job, Eli. You deserve a cookie."

"Do you have a cookie?" he asked, hopeful.

"No."

"Oh."

They stared at each other, distracted by electricity and cookies, but I was ready to get back to work.

"Hey, guys," I said, trying to reel them back in. "How about those real estate listings?"

I'd just described the cabin as I remembered it for the third time. We each dug into our pile of printed listings, scattering papers from one end of the room to the other, when the lights in the room began to flicker.

"Jo?" Lucy said, a slight waver in her voice. "Is that you?"

The warm flow of electricity through my body shook like Lucy's voice. As soon as it began to go, I missed it. But I wasn't causing the lapse. "No, not this time," I said.

"The lights here never go—"

But before Eli could finish what was probably going to be a hopeful statement, the lights flickered, surged, and then went out entirely. The power of the surge made me jump to my feet, and my hair stood on end, crackling with static.

Lucy cried out. I would have but I was still reeling from the jump-start. I felt like I could run a marathon.

"What just happened?" Eli said, looking around. With all the candles we had in the room, we could still see each other, though the light danced and flickered and threw monstrous shadows against the wall.

"Power went out," I whispered. I struggled to stand still, my muscles and nerves all fired up and ready to move.

"But the power here never goes out," said Lucy. "And it's not even snowing."

"I know," I said, looking around the room. "Something's not right. Can you go look in the hall. Is it just this room?"

As though in answer to my question, the hallway filled with the voices of other students, calling out to each other amid the sudden darkness. Lucy turned to me. "Definitely not just us."

A breeze flew in through the window, blowing a candle flame higher. Eli walked to the window in the flickering light. He slid it up higher. "The moon's so bright," he said. "It's lighter outside than in."

The air around me crackled and snapped. Something was wrong. I could feel it in a way I'd never felt anything before. I crossed the room in two big strides, and without knowing why I pushed Eli aside.

"Hey..." he said, just before a stone, a small boulder, really, came pummeling through the open window. The thin screen was an inadequate barrier, and it hit me square in the chest. I flew back from the force and tumbled to the ground, holding the rock like a star receiver catching the winning touchdown pass.

"Jo!" Lucy shrieked, and ran to me. "What the hell? Are you okay?"

She grabbed me under the shoulders and began to haul me to my feet, but I was ahead of her. I hopped up, still holding the boulder.

I opened my mouth to speak, but Eli interrupted. "Guys, help. Get a blanket, a towel, something!"

I turned my head. When I knocked Eli aside, he'd crashed into a small cluster of candles on my desk. One had fallen over, hot wax dripping down the desk leg. Worse, though, was the flame that had alighted on the curtains my mother and I so carefully selected and hung on the day I moved in. The flame now danced as it moved up the curtain's thin cotton fabric.

"Oh God," I said, dropping the rock. I ran to the bathroom while

Lucy ran to the flames to help Eli. I yanked a towel off the rack and turned on the shower. Keeping my torso away from the water I stuck the towel into the stream. Electricity sparked around my fingers, but I ignored it. The towel soaked, I ran back to the flames. Eli and Lucy had no luck batting at them with my comforter.

"Look out," I cried, and I swung my wet towel at the curtains. The flames sizzled and smoked as I swung again and again. Soon, they died down to a low, shimmering smolder. Eli stopped my arm from swinging, and then tugged the remaining fabric down from the curtain rod. He stomped on the dying embers.

"That was close," he said, as Lucy collapsed on the bed. "What in God's name is going on?"

"I don't know, but…"

Once again, I was cut off, this time by the shrill cries of the fire alarm as it roared to life throughout the building. Never one to enjoy a good, high-pitched alarm, I brought my hands to my ears as the sound cut through my head in a whole new way. "Make it stop," I shouted.

"It's the smoke from the fire," said Lucy. "We have to go. Quick, blow out all the candles!"

"I can't go out like this," I said. "People will see me!"

Our voices grew louder and louder to be heard over the alarm's shrieks.

"I don't know what to do!"

Meanwhile, Eli went around the room, blowing out all the candles and stuffing them into drawers and closets. He shoved the remnants of the burnt curtain beneath the bed. "Lucy, get your coat," he said, ignoring our panic. When she didn't respond, he added, "Now. We'll meet you in the hall."

She ran to her room through the bathroom in the sudden, loud, and velvety darkness.

I turned to Eli. "What about me?" I said. I hated the pleading I heard in my voice, the fear. I hated needing anyone to tell me what to do, but I was out of ideas. "Are you going to shove me under the bed too?"

"No," he said. "They'll search the rooms to see what set off the alarm. You have to get out of here too."

"But I'm falling apart!"

"So we cover you up," he said. "Don't worry, you'll see."

And he reached over and picked up a blanket from my bed. He draped it over my head, then wrapped it under my chin, kerchief-style. "Here," he said. "Hold it like this. We'll keep you in the shadows. No one will even notice you."

He reached through the blanket, took hold of my arm, and led me, the reluctant one this time around, out into the teeming chaos of the hall.

OUTSIDE, STUDENTS CLUSTERED AROUND EACH other, huddled together for warmth. Eli, Lucy, and I stood apart, in silence, beneath a copse of trees. As I watched people hold onto each other, clinging together to conserve body heat as firemen entered the dorms, I thought about what this would have been like the week before. I pictured the three of us, on a normal night. Eli would have stood in the middle, and he'd have held Lucy and me close, an arm around each of us. We'd have been like the three amigos, all snuggly and warm and normal. Just like all the kids around us.

Instead, we stood apart, and though Lucy and Eli stood protectively between me and the rest of the Calvin Hall student body, no one touched. Lucy hopped up and down in the cold, her own comforter pulled tight around her, covering her coat, her hat, her arms and legs, as she froze, untouched in the night.

Eli had been wrong. To me, standing in our self-contained silos, we were as obviously hiding something as a kid sneaking out of a candy store with a fistful of licorice.

I felt more alone than I'd ever felt. I wanted to cry. I wanted to scream. I wanted to hit something so hard my hands would bleed.

I wanted my blood back. My normal life. My old problems: fights with Eli, trouble in Chemistry. I was sick of this new life, this new normal, and I'd have given anything to be up in my bed, safe and warm and no longer undead.

But it wasn't meant to be, and even our new normal was soon interrupted.

"You kids causing more trouble?" said a dark, husky voice behind us. "Somehow I'm not surprised to see you here."

We all jumped and turned.

"Crap," Eli whispered. I heard him, though, and I shot him a warning look that he probably missed in the darkness.

Officer Strong stood, leaning against a tree, watching us. I melted backward as Eli and Lucy stepped forward.

"Officer Strong," said Lucy. "So nice to see you again. Aren't you freezing? I'm freezing."

Eli was less friendly. He only nodded in the officer's direction.

Strong looked right at me. "I've been keeping an eye on things around here," he said. "Don't want you to turn up missing again, do we, Miss Hall? I see you and your boyfriend have patched things up?"

I gave Lucy a look, begging her to take over, but she hesitated. So I nodded. "Yes," I said, as brightly as I could muster. "We had a long talk after you came by this morning. It was a stupid fight and we're back together."

Why do you care? I silently asked.

Strong turned his gaze on Eli, who stepped closer to me, though he kept his arms pinned at his sides. "So," Strong said. "I don't have to expect any more phony reports."

Lucy laughed. Hard. To my ears it sounded fake, but I knew her better than most, and I hoped Strong wouldn't notice. "Oh, Officer Strong," she said, and walked closer to him. "You're so funny." She slid her blanket back from her head, letting it fall prettily around her shoulders.

She looked like a snow queen, and he finally noticed. "Lucy," he said. "I'm sorry, I didn't get your last name earlier." He smiled at her. "You look different from earlier, don't you?"

I'd seen that look on the eyes of plenty of boys and men before. Lucy had that effect on them. She noticed it too.

"It's probably because I've showered," she said, tossing her head and laughing. "So tell me, are you stalking me?"

I thought I saw a dark cloud pass before Strong's eyes, but it was probably just a flicker of light.

Nearby, the fire truck turned off its sirens and the firemen climbed back in. A cheer went up among the students as lights suddenly blazed forth from Calvin Hall. The crisis had ended; the power was back on.

Strong laughed. "No, I'm just making sure nothing else goes wrong for your friend here," he said. "They like me to keep an eye out after a report like the one your boyfriend filed goes down. It's not that unusual. Especially in light of…" He trailed off, staring around him as other students began filtering back into the dorm. He held out a hand to keep us there.

"In light of what?" Eli asked. He sounded aggressive, angry.

Strong shot him a warning look. "Watch it, buddy," he said. The he glanced around again, the look of someone convinced he was being followed. "I guess I can tell you three this. Can I trust you to keep a secret?"

We exchanged looks, the three of us, and all nodded, solemnly, like little children taking a sacred vow. Lucy even held up a hand, pinkie outstretched, in typical pinkie-swear fashion. No one else swore with her, though.

"All right, then," Strong said, dropping his voice a few decibels lower. "Let's just say that Miss Hall's disappearance isn't the first disappearance that's been reported among young, college-age girls recently. And let's just say she's the first one who's turned back up, seemingly fine. But let's also say that the police chief is worried, and asked me to keep a special close eye on Miss Hall, and also on the ambassador's daughter. Lucy, I hear that's you?"

She nodded. "Yes."

"Because if an ambassador's daughter turns up missing, it would mean big things, even bigger than we know, could be afoot. So it's my job now to keep an eye on you both, to make sure nothing further goes wrong."

"But Officer Strong," I said, my voice strained and tense, "I was never missing. I *told* you that."

He gave me a look, eyeing me up and down. I pressed myself further back into the shadows. The chaos surrounding us had died down as all the students reentered the building, and suddenly we four stood alone outside the dorm, in the darkness.

"I don't think I believe you, Miss Hall," Strong said, and then he turned his glare on Eli. "I'm not sure I believe any of you. But until I have proof, I can't do anything but watch, and wait, and make sure things move smoothly from here."

With that, he turned on his heel and strode off into the night, his boots crunching in the snow.

"What the…" Eli said.

"Heck," Lucy finished for him.

I let my blanket fall to the ground and covered my face with my hands. Closing my eyes, I willed my thoughts to stop churning. Nothing Strong said would matter, if only we could find the people who did this to me and convince them to turn me back into a normal girl. Then we would be fine. That had to be the priority.

When I dropped my hands, I saw Lucy and Eli staring at me, their skin pink and vibrant and alive in the cold. They looked concerned.

"Screw it," I said, taking each of them by the arm and heading back toward the building. "Screw it all. Let's get back upstairs. There's still that boulder in my room we need to deal with."

From the OoA files, dated February 15
Memorandum:

Efforts to apprehend Subject 632G-J have been unsuccessful. She is proving wily, whether she realizes it or not. She remains in public places, heavily surrounded by other students and faculty.
If we are unable to return her to the lab and our study within the next 48 hours, damage to her person will become irreversible; we will be faced with no other option than termination of Subject 632G-J.
Retrieval efforts redoubled. We must bring her in quickly and silently. She is a valuable success story that must be studied further.
Additionally, new subject identified. She will be Subject 679G-L. Photo to be provided with official Subject Memorandum.

BACK IN THE comparative safety of my room, strong breezes blew my remaining curtain like an unmoored ship's sail in a squall. Eli hurried to close the window, hiding the gaping hole in the screen with a pane of cloudy glass. Beside me, Lucy shuddered.

"There it is," she said, and I followed her gaze to the large, smooth rock in the center of the floor. Tied to it, like something out of an old gangster flick, was a piece of folded paper.

"Don't touch it," said Eli. "It could be laced with something."

"Laced with what? Something to make me deader? Doubtful. So, my note. My rock. Mine."

Eli glanced at Lucy. She wouldn't meet his eyes, but she nodded, and so did Eli.

I approached the rock with caution. I wasn't afraid of any hidden disease for myself—I'd have hugged a leper, just because I could—but I had to admit there was a chance the rock concealed an explosive device. I didn't want to blow up my friends.

To that end, I paused. "Why don't you two wait in Lucy's room, okay? No arguments. Let me look at it by myself for a sec, just in case."

"In case of..." Lucy began, but Eli grabbed her arm.

"She's got a point. I think we should listen."

But they both stared at me, concerned and weary, as they backed slowly away into the bathroom. I waited until I heard the bathroom door on my side click, and then the one on her side as well.

I knelt beside the rock and picked it up, bracing for some kind of detonation that would end my misery right then. Nothing happened. No sound came louder than the rustling of notebook paper beneath my own papery skin.

The string attaching the note to the rock was basic, everyday twine. I'd seen string like that at Eli's before. He and his roommates used it to tie up collapsed cardboard before their monthly trips to the recycling center. I knew I couldn't untie it, not with my fumbling fingers anyway, so I stood up and walked to my desk.

I had a pocketknife in the top drawer, given to me by father before I headed east the year before. "You never know when you'll need a knife," he'd said.

"Thanks, Daddy," I whispered as I slipped the blade out and locked it into place. I set the rock down and ran my fingertip over the blade to test its sharpness. The blade slid right into my finger, without hesitation, and I dropped it.

"Jo," said Eli, his voice muffled through two thick doors. "Are you doing okay in there?"

"Never better," I called back, a reflex-reaction, as I stared at the clean line etched into my fingertip. The cut went deep into the pad, and when I pulled the skin back, I saw the white, parched muscle below. I felt no pain as I stared in silent sadness.

"I miss having blood," I whispered to myself, staving off the urge to pop my injured finger into my mouth. That gesture wouldn't be necessary anymore.

Then I nodded to spur myself back into action. "I'm opening the note now," I called, picking the knife back up and slicing through the thin twine. I unfolded it, my fingers shaking, and glanced at the contents. "It's….um….they have really bad handwriting."

Eli burst back through the door. "That's all you have to say about it?"

Lucy followed. "What does it say?"

"It says you're in danger. It says you should go now." I dropped the note on the desk and went back to my bed. Eli and Lucy ran to where I'd left it. I let them read. It would only take a second.

For there, scrawled in handwriting barely legible, in a thick, coppery ink that I wasn't convinced wasn't blood, was a cheap joke, a kick in the gut while I was already down, and a threat against the two people who were trying to help me survive:

I'll get you, my pretty. And your little friends too.

"SCREW 'EM," SAID ELI.

Lucy took the note to our bathroom and burned it in the sink, setting it on fire with the same matches she used to relight the scented candles in my room.

"But that was evidence," I said, weakly, while I sat in my bed, too overwhelmed with grief and fear to move.

"Evidence of what? Of their sick sense of humor? Or of their intent to get Eli and me, too? Either way, I'm with him. Screw them. Let's get back to work."

So that's what we did. We searched hundreds of real estate records for the mountains surrounding campus, but nothing looked familiar to me. Hours later, without having made any actual progress, Eli left, promising to return in between classes the next day. Lucy, looking deflated, headed through the bathroom into her room. They were tired,

I could see that. I was, too, on some level. Tired, frustrated, angry. But my body and mind, even after lying still and unplugged for hours, refused to rest. It just kept on ticking. Chugging. Thinking. Working. No matter how much I wanted to sleep, it didn't happen.

I tossed and turned. I read a bit of *Romeo and Juliet*—required reading for Professor Lewis's class that week—but then I went back to the computer, staring blankly as I flipped from house to house to house.

Finally, around five a.m., I gave up and got out of bed. In the flickering candlelight, I pulled off my clothes and stood naked in front of the mirror. The flames cast shadows against my body, adding dents and dimples to my already mottled frame.

The day's activities had been unkind to me. The staples on my stomach tore away from the skin in some spots, and two in a row had pulled completely out near the bottom, opening a gaping hole in my lower abdomen. The bandage around my electrical cord was dingy and gray, fraying around the edges. I yanked it off, disgusted by the sensation of crust detaching from skin, and then I grabbed a nearby coil of gauze and started to cover up the hole in my stomach.

When I was done I stared some more. My arm hung at my side, splinted but still crooked. The fingers on my right hand were black, ugly. On my left hand, one finger was attached by duct tape, thanks to Lucy's clumsy handiwork. And everywhere, my skin was gray and hard, like marble. I hadn't lost weight since the morgue, but I looked skinny and malnourished as my body began to collapse in on itself. And my eyes were the worst: white where they'd once been blue, pupils dilated and vacant, obvious even in the dull candlelight.

I was dead. I didn't need a mirror to tell me that.

What I needed to find was someone to help me. To fix me. That was all that mattered.

Because I wasn't ready to be dead. Not then. Not yet. And since my friends were sleeping, I decided to take matters into my own hands.

Slowly, in the dancing candlelight, I pulled on a pair of baggy sweatpants, roomy enough to accommodate my bandages and cord, then a T-shirt and hoodie. I slid my feet into a pair of boots, and left my room.

Let Lucy sleep, I told myself, glancing at her door as I slipped in silence down the long hallway and headed for the stairs. *She needs the rest.*

Outside Calvin Hall, night sat heavy atop the snow. The moon was set, but stars danced in the clear black sky. The whole campus was asleep. I passed Strong's police car, parked in the fire zone in front of the dorm. The car was running, puffing plumes of exhaust behind it like a sleeping dragon, and he sat inside. His head was tilted back against the headrest and his mouth hung slack, a tiny pool of drool glistening in one corner. As he breathed, deep, heavy breaths, the puddle wiggled, dangerously close to spilling over his bottom lip. I stood and watched, entranced for a moment, until the mountains beckoned.

Come here, they said in voices deep and dreamy. The voices of those who came before, I thought. Our forefathers. *Come here and we'll take care of you. We'll show you the way. Let us help you.*

I wanted to believe. I trudged through the snow in the direction from which I'd come the day before: down the hill, behind the English Department, then back out into the wilderness. It was nice, feeling neither cold nor fatigue. I was a machine. So long as I was properly charged, I could keep going and going and going.

So I did. Alone in the dark, I was no longer afraid. I walked slowly, methodically, carefully retracing my steps, but taking time to look around me. I absorbed the dark, the wild beauty of the mountains around me. I would accomplish everything.

I climbed to the top of a hill a mile away from campus. Though I was surrounded on all sides by mountains, I had an unparalleled view of the sunrise. I froze, gazing out over the mountain ranges. The sun's fingers were a thousand shades of yellow and pink and gold as they reached through the deep blue sky between snowy mountain caps. I could see for miles, and the vastness of the world reminded me how far I'd run on that first night in the mountains. The memory of that night suddenly felt freeing; I could have gone anywhere, done anything. It seemed, in retrospect, that I wasted the night that never ended. I huddled in a cave instead of drinking in nature. I could have been drunk with beauty, but instead I cowered. As I looked around, I realized I never needed to be afraid again. Not when the world was so beautiful and fresh and welcoming.

I was exhilarated. I raised my arms to welcome the coming dawn, and drew back my lips in a cry of joy.

But then my thoughts went dim. My body grew heavy. In an instant, I felt it: I was running out of power.

I didn't have a lot of time. This shutdown was coming on faster, fiercer, as though it wanted nothing more than to rob me of the fleeting joy I'd felt. I fell to my knees.

I need help. I pulled my dead cell phone from the pocket of my hoodie and held down the power button. Nothing happened. Though I'd charged it for hours after we returned home from Eli's, it stayed dead. Cold. Destroyed by the winter weather. *Come on, come on... START.*

Nothing.

As fog clouded my dying brain and fear set into my absent heart, I had an idea. I unzipped my hoodie with fingers grown thicker and clumsier as my body shut down. I lifted my shirt. *Please work.*

I held the phone tight, and I touched it to one of my metal nipples.

Sparks lit the air and sizzled when they touched down amid the snow. In my hand the phone clicked, and vibrated, and then, miraculously, it booted. But it was slow, so slow. Just like me.

"Call Lucy," I croaked, as soon as my phone would accept a voice command. My cold fingers were ineffectual on the smooth touch screen. The ringing was music in my ears.

She picked up immediately and her voice sounded, muffled and sleepy. "Hello? Hello?"

I tried to talk, but nothing came out. *"Call Lucy" might be my last words.*

"Hello? Jo? Is that you? Jo?" I heard a door slam. "Jo, why aren't you in your room? Where are you?"

Save me, Lucy. I don't want to die.

I moaned. My brain shouted words in my head, but my vocal cords couldn't form them.

The last thing I heard before my power went off was Lucy. "Jo, where are you? Never mind. I'm coming. I'm coming!"

Above me, the sky burned with the colors of a wildfire as I closed my eyes.

THE NEXT THING I KNEW was warmth flowing into my body. My eyes fluttered open, and the faces of Lucy and Eli slowly came into focus. We were in my room again. I was in my bed. I saw my remaining curtain billowing in the breeze from the open window.

"Look, look, she's waking up!" Lucy's eyes were red and tearstains striped her cheeks, cutting white, freckled paths through a thick layer of grime. "Oh, thank God, she's waking up. Jo? Jo? Can you hear me?"

I tried to respond but couldn't quite move my mouth. I blinked.

Lucy sighed as if she'd held her breath for hours. "She blinked. Jo, if you can hear me, blink twice."

I blinked twice.

"Hooray!" Lucy said, then leaned over and dropped a kiss on my forehead. "I think you'll make it. You just lay still and keep charging."

As if I had any choice.

They moved out of my line of sight, but they spoke about me as if they thought I couldn't hear them. I heard every word.

Eli's voice had a knife-sharp edge to it. "Okay, so she's awake. I'm out of here. You two are on your own for the rest of the day. Think you can stay out of trouble?"

"Come on," said Lucy. I couldn't see her, but I knew the look on her face. Her eyes would be big, her cheeks flushed pink. She always looked like that when she was begging. "Don't be like that. She didn't mean anything by it."

"She left her room in the middle of the night, *by herself*. I don't care what she meant by it. She was stupid. She could have *died*. I mean, that's what got her into this situation in the first place, right? And now, well, I'm done wasting my time on someone who keeps trying to get herself killed."

"Eli!"

"Besides, it's not that she *could* have died. It's that she *is* dead. We know this. Nothing we do now is going to change that."

"Eli! She can hear you!" Lucy's voice was thick with tears again.

"So what if she can? It's time she knows the truth." The door opened. "And anyway, we broke up the night she disappeared. She only came back to me because she needed something. I can't keep wasting my time on a girl who walked out on me."

"Come on, stop it," Lucy said. "You know Jo loved you, and you know this isn't ending here. Maybe someone can help her, fix her. Change her back, even. But that won't happen if we don't help her. Come on, Eli. Please don't go. Not like this."

"No one can fix her." He was quiet for a moment, but then he spoke in a louder voice that reminded me of the fight that had started my journey. "Listen, don't call me later, okay? I have exams, work, and now I have to do it all on two hours of sleep. Thanks a ton, Jo. For nothing."

He slammed the door.

Lucy appeared back in front of my face, tears rolling down her cheeks. "Don't listen to him, Jo, okay? He doesn't know what he's talking about. And maybe he's wrong. Maybe if we find who did this, they *can* fix you." She laid her head down on my shoulder, but sat up quickly again. "God, you stink. It's not like anything I've ever smelled before."

Lucy sat on the edge of my bed, wiggling until her back was to me, and all I could see was her wild, tangled ponytail, bobbing as she spoke. "He's just mad, Jo. He didn't really mean those things. You scared him, that's all, so that made him get mean. I wish you'd seen him when we were looking for you. He was like a machine—so intense, so determined. He loves you, Jo. If you had seen him, you'd know exactly how much. And so don't listen to those mean things he said. They're not true." She sighed a deep, shuddering sigh. The bed shook as she reached up to stifle a sob and also to wipe her own tears away.

"God, Jo, I don't know the last time I've cried this much in the same twenty-four-hour span. I hate it." She sniffled, and it was wet and thick. Snotty. "I'm done crying now, Jo. You hear me? I'm done. Because I don't accept that we won't figure this out. Together. Only us if it has to be that way, but I know Eli will be back too. He loves you. And this story will have a happy ending. Do you hear me, Jo? Happy. So remember that."

Lucy stood, her tall, slender frame filling my line of sight. She turned and leaned over me again, and let her hand linger over my forehead, stroking my hair and tucking a lock behind my ear. She smiled, very faintly, though her eyes remained wet. "When you get back up, we're going to have to do something about your nose. But don't get up now, okay? For now you need to rest. Recharge. I'll be back, okay?"

She walked through the bathroom to her room, leaving the doors open between us. She rustled around over there, opening and closing doors and closets. When the rooms grew silent, I assumed she went to sleep.

I wanted to get up, wake Lucy back up, call Eli and beg him to come back. I wanted to tell them that I, too, knew it would all be okay. And that I was sorry I'd dragged them into this.

But my body wasn't charged. All I could do was lie there silently on my bed and wonder: *What happened to my nose?*

Chapter 9

I WAS INCAPACITATED FOR most of the morning, able to move my arms and my head, but little else. Eli wouldn't return my calls, and Lucy was like a mother hen, clucking around my room, afraid to let me out of her sight.

"I thought you *died*," she said, more than once. "When we found you, we thought you were *dead* for good this time. We followed your tracks. You were lucky you didn't go too far. Eli and I were able to carry you home."

"I know. I'm sorry. For everything. For dying," I said, mumbling on purpose, hoping she wouldn't understand me, but also hoping she would.

"You should have seen Eli," Lucy said, continuing as though she hadn't heard me, even though the pained look on her face told me she had. "He was like Superman, carrying you over his shoulders. He was crying, too. I think this is breaking his heart, Jo. I think that's why he said those things he did. He didn't mean them." She looked down at me, begging me to believe her, as though by repeating herself she could make the words more true. But I thought I knew better. Eli was right. We'd broken up, and then I went and dragged him and Lucy into danger. That had been my choice, my doing, and it was the worst thing I'd ever done.

"Right," I said. "He's just sad. Not angry at me for being the stupidest person alive. Not mad at me for getting him into this."

Lucy ignored me. "And then when we plugged you in and you didn't come back right away, then we *really* thought you were dead. But we just kept hoping. I think Eli even said a prayer, can you believe that, Jo? He said a prayer, and I swear, right after that was when you opened your eyes. It was almost enough to make both of us believe in…well, in something. And I swear, he wasn't mad at you. He just didn't know how to tell you how bad you scared him, and how relieved he was. You know?"

A sigh was a useless gesture for me, but old habits die hard…just like people. "Whatever. He's mad, and we both know why, but can we get back to the search?" I asked. "When I was staring at the mountains last night, I realized how far I ran when I first left the cabin. I think we need to expand our search criteria, go a few miles further out than we've been going."

"Jo. You were dead. Now that you're back, you should rest a little more, okay? The search can wait. Another hour isn't going to change anything for the better or worse. I promise." She bounced out of the room, knowing full well my computer was out of reach and I wasn't strong enough to get up on my own. I was a prisoner in my own defective body, and it was starting to make me angry.

"Luce!" I called after her. "Luce! Come back." But it was no use. She was protecting me, and not allowing me to protect her in the one way I thought I could.

An hour later, I still lay, immobile, frustrated, and angry. Lucy came back into my room, holding her cell phone. Her eyes were big and surprised.

"What?" I said, more than a little testy.

"Can you get up yet?" she asked.

"No. Thanks for asking. I still can't move at all, in fact."

Lucy looked relieved. "Oh, good. I have to go out for a few. Now I don't have to worry about you running away again. I'll lock you in, though, so I know you're safe and sound. I'm sorry to leave you, but I have to."

Without giving me a chance to protest, she flew out through our bathroom. Minutes later, I heard her door click shut. She'd gone out, and hadn't told me where.

Knowing she was gone made me even lonelier.

I lay in silence on my bed and counted spots on the industrial ceiling. I tried to remember every detail about the morgue, and the path I took when running from it. I was sure somehow I could reconstruct that path, backwards, if only they would let me. And if only my body would let me.

After a while, I began to feel my toes. I could wiggle them again. And then I could feel my feet, my legs, and even my hips. I still couldn't move gracefully—but let's face it, grace had never been my strong suit—but I could sit up. My computer sat atop a pile of blankets at the end of the bed. I hooked the cord around my foot and slid it up to my hand. Slowly, I used the cord to pull the computer to me, and I pulled it onto my lap and lifted the cover.

Jo1995: Did something real dumb last night. Huge apology to @LucyGoosie and @EliPete21. You two are the best.

LucyGoosie: @Jo1995 @EliPete21 Anything for our girl. You smell. Doesn't she, E?

Jo1995: @EliPete21 Please call me. Please?

Jo1995: @EliPete21 Hello? Hello McFly? Bueller? Bueller?

Jo1995: Shit.

Hi Mommy,

I miss you. I love you.

Love, Jo

Jo,

What's wrong? Do you need Daddy and me to come up?

Love, your worried mother

Hi Mom,

Sorry, I guess I was just feeling a little homesick. Don't come, not yet. Maybe soon?

Love, Jo

Dear Jo,

Just checking up on you. Will we be seeing you in class this week? Did you ever go to the clinic? Are you having any new symptoms I should know about?

Take care,
Sondra Lewis
English Dept.

Dear Prof. Lewis,

I'm doing ok, thanks. I don't think you'll see me in class this week, though. I didn't go to the clinic. I'm on the mend, it's just taking some time.

Thanks again for your concern, and the soup. It was yummy.

Jo Hall

Dearest Jolene,

Oh, how I miss seeing your face. I was only able to look upon it for three days, but it is such a lovely one. A lovely face, a lovely body. Such a fine specimen you were, seated in my laboratory. But now you're gone, far from me.

I never dreamed your first move after reanimation would be to leave me. I never dreamed I'd lose you so quickly, my Jolene.

I only want to help you. I can help you. You awoke too soon, you see. I didn't have a chance to finish the process. As you are now, you're a monster. But I can complete you so no one will ever know the difference between you and a living, breathing individual. You can retake your normal life, with my help.

Right now, you are a work half-finished. With my help, you will be a masterpiece, my darling girl.

Please. Come home to me. Let me help you. No one else can help you as I can.

My partners are not as kind as me. I hear they've sent you a message, that you're being watched. Let me assure you, if you come home to me, I will do you no harm, nor will I harm your friends. I promise you will get no such assurances from my partners. They are not happy at your escape, and will do anything to bring you back…in any shape. I trust you know what I mean.

But me? I love you. You are one of my greatest successes. Or at least you will be. Come home, dearest Jolene.

With loving affection,
Your creator

P.S. If you'd like to find me, there's no need for fuss or silly internet searches. I am at 2959 Primrose Path, your home. Do you remember it? I do hope to see you here soon. My dearest Jolene.

I SNAPPED MY LAPTOP CLOSED and jerked my hand away as though it bit me. In a way, it had.

"Lucy," I tried to call, but my voice was weak still and the doors between our rooms were closed. My cell phone was on my desk, well out of my reach as I still wasn't strong enough to stand.

I reopened my computer.

The email was still there, staring at me. "Dearest Jolene," it called me. It taunted me. "Your creator."

I opened a Google search and typed in the address. 2959 Primrose Path. I clicked Enter.

There it was, right in front of me. A real estate entry for the property at 2959 Primrose Path. Thirteen miles from campus, high up in the foothills. I clicked over to Google Earth to be sure, zooming in with their street view until I was practically at the front door.

This was it. The welcome mat. The friendly swing. The homey

front porch.

"Lucy," I said again, but Lucy still didn't hear me. I tried to shout. "Luce!" No response. Then I remembered: Lucy wasn't home.

I read and reread the email while I awaited her return, and the return of my strength. I knew every word by heart within minutes, and fear and anger helped bolster my decrepit limbs. When I finally heard the door to Lucy's room slam, I shouted. "*Luce!*"

It took a while for the door between my room and the bathroom to open, though. Had I been able to, I'd have paced a track in the carpet in my room. When Lucy appeared in the doorway she looked pale, and I leaned forward. "Are you okay?"

She smiled, though her face remained wan. "I'm fine. I think my stomach is mad at me from the total grease-fest yesterday. But that's not important. What's going on in here? You sounded upset." She walked to the bed and sat down beside me, her face betraying how she really felt at reexposure to my scent.

"Here," I said, turning my computer screen toward her. "Read this."

More color drained from her already-pale face. "Oh my God. Is this for real?"

I nodded. "I think so. Nobody knows about me but you and Eli. The address, here." I pulled up Google Earth again. "That's it. That's the house." I swallowed a mouthful of nothing. "The laboratory."

Lucy shuddered, shaking the bed. "Your creator? Ugh, that's creepy. I don't trust this. You can't go."

"What choice do I have? Seems like the others are just biding their time till they catch me anyway. They know where I am."

"Yeah, but…"

"No buts," I said. "We're beyond buts."

"No we're not. There has to be another way." She paused and thought, then snapped her fingers. "That's it. We call Strong. I'm sure he's close by, and I think it's time to call in the professionals." Then she smiled a secret smile, meant only for herself, but I couldn't help but see it.

I snorted. "Strong? What's he gonna do? Fix me with his bulging biceps? Come *on*, Luce. He can't help me! This person, the creator, might be my only hope. I can't keep living like this."

Lucy shook her head violently. "Maybe he'll go to the house? Scope it out?"

"We can't tell him, Luce! I'm not ready to die." Despite the lack of tears in my body, some of my physical reactions worked just fine. My lower lip trembled as I tried to quell the hysteria building inside my stomach, or whatever was left of it.

"He wouldn't…" But she trailed off. She knew what he'd have to do. What just about anyone *official* would have to do.

She stood up suddenly. "I'll be right back." Lucy ran to the bathroom and slammed the door behind her.

While she was gone, I reread the email. Again. *My creator. Dearest Jolene. I can help you. I'm the only one who can help you.* I remembered waking up on the steel bed, naked and alone. I thought about letting this person finish what they started and then coming back to resume my normal life. I wondered what normal would even look like for me. I wondered, for a long time while the fan in the bathroom whirred and clanged, what exactly it was that they started. I thought about my parents, and wanted to see them so desperately, my absent heart ached.

By the time Lucy returned, nursing a ginger ale from the hallway vending machine, I'd made my decision.

"We're going." I said. To prove my point I swung my legs over the side of the bed. I pushed. I pulled. I stood. I had my power back. "At least, I am."

She nodded, sipping carefully from the can. "In that case, we better call Eli." She reached out and tossed me my cell phone.

"No, absolutely not."

I almost dropped the phone. "But I…I need you! Please?"

"What the hell do you think is going to happen, Jo? This person is going to welcome you with open arms? Fix you? Let you come on back to your normal life? No way, Jo. You're going to get yourself killed!" He was angry, but whispering.

"Where are you?"

"Dickson Hall. I was in class, Jo, like a normal person. I'm exhausted, thanks to you. I'm stressed out, thanks to you. And I'm not obligated to help you anymore." He sounded like he was reading from a script, and I wondered how many times he'd rehearsed this little speech while sitting in class that morning.

I took one of those deep breaths I didn't need, but that somehow made me feel a little more human, a little more alive. "Please? I need you."

"I have a mid-term in an hour. I finish this class, and then go right into a mid-term. For which I didn't study, I should tell you." He paused, and in my mind I saw him looking at his to-do list. "After that I have a bio-chem lab, and if I don't ace it, I'm going to be a C in the class at best. So it's not a good time for me."

"Right. Okay. Thanks anyway." I felt flat, deflated. My voice shook. "We'll be fine."

"Yes, fine. Right. That's exactly what you'll be." He hung up the phone.

I sat in the bed and stared at the silent phone in my hand. "Asshole!" I said, and I wound up my arm to toss the phone into the wall.

Lucy caught my hand. "Easy there. I guess we can't count on Eli?"

I shook my head, too upset to talk. I wished I could cry, but no tears could come. Of course.

Lucy slid her arm across my shoulders and gave me a little squeeze. It was the closest thing to a hug I'd had in days, and I leaned into it, trying to make it last. "Well," she said, pulling her arm away and looking slightly green. "I guess we're in this together, then. Just the two of us."

"Are you sure? This could be dangerous." I didn't want to put Lucy into any more danger than I already had.

"Danger's my middle name," she said, and she grinned. Fear stood bright in her eyes, but I knew Lucy—there was no stopping her once she had her mind set.

We spent the next hour rigging up a car charger for me so I could continue charging away from our home base. We took a phone car charger and cut the end of it off, exposing some of the wires. Lucy found an extension cord in a janitorial closet down the hall, and we cut the end of that off as well. Then we took the "innie" end of the extension cord and spliced it to the "outie" portion of the car charger, wrapped the spliced part with electrical tape like Eli did on my back, and we called ourselves brilliant.

We giggled while we worked. We argued over the best way to cut, the proper splicing methods. For the first time in days, both of us felt normal. Neither of us wanted it to end, so we took our time and were extra careful, wrapping the tape around and around, testing the sparks against my metal nipples. But all good things must come to an end, and soon it was complete.

I moved about the room using furniture to support myself, pressing against desks and bed posts for balance and strength. When Lucy saw, she laughed. "You look like an old lady," she said, snorting. "I mean, really, do you want me to get you a walker?"

"Shut up," I said, though she wasn't far off from the truth. Still, though, I was happy to realize: the more I moved, the more limber I became. I felt myself growing stronger.

We packed a few supplies for our journey. Pepto-Bismol for Lucy, whose stomach still bothered her. Another ginger ale. A field hockey stick that we thought might be handy in emergencies. And, of course, my car charger.

"So what do we hope to accomplish?" she asked when I sat down to recharge before we were ready to go. "I want to know your plans before we head out into the abyss."

"The way I see it," I said, "there are two things that could happen. First, maybe this creator guy really wants to help me. I don't know why he did this, but maybe there's some better plan for me, you know?"

Lucy sighed. "Maybe. But do you really think so?"

"No. More likely, they're going to try to kill me. I don't know why, but that feels more right. Still, I can't *not* know why they did this to me. I have to go. And no matter what, if things get messy, we get out of there, and then you can call Strong."

She patted me on the arm, and then gave me a quick squeeze. "I'm not ready to say goodbye yet. We'll figure something out. Something that doesn't involve calling Adam." Lucy sniffed, then stood up. "Okay, I'm going to get my car. It's in the lot on the far end of campus. It'll take me about thirty minutes to get there, probably, in this snow. Wait here, charge up. I'll come up and get you when I'm back. We're…not going to have an easy time getting you past the front desk anymore. I'm thinking you need a scarf. And the ski mask. And a hood."

I glanced in the mirror. She was right. The night before, while I lay motionless in the snow, my nose had blackened from the cold, and a large chunk of it had fallen off. I was becoming a monster. "Yeah. All of the above."

Lucy sighed. "Your smell's getting even worse. I'm not kidding. When we come back, unless this creator person can perform miracles, we're going to need a whole new level of smell control." She walked through the door to my room and took a deep breath of the comparatively fresh, always-stale hallway air. "Be right back, Stinky."

Under normal circumstances, the thirteen-mile drive to 2959 Primrose Path should have taken about forty-five minutes. But with several feet of iced-over snow covering most of the steep, windy roads through the mountains, and Lucy's little Honda, which hadn't been out of the parking lot since we'd returned to school after winter break, the drive went less than smoothly.

Lucy's GPS didn't help. "Turn right," it said as we neared our destination, and Lucy looked doubtfully at a snowy street that inclined to near vertical.

"I don't think I can," she said in a hushed voice.

"Don't, then. The GPS will adjust," I said, shrugging. The warm, steady hum of electricity through our converted car charger was a balm that kept me mellow and calm. Laid back, even. Strains of Bob Marley filtered out through the radio speakers, and I leaned my head against the headrest. "Every little thing…is gonna be all right."

Lucy slowed the car to a stop, pulling it off to the side of the road and eyeing the turn with suspicion in her eyes. I grew more nervous watching her, and suddenly my decision to go in search of the person or people who had done this to me seemed much less sound.

"Maybe we should turn around, Luce. What do you think?"

Lucy turned to face me with sudden fury in her eyes. "Are you kidding me?"

"What?"

"I said, are you kidding? We've come this far, Jo. I didn't want to come, but here we are. And you want to give up? No way. We see this through to the end. Together." Then she bent over, toward the steering wheel, holding her stomach. "Ouch, crap."

"Are you okay?" Panic swelled inside me. She didn't answer immediately. "Talk to me, Lucille!"

"It's just my stomach," she said, sitting up straight again. "It cramped. I'm okay."

"Your car can't make it up that road, and you're sick. These are bad omens. You need to be back at the dorm, in bed."

Lucy just rolled her eyes. "Eff it," she said, and turned the car back on.

She turned the blinker on and jerked the car back onto the main road without looking. There was only one car on the road, driving toward us. It honked as the Honda fishtailed slightly toward it. Lucy flipped the driver off.

For one blessed, quiet moment I thought Lucy was going to take us home. As she started to turn the wheel, easing the car into a U-turn, I would have breathed a sigh of relief if I'd had any breath in my lungs to exhale. Home sounded good.

But then she turned and gave me one more glance. "Screw it," she said again, and then, midway through the U-turn, she cut the wheel further and floored the gas pedal. "We're gonna get you fixed if it kills us!"

The Honda surged forward, its nose pointed toward the vertical side street. It slid around, almost out of Lucy's control. We flew up the steep hill, barely staying on the road, but moving forward, at least for a minute.

Then all forward motion ceased. The car slid back the way it came.

Lucy screamed. I screamed, too, my voice raspy and weak beside her shrill one.

I turned around as best as my stiff neck would allow. Behind us, on the main road, stood a long, gray van. No windows in the back, chains on the tires, dark, tinted glass on the driver's side. It looked threatening, and I felt like I'd seen it before.

I screamed again. I didn't want to crash into that van. It was bad news.

Lucy took her foot off the gas pedal when we began our descent, and she pulled both knees up to her chin, curling herself into a ball of panic.

"Lucy!" I shrieked. "Hit the gas! Hard as you can! Go! Go! Go!"

We each screamed, a cacophony of terror. As if in a dream, I watched Lucy move in slow motion, her arms and legs cutting through thick, invisible ether as she slid her foot down to the floor and pressed the gas pedal.

"Harder," I cried. "Harder!"

For a moment the car filled with the squeal of spinning tires trying to find purchase on the icy street below. Smoke rose on both sides of the Honda. Still, we went down the hill on a collision course with the gray van that filled me with dread.

Finally, after breathless moments filled with screaming girls and burning rubber, the tires caught clear pavement, and the car stopped sliding and shot forward like a bullet. We flew up the hill, past the spot that caused our initial slide, and away from the van that waited below us.

We rounded a corner and the road evened out some. Still screaming, Lucy removed her foot from the gas. The car slowed and rolled to a stop. Finally, Lucy stopped screaming. So did I. We were out of the danger zone. The van would never make it up the incline; we shouldn't have, that was for sure.

But had we gone straight into another danger zone? There was no way to know for sure, so we crept silently along the winding roads toward Primrose Path. As we drove, the wind picked up and dark clouds blotted out the sun. Soon, it began to snow.

From the OoA files, dated February 16
Memorandum:

Agent 55 continues attempts to extract Subject 632G-

J from her dorm.

During this time, Agent 55 identifies Subject 645-L as a new possibility. Her mother is of high position with the State Department. Tall, attractive, red-headed. Agent 55 has begun to work to pull the new Subject in; however, at this time, she refuses all advances at private contact. Attempts to pick her up in Agent's car were denied. Public meeting places are all Agent 55 has at this point. Attempts will continue until extraction is complete.

THE SKY BURNED black but the rest of our world was bleached white with snow as Lucy pulled the Honda up the driveway at 2959 Primrose Path. If blood still flowed through my veins, it would have frozen solid at the sight of the innocuous-looking cabin. A ghostly stomach pain gripped my abdomen in a vise, and I wanted more than anything to throw up. But there was nothing inside me to evacuate.

"Is this it?" Lucy whispered, letting the car roll to a stop. The windshield wipers worked double-time to clear the small area on the frozen windshield through which we peered.

I could only nod. My vocal cords were unresponsive.

"I wish Eli had come," she said.

"We can turn around," I managed to say after a long moment in which we both stared at the front door with the welcome mat turning white with gusting snow. "There's still time to go back."

"In this storm? We'd crash before we made it ten feet down the road. Going up is one thing, going down is something else entirely. We have to stay, at least for a little while. Besides, what about the van?"

The memory of the gray van, waiting for us at the bottom of the mountain, made me shudder. I wondered if I had goosebumps beneath the layers of clothes I wore to hide my tattered body. *Probably not,* I thought, and then I forced myself to focus. "We can go down the road, just a little. Wait out the storm in a different driveway. I have a bad feeling about this."

Lucy shook her head. "I'm not backing out now. If you don't want to go in, I'll go by myself. I want to see the people who did this to you, face-to-face."

I eyed her.

Lucy was still pale, either with sickness or with cold. I wasn't sure which, but her skin was milky, devoid of its usual pink, cheerful flush. She also looked misshapen, all folded up on herself in the driver's seat of the Honda, her head swallowed up in an oversized pink hat. She'd not been able to shed her thick down jacket to drive. My stench necessitated open windows so she wouldn't asphyxiate, and the air outside was frigid. Her gloved hands held tight to the steering wheel, and I imagined her knuckles stretched white within the knitted wool.

In short, she looked awful. Terrified, sick, scared—whatever it was, it wasn't good. And as such, her determination shamed me. I hadn't come this far to let my best friend fight my battles for me. Add to that, deep inside, I still clung to the idea that the composer of the email, which had led us to Primrose Path, wanted to help me. Maybe it was still possible for my story to have a happy ending.

Lucy groaned and curled up tighter for a second. "My stomach needs to knock it off," she said, scrunching her face in pain. "I'm ready to get out of here."

Sick but still fearless, that was Lucy. Well, I could be brave too.

I opened the car door and stood, turning my face into the onslaught of tiny, icy snowflakes. I looked back to Lucy, still seated in the car, and gave her a half smile, aware of a crack opening in my frozen cheek as I tried for what used to be my most winning facial expression.

Lucy laughed, suitably horrified. “Oh, crap, your face!”

“Never mind my face,” I said, smiling more broadly. The crack widened to my ear. “I’m ready to go meet my goddamn creator. Are you?”

She stood up beside the Honda. “Like a frat boy in a sorority house.”

I laughed. It felt good to laugh. There was no other way to release the emotions at war within me. “Let’s go.”

Clutching each other, we walked through the shrieking winds, our boots silent in the powdery snow. Lucy’s hat flew from her head, the pink cloth disappearing over the side of the mountain, and off a cliff behind the cabin. She started to squeal but clapped a hand over her mouth. “We should be quiet,” she whispered.

“Screw that.” I walked up the front porch steps, my legs stiff and inflexible from the cold, pretending the cracks and pops I heard weren’t permanent damage. There was no way to silence the clomping sound my heavy, uncoordinated feet made on the frozen wood, so I didn’t even try. Instead, I walked up to the solid front door and banged on it with all the strength I could summon from my wrecked arms.

“Hey, in there!” I shouted, my voice raw, inhuman. “Hey! It’s me! It’s Jo! Jolene! You wanted to see me, so let me in!”

Lucy jumped back, startled.

I turned back to her. “Well, I just figured, might as well let them know I’m home.” The words surprised me as I said them, but I meant them. Home. The cabin *was* a home to me. Sort of. If you looked at things a certain way, I was practically *born* there.

Home.

“Somebody let me in!”

No one came to the door. I tried again. “Come on, you in there! You told me to come! Answer your door! Come on!” I banged harder, pulling off a glove in the hope that my bare, marble skin would make more of an impact. It didn't, and pieces of me rained down amid the snowfall.

Still, there was no answer.

Beside me, Lucy stood almost knee-deep in the snow, her body shaking and shifting against the sub-zero temperature. The tip of her nose was turning white as the snow worsened. We were in a blizzard, nearing whiteout conditions, and could barely see the car, not ten feet away. If we shifted our feet, they emerged from the powder, but like bare toes in the surf were almost immediately covered again with the next gust of wind.

"We have to do something," Lucy shouted over the howling wind. "I'm so cold! Maybe we can wait out the blizzard in the car?"

"You'll freeze to death!"

I reached down and tried turning the doorknob. It moved easily beneath my hand, and with a loud click, the door slid inward. We rushed inside. I slammed it behind us, closing the storm out, and Lucy and me inside.

We stood in near pitch-darkness, with only the faint light of a computer screen illuminating the room at all. In the disorienting mix of darkness and green-tinted light, it was harder to match the room to the foggy memory of my awakening, but I knew I was in the right place. Microscopic hairs on the back of my neck jerked to attention.

Lucy took a few steps forward. "Maybe there's a light."

"Wait, no," I started to say, but had barely formed the "w" with my dry, brittle lips before I heard a crash. The faint shadow of Lucy, outlined against the computer screen, tumbled head over heels to the ground.

Her scream built slowly at first, but once begun it rose steadily into a shrill, panicky shriek. I ran with my hand trailing down the wall, fumbling and stumbling, searching for a light switch. I found one and flipped it up.

Light flooded the room from circular, stainless steel fixtures hanging on the ceiling. It reflected off metal tables, bouncing off cabinets lining the far wall. But the light was cruel, forming multiple spotlights that rained down upon bodies, prostrate on the tabletops. They were girls. Dead-looking girls, each in their late teens, early twenties. Each wore like a badge of honor a mangled, stapled incision running down her entire abdomen. Each looked exactly like I must have looked when I awakened on the lone, empty table.

Lucy lay on the ground beside an upturned table, struggling beneath the weight of another girl's body. It was supple, arms and legs bending and wrapping around Lucy's inert figure as she fought and cried and wailed in terror. The table, heavy and metal, pinned them both to the ground.

"Jo! Help me! Please, Jo, get it off! Get it off!"

I rushed to her, but my knees gave way beneath me and I fell to the floor beside them. Lucy stared at me, tears in her eyes. "Please, help." She sounded meek, defeated. I didn't blame her. She'd just lost a wrestling match with a cadaver. "Please. I think she's dead."

Grunting with effort, I pulled myself back to my feet and grasped Lucy's arms. I pulled, and I tugged, but she was stuck. My mind raced, and my eyes darkened with fear. The light in the room faded. I couldn't see. My hands found the table's leg, and my fingers closed around the smooth, cold, metal. I pulled. The table moved, ever so slightly. I pulled again.

The table and I tumbled back, crashing into the wall, where I landed in a heap of arms and legs bent at impossible angles. I sat in silence as the room came back into focus. Two feet away from me sat Lucy. She was free.

"Thanks," she said, panting heavily. She disentangled herself from the dead girl's limbs.

"Any time."

"You okay?"

I nodded, and then leaned forward to lay my cracked cheek against her sweat-damped hair. "Yeah. Are you?"

"Uh-huh. I might have broken my ankle, though. I'm not sure. The table landed on it."

"Crap."

"Yeah. Sucks."

"Well, the good news is," I said, shrugging, "we know nobody's here. We made enough noise to even wake the dead, *if* they were ready to be awoken."

Lucy eyed the body beside here. "That's not funny, Jo."

"Yeah. I know."

We sat in silence for another minute. Lucy pulled herself out of my grasp to lean against the wall beside me instead. She looked around the room, taking her time to linger over each table and the body atop it. One hand slid up to cover her mouth. Finally, she turned to me with tears in her eyes. "You know, you told me. You told me about this place, but I didn't believe you. How *could* I? This is…unbelievable."

I nodded again. "I know."

"Who *are* they all? Where are they from?"

I shrugged. "Who knows? College girls, like me? Townies? No way are they all local though. We'd have heard if this many local girls were missing."

"What if no one knows they're missing? I didn't know *you* were missing." She took my hand in hers. "I'm still so sorry about that."

"Quit apologizing." I glanced around me, and quickly counted the cabinets against the wall. "There are twenty-four drawers. We should see if they're full."

Lucy struggled upright, balancing against the wall and favoring her right foot. I reached out an arm and pulled her to me. Leaning against each other we hobbled to the cabinets, taking care not to bump any of the bodies on the metal beds. Each was plugged into a socket in the floor, and their cords threatened to trip us up with every step. With time and extra care, we made it to the wall of cabinets unscathed.

The wall itself was intimidating. *Twenty-four bodies might lie in these drawers*, I thought. *Twenty-four more girls.* Lucy gave me a look, and I lifted an arm. I yanked on a cabinet handle, but it resisted. It was locked. Lucy tried a different one. Locked.

"I want to know what's in there."

"More bodies, I'm sure," said Lucy. Then, as if having an epiphany, her eyes lit up. "This is bad," she said. "No one here is going to help you."

"Yeah," I said, nodding. "I think I agree now. We should leave."

The wind howled outside the cabin, and then, within, we heard a loud, echoing click. The hair on my arms rose as a surge of electricity crackled around me. I rushed to the door on unstable legs and reached out for the doorknob. Sparks crackled as my fingertips approached the metal knob. I ignored them, and grasped and turned.

For the first time in our surprisingly odd relationship, the doorknob was locked. I tried again, twisting, rattling, pulling, and shaking it in desperation. It wouldn't budge.

I turned to Lucy. "We…can't…"

To my surprise, she only shrugged. "We couldn't leave yet anyway," she said. She pulled out her cell phone. "We need evidence. We need Ad…Officer Strong."

"Yes, but now we really *can't* leave. Like, physically cannot leave."

"Don't worry. We'll find a way. We're the good guys, and the good guys always win in the end."

I wasn't so sure, but I had no choice. I tried to believe.

"Do you have a signal?" I asked, pointing at her phone.

"No, but I'm a good photographer, aren't I?" Lucy walked to the body on the ground and knelt beside it. She reached out a hand and touched the girl's chin, pointing the face toward her. "She's warm," she said. "Not cold like you." As I watched from my place against the cabinets, she snapped a picture with her phone.

Then she walked to the next girl, still on the table, and snapped another picture. Then to the next girl, and the next.

"Brilliant," I said.

"I can send these to Adam when we get out of here. I mean… Officer Strong. Whatever. Maybe it'll help let these girls' families know what happened to them. I don't think they're going to make it home."

I nodded, and didn't point out: I probably wasn't going to make it home, either. No one was going to save me, at least not in this godforsaken laboratory. My quest for self-preservation was falling apart around my ears…and including my ears. I reached up and sure enough, one was gone.

Oh well. Just one more thing to fix.

But maybe, just maybe, I could help make things right before it was my time to go. "Yes. Let's help them."

WE WALKED FROM GIRL TO girl. I adjusted the stainless steel lamps hanging over each body while Lucy took their pictures. There were twelve girls in all, including the one who'd fallen. All were silent, immobile, and all were plugged into the electrical sockets in the floor beneath them. We had no way of knowing if any of them would wake up like I did, but it didn't look likely. According to Lucy, the smell in the room was overwhelmingly of death and decay, and more than once she dry-heaved over a rusted trashcan.

I, of course, couldn't smell a thing.

Each girl was lovely in her immobility, like Snow White in her glass coffin, awaiting her prince. There was a brunette with pale skin, dots of pink just barely marking her cheek with a slight sign of life. A redhead with freckles covering the whole of her face. Several blondes with orange-tan skin. Not one was overweight, not one was anything less than beautiful.

I thought of myself prior to my own transformation into a half-dead monster-robot-cyborg-*thing*, and I realized exactly how beautiful I had once been. Young, vibrant, imperfect for sure, but maybe all the more beautiful for my imperfections. It takes dying, or something close to it, to get a teenage girl to realize her own beauty, I guess. At least, it did for me.

I turned to Lucy, so focused on getting the pictures of the girls *just right*, and took note of how beautiful she was, as well. We'd often been stopped while walking on campus by boys who would stare into her blue-green eyes and say nothing more than a vague hello.

"You're not safe here," I said, looking around the room. "You're a target."

"I *know*."

"Let's *go*! Find some other way out."

"Not yet. I'm not finished."

"Lucy," I said, forcing a useless sigh. "It's too late for me now. Seeing all this? It lets me know that. So now I have one job." I glanced around the room, at the lifeless girls on the tables. "I have to save you. But I can't do that while we're here."

"You know…" Lucy said.

I never got a chance to find out what I probably *didn't* know, though, because right at that moment, a bigger, more tremendous power surge ripped through the room. Light bulbs burst in their stainless steel cylinders. The computer in the corner buzzed and beeped in an alarming way. I was almost blinded by the light that flooded the room, and Lucy dropped to the floor, shielding her eyes and covering her head. Then once again static crackled around us, as loud as any thunder in a summer storm.

Too bad this thunder came in the dead of winter.

It ended almost as soon as it started, and we lifted our heads.

"Goddammit!" Lucy said. "This place is a funhouse of terror, isn't it?" She pulled herself to her feet, slowly and carefully, gripping the nearest table for leverage, her phone still clutched tightly in her other hand.

"What's next?" I asked, my voice shaky and weak.

As if in answer to my question, the lights went out, and Lucy and I were once again plunged into pitch-black. This time, even the computer screen went dark. We screamed again.

We couldn't help it. In the darkness, surrounded by death, we screamed like helpless, little girls. I hated it.

Beside me, something moved. "That you, Luce?" I spoke into the darkness, loud enough that she heard me and ceased shrieking.

Her voice came from afar. Neither of us had kept still during our screaming; we'd fumbled around, trying to find each other, but failed. "No, I'm over here, next to the wall." There was a dull thud. "What was that?"

I knew. I hated that I knew, but I did. "The girls. They're waking up. The power surge woke them." I sounded freakishly calm, even to myself. But I was surrounded by girls like me, and they were waking up. I could *help* them.

"Jo! Something's touching me! Jo! It's cold!"

"It's okay, Luce. It's just the girls." I looked around me, and even in the darkness I could see their unsteady shapes, rising from their tables. My eyes were adjusting rapidly to the lack of light, and I found if I squinted just so, I could see pretty well. "Girls, it's okay. Lucy, it's okay. Everyone, we're going to be okay." I remembered how scared I'd been when I'd awoken. "I'm here. I'm Jo. I'm just like you, and I can help you."

From around me came the rustling and banging of stiff,

uncoordinated bodies sitting up and sliding off tables. There were crashes as some rolled and fell to the floor. Just like I had. And still I stood, motionless, speaking, watching. "I'm here to help. You're going to be fine." I spoke with a confidence I didn't know I possessed.

I felt a hand on my arm. A girl stood beside me, unsteady and unsure. She was one of the blondes, and even in the pallor of her partial death, even in the darkness, she was beautiful. Her skin was supple, where mine was taut and gray. She reached with her other hand and held my arm in both of hers.

"Lucy," I whispered. "Luce, come over here."

"I can't," she whispered loudly. "I think I'm stuck. I can't see you. Where are you?" She'd moved further down the wall, toward a corner, clearly not feeling the kinship that I felt with the girls. There were five of them between us.

I covered the hands on my arm with my own, and squeezed. "I know you're scared," I said to the girl attached to the hands. "But I'm here. It's okay."

Around us, the girls stumbled as they walked. They seemed to be targeting Lucy and me, which made sense. They were scared. They needed comfort. Then one let out a moan, and I smiled, remembering my own experiences in relearning speech.

"It's okay," I said to her. "Go ahead and moan if you need to. You'll figure out how to make words again in a minute. Keep practicing."

Around me, other girls took up the moaning. The sounds were guttural, primitive, and I wondered: *Did I sound that bad?*

"Jo?" Lucy's voice cut through the moans, though it was meek, shaking. She was terrified.

"Calm down, Lucy. We're going to help these girls, aren't we?" I squeezed the hands on my arm again, patting them as comfortingly as I could.

The hands on my arm began to squeeze. The blonde girl attached to them began to moan, quietly at first, and then louder, her voice blending with those already filling the room. She squeezed harder.

With horror, but without pain, I felt the fingers penetrate the flesh on my arm, reaching through until they hit bone. I felt the brittle bone break.

"Stop," I said. "Don't do that!" I tried then to pull her hands from my arm. I couldn't. The girl moaned again.

It sounded different, though, than I remembered my own voice sounding when I first tried to speak. These moans were more animal, less human. Feral. Vicious.

And suddenly, I was scared. Really, truly, indescribably terrified.

CHAPTER 11

GOO OOZED FROM the new lacerations in my arm, clinging to the fingers of the girl who held me in her vise-like grip. I was surprised; really, I thought I was all dried out by then. Fluid exiting my wounds was as baffling as the fact that the girl was trying to hurt me. My mouth opened, forming a silent O as I stared at her.

The other girls took up the moans. Animalistic, sub-human moans. The guttural sounds told me these girls weren't waking up like I did. They were waking up as something else.

Lucy screamed. Louder than before, and more shrill. It cut through me like a warm knife through butter.

She lingered in the corner, surrounded by four girls, each shuffling toward her. She stood propped against the wall, holding out one hand like a football player stiff-arming an opponent.

A girl leaned in toward Lucy, her mouth open wide. In the dark, her teeth glistened. They looked sharp. *Did they sharpen her teeth? To points?*

They did. Lucy screamed again.

The girl gripping my arm leaned toward me in the same way. Mouth open, ready to bite.

"Oh, hell no," I said. "I'm nobody's breakfast."

I reached up and shoved my free hand into her gaping mouth, as far back as I could push it. She clamped down on my wrist, but it didn't matter. I couldn't feel anything. So I kept on pushing my arm into her mouth until my fist reached the back of her throat.

I had no idea if the girl could feel anything, but she had a gag reflex.

She yanked her head away and let go of my arm, reeling back until she stumbled, cracked her head against one of the tables, and fell to the ground. She didn't get up. I was free.

"I'm coming, Luce!" I shouted.

I ran, as best as my battered legs could, to my best friend. The girls between us were all focused on Lucy, readying themselves for an attack. They sniffed, they leaned in, they moaned, and she screamed.

I dropped one shoulder and slammed into the first girl. Domino-style, she fell into another, who took out another, until there was just one girl in my way. She was the closest. She moaned, and lunged.

Lucy dropped to the ground, and the girl crashed into the wall. I slammed into her from behind, and we both fell to the side. She tried to bite me, but I shoved her aside, pushing her halfway across the room as if she weighed nothing more than a notebook.

"You all right, Luce?" I said. She lay on the ground beside me, trembling and coughing.

"Yeah," she said. "How'd you do that?"

"Don't know."

Adrenaline? I thought, forgetting that I probably had none. I shrugged, then pulled myself to standing and helped Lucy up. Around us, the girls regrouped for another attack. "We need to get out of here."

"You think?"

I slid an arm under hers, and she leaned on me. Together, we walked about as well as the freshly awoken monster girls. Which is to say, we were clumsy. At best.

But we had a bit more determination than the others as they continued their pursuit. I'd knocked many to the ground, and some were still too clumsy and disoriented to get up. They created numerous speed bumps, tripping up those girls who remained on their feet.

We also had a head start, heading away from the locked front door toward another door in the back of the room. We had no idea where it would lead, but I hoped it would be better than facing more robot-monster-girls.

Together, Lucy and I half-hopped, half-limped to the other door. We reached it with barely any wiggle room between us and the slobbering, drooling group of hungry girls.

THE STEPS BEHIND THE DOOR went down. Way down. They were steep, and lit by fluorescent lights on the slanted ceiling. But those lights flickered dangerously, as if they wouldn't remain lit for long.

Every so often, the single, solitary door standing between us and the girls upstairs rattled and shook. They were coming for us, and there was no lock. The door never opened, though.

I guessed the girls didn't remember how to turn doorknobs yet.

Lucy and I walked down, as quickly and carefully as we could. And down. And down. On our way, we stumbled, we tripped, we caught and clutched each other as my knees and hips gave out, and Lucy's bad ankle refused to support her weight.

It felt like the stairs would never end.

"Do you think someone's down there?" Lucy whispered.

"I have no idea," I said. "But what choice to we have? Do you want to go back up there? Those girls tried to eat us."

She shook her head, bit her lip, and walked on.

After fifty steep steps—I counted—we reached another landing. A huge room opened before us when we slid open another unlocked door. More fluorescent lights filled the room, though a faulty one in the center offered a strobe effect like a bad nightclub on a hot summer's night.

Lucy closed her eyes and smiled as we entered the room. She placed her hand on my shoulder, letting me guide her, and she checked out for just a minute.

Her voice was dream-like. "I can almost hear the bass," she said. "Remember last semester when we…"

"Danced on the speakers at the club? Yeah, I remember." And I did.

I was alive. Whole. Beautiful. Lucy and I snuck into a dance club using fake IDs and a cheap pickup line on the bouncer. We wanted to dance.

Boys snuck us drinks, and we were intoxicated with the atmosphere. It was electric.

Lucy climbed onto a giant speaker beside the DJ booth. All eyes in the room were on her as she danced and swayed. After a minute by herself, her eyes scanned the floor, locking on mine. Her best friend.

When she reached out her hand to me I took it. I let her pull me up beside her. I let her slide against me, and I let her dance. Soon I danced, too. Our hips shook to the thump thump thump of the beat as it rattled beneath our feet. Our bodies moved together, hands entwined, eyes locked only on each other.

We danced until the club closed. Until bouncers forced us down from our tower thrones. Until we were so hot and sweaty and thirsty we thought we'd die.

Together we stumbled home through the snow, back to Calvin Hall, where we collapsed in Lucy's bed with our shoes still on our feet. We giggled and held each other and told loud, silly secrets until the sun came up, when finally we slept.

When I awoke, hours later, we were still holding hands.

BUT WE WEREN'T AT THE club. We weren't even in the dorm. We were in a flickering basement room beneath a morgue disguised as a rustic mountain cabin. And we weren't alone. Above us a group of monstrous girls waited to destroy us.

It was time to take stock of the situation. Looking around me, I saw a cot, centered and lonely, bland and militaristic, leaning against a wall on the far side of the room. I walked to it and ran my hand along the smooth metal frame. *My "creator" slept here*, I thought. *I wish I could burn it.*

Lucy hobbled over behind me. "It smells musty down here," she said. "And like death. Like you."

"I guess I should be relieved you're still distinguishing between the last two."

It came out sharper than I intended, and Lucy put a hand on my damaged forearm. "Jo. Don't be like that." She paused, and then squeezed, her face contorting with disgust. "Yuck. What happened here?"

"One of those girls got me. I think it's broken."

"Definitely broken. I just touched your bone. It was pretty jagged."

"You're not gagging?"

She sighed. "I guess I'm getting used to it. What's that over there?"

We walked to a long teacher-desk, all wood veneer on top and mint-green metal on the bottom. The rusted chrome door handles each hung by a single screw, as if the other had been requisitioned for some other use. I ran a hand along my abdomen. *Wonder if it's in here.*

I didn't wonder for too long. The top of the desk was littered with tantalizing-looking papers and notebooks and office supplies. Lucy reached out to steady herself and knocked a notebook to the ground. "Oops," she said as she leaned over to pick it up. "Clumsy me. Now I guess I have to read it. See what the hell's going on here."

I nodded. She opened the notebook and started reading, her eyebrows furrowed together to form a tiny crease of concentration. I grabbed a stack of paper close to me and began to flip through them.

They were memos, mostly, and a couple of letters. There was a thick manila folder deep within the stack, on the cover of which was written, in blood-red marker: *OoA—Soldier Design Documentation.*

Soldier? I thought. *What soldiers? How do you design a soldier?*

Images of camouflage and guns filled my head for a moment as I set the other papers down on the desk and flipped open the folder.

On the first page were two crude outlines of a woman. The major organs like the heart, lungs, and brain were there in the first drawing, along with lines that had to represent veins and arteries.

In the second, the heart was replaced by a box around a positive and a negative symbol. Dots down the front of the abdomen seemed reminiscent of the metal nubs that poked out through my own skin. Arrows and handwritten notes covered the pictures, and most of the notes had been crossed through in darker ink. It looked as though whoever had taken them had been frustrated, slicing and dicing their own notes.

Or they've been corrected by a teacher, I thought. I'd received plenty of papers back from professors, covered in similar cross-outs and arrows and notes.

I flipped to the next page, and the next. More drawings, and then formulas. Information on chemicals, and I saw the words "embalming fluid" multiple times. My knowledge of the periodic table of elements wasn't up to snuff, but I could see dozens of chemical formulas listed on each page.

Lucy leaned over my shoulder, and I jumped.

"Radium?" she asked. "Barium? What the hell are you looking at, Jo?"

I snapped it closed and offered it to her. "Design documents," I said. "Someone's designing people. I guess they designed me." I looked around the room, and a bulletin board nearer to the bed caught my eye. It was covered in photos.

"Do you see…" I started to say, but Lucy was ahead of me, already stumbling toward the photos.

Dozens and dozens of girls were posted on the wall. Small snapshots, mostly taken from afar. There were girls at local places: the nail salon and the grocery on campus. Others came from as far away as Boston. In the photos, girls smiled, laughed, and chatted with others. They held cell phones, smoothies. They were all young, all beautiful, all well-dressed and well-coiffed.

Just like me, I thought, nodding silently.

Across the top couple of rows, each photo had a little red X in the upper right-hand corner. I followed the path across and down the photos with my finger. X, X, X.

"I think they're all dead now," I whispered to Lucy.

She didn't respond. Lucy stood, her hand covering her mouth, her skin devoid of color. Anxious to see what had upset her, I sped up my journey through the photos.

First, I found myself.

There I stood, leaving Eli's apartment building on a sunny winter day. I looked perfect. I had been perfect, back then. In the photo I smiled, almost as though I knew someone was taking my picture, although judging from the framing it was taken through the windshield of a car.

In the corner of my photo, there was a question mark, circled. No X for me.

I guessed I was a big question mark for them. That was fine; I was a big question mark for me, too. "I found me," I whispered.

"Keep looking," Lucy said, sounding choked and muffled through her hand. She reached out and pointed, her finger shaking.

Down below, after the X's ended, were more girls. More targets, I guessed. And there, leaving the Rat only the day before, looking for me, was Lucy. She'd made their wall. She was definitely a target. Beside her was a picture of her mother. The ambassador.

I jumped back as though the picture had bitten me. "No," I said, but she nodded again.

"No," I said again, more firmly. "No. I will not let this happen, Lucy. No matter what else goes down, this...*this*...will not happen to you."

She nodded, but her hands shook. I pulled her away from the photos, toward me. I wanted to hold her.

But then something caught my eye. Another photo on the wall was circled, with an exclamation point gracing the corner. It seemed like... "Luce!" I said. "I think they succeeded."

"What?"

"Look," I said. "There's me. I'm a question mark. Everyone else has an X. But look! She's circled. She's got an exclamation point. That can only mean one thing, right?"

Lucy's hand dropped from her mouth. "But what *does* that mean? They succeeded in what?"

"I don't know, but I'm damn well gonna find out. Grab those papers you had. Get the notebook. We're taking it all, and we're getting the hell out of here."

We gathered all the paperwork we could carry, shoving papers and notebooks deep into the oversized pockets of my oversized parka. We could sort through it all later.

"So, HOW DO WE GET out?" Lucy said. She gestured toward the steps. "I'm not going back up there."

I shuddered, remembering the surreal feeling of my hand in another girl's throat. "No," I said. "Definitely not. There has to be another way. Do you have service yet? We need Officer Strong." The officer's involvement would spell the end of me, of that I was sure, but that fact was suddenly secondary to me. First and foremost, I needed to get Lucy to safety.

She shook her head. "I already tried. No service."

"Crap."

As if on some unknown, unseen cue, the lights went out again, and we were plunged once more into pitch-blackness.

"Crap!" I said, more forcefully this time.

I took Lucy's hand. "Can you use your phone as a light? So we can find our way out?" I glanced around. "I mean, I can see, sort of, but a light would help."

"Yeah. I can't see a damn thing." She pulled her phone from her pocket and unlocked it. Its light was bright and provided comfort, and the ability to not knock our heads off on low-hanging shelves. We inched our way along the wall, Lucy's free hand gripping my shoulder, toward a door at the far end of the room.

"Hello, ladies," said a voice. It seemed to come from all around us, from a hidden sound system put to good use in freaking girls out. It worked. Lucy and I clutched each other and froze in our tracks.

The voice came from everywhere, burying us with its weight. Loud, throaty, mechanized. A computer speaking with a human's syntax, with no gender, no identifying characteristics.

It was the voice of evil. My knees went weak.

"This is bad," I whispered, as if Lucy needed me to tell her that.

"Hello, ladies," it said again. "You do know it's proper manners to say hello when someone greets you, don't you?"

I searched the room, looking for something to show us from where the voice came. I held Lucy's arm with my decrepit hand. I felt like a girl under a magnifying glass, pointed into the sun.

For her part, Lucy went suddenly calm. She fumbled with buttons on her phone, squinting in the faint glow of its screen. I didn't know what she was doing until I saw the red light on. *Lights, camera, action.*

"Hello." She spoke into the darkness. Her voice was strong, powerful. "Who are you? What do you want with us?"

"You don't think I'm so silly as to identify myself while you have a camera rolling, do you? I credited you with more brains than that. It's one of the reasons I decided I want you. I've enjoyed watching your ingenuity while caring for your little friend."

"Screw you," I said, maybe a little louder than I intended.

"Not helping," Lucy whispered. "Don't antagonize them."

The voice agreed. "Now, now, that's not how we speak to our friends. I'm your creator, and therefore your friend. I love you, and I'm so glad you've come home to me."

One minute the voice seemed to come from above, the next from below. I spun my head around, trying to see something, anything, that would tell me how to get us out of there. *Keep it talking,* I told myself.

"What did you do to me?"

"Jo, dear, I thought you already knew. You read our memos, didn't you?"

I shook my head. "I had a hard time reading in the strobe light. You know, you guys really should fix your fluorescents. Those lights flashing like that? That can cause migraines. Or seizures."

Beside me, Lucy giggled. "I bet you guys have lots of migraines, right? Since you're all kinds of psychotic?"

"What are you doing?" I whispered.

"Don't they usually go hand in hand? Migraines and psychosis?" She covered her mouth with her hand as she spoke.

"I don't know. I thought we weren't antagonizing them." If I'd had a heart that still beat, it would have been pounding right then, I knew. This banter wasn't helping.

"I changed my mind," said Lucy, growling a little. "They deserve to be antagonized."

"Hush…"

"*Ladies!*" boomed the voice. "Ladies, please, stop this bickering. This is neither the time nor place. Jolene. Dear. You have caused us more than a little trouble. We've spent the last two days searching for you, aching to find you, hoping all our work wouldn't be for nothing. As I'm sure you've noticed, it's not easy, creating you girls. Even with the proper supplies, and blueprints, there are accidents. Some girls don't take to the process as well as you did. You did so well, in fact, you woke up before we could finish you. You're a work-in-progress, and I'd like to see you complete. I think you'll be a masterpiece."

The voice paused, and an echoing static filled the room for a second. Lucy let go of me and pressed the heels of her hands to her ears, her face contorted in pain. When the static stopped and the voice continued, it sounded different, like another person was speaking behind the fog of mechanical distortion. "And now, the beautiful Lucille has returned you to us. This is *not* the time for you ladies to fight. *This* is the time to celebrate. *This* is the time for me to get back to work on you, Jolene. To return you to the state you were in prior to your little adventure. I've been watching while you explored our home, waiting for my friends to come join me. We can fix you, right here, right now, if only you'll give yourself over to us peaceably. And Lucy, well, my dear, it's almost time to get started on you, isn't it?"

"No," I said. I let go of Lucy and stepped away from her, putting some distance between us. I wanted to need a deep breath. I wanted it so badly. This seemed like the kind of moment that required a deep breath, a pause before I spoke. But I didn't need it. "Can you actually fix me?"

"Oh yes," said the voice. "You're not yet beyond repair. We can rehydrate, re-skin, re-humanize you. Is that what you want, Jolene?"

Behind me, Lucy squeaked. I turned my head. "What?"

She covered her mouth with her hand again, and her voice came out muffled. "Don't trust them," she said. "Please. I won't let them take you. Please don't let them do this to me. We have to fight."

I nodded, but took another step away from her. I looked up to the ceiling, where I hoped the hidden cameras were placed. "It's what I want, more than anything in the world."

"More than anything?"

Lucy squeaked again.

"Yes." I hung my head in shame. It was true. I still wanted, really wanted, to get my life back.

"Well, then," said the voice. "That's more like it. I'm so glad you're home, Jolene, dear. Now it's time to say goodbye to Lucy, isn't it?"

Lucy began to cry, heaving great, angry sobs beside me. I reached out to calm her but she pulled away.

She didn't realize I had a plan. It was the only way to save her. I let my arm drop, and I looked back up to the ceiling, still trying and failing to find the source of the voice. I spoke again. "Peacefully, of course, with one condition. I'll go with you, quietly, calmly, right now. But only if you let Lucy go." I hoped my voice sounded as firm as I intended it.

"Of course, Jolene," said the voice after a pause. "Whatever you say. Just say your goodbye and it's time to go."

A voice in my head said *no, no, no.* I did it anyway. As though I was dreaming, I felt myself open my arms to Lucy.

She held back. "No," she said, tears ruining the way her pale skin glowed in the darkness. "No, Jo. Have you not seen this place? How can you trust them?"

I pulled her to me anyway, moving through fog. I buried my face in her hair. I wished so hard I could smell her, then. Her shampoo, her perfume, her lotion. The smells of my life since our first day in the dorm.

She sobbed and clutched at my arms, my shoulders, her fingers digging into my ailing flesh. "Don't go," she cried. "Please, don't do this. I'll never see you again. Don't give up."

"It's the only way to save the both of us," I said. *I hope it's true, I hope it's true.* "You're going to be safe. You heard him. Safe. And they're going to fix me."

Hope rose in my chest, my throat. *It could happen. Our happy ending could really happen.*

I peeled Lucy off me. "I'm going to see you again," I said. "Soon. But just in case, I love you."

She fell to her knees. "They're lying," she sobbed. "How can you not see that? They want me, too, and they're going to kill you."

I had to let her go. I had to try. I lifted my head high and walked to the door. It opened easily in my hand. The sounds of Lucy's cries filled my ears as I stepped across the threshold. I let the door close. There was a click as the door locked behind me, and lights surged on.

Then the sound of moans, insistent and hungry, filled the room where Lucy stayed, as the other door opened and the monster-girls came pouring in.

Lucy screamed. "No! Jo! No!"

Design Doc 36-J
Iteration 7

There is, and always will be, a fine balance between being a free-thinking individual, and being a mindless soldier.

That lesson can be seen clearly in Iteration 6.

When allowing subjects to maintain full control of their unmodified brains, we have witnessed erratic behavior upon reanimation. One subject awoke early, escaped, and has proven difficult to capture. Said reanimation was premature and unexpected, and subject was alone upon arising.

Subject has proven herself resourceful and intelligent beyond all expectation. When we control the reanimation process, including indoctrination into the cause, subjects with unmodified brains may become our most powerful resources, as we have seen before.

However, as subjects retaining semi-normal brain wave activity require much more care, maintenance and control, we are now experimenting with cerebral modifications, the likes of which have never been seen in our experiments before. The results of Iteration 7, however, were not quite what we expected.

Instead of being innocent, childlike, thanks to their modifications, the girls (who reanimated much more easily and predictably and on command than their full-brain cousins) awoke in a vicious state. They were feral. Insatiable. Led entirely by the id. Similar to zombies of the old horror movies.

While our ultimate goal will be to find a middle ground, Iteration 7 was not a total failure. Those feral creatures will have a prominent place in our army. Their hunger, their lack of regard for their own safety, and their potential to do damage combine to make these subjects exceptional foot soldiers. We will maintain the brain scans from these Subjects (all of whom have, by now, been terminated) and plan to recreate subjects such as these at a later date.

In the meantime, for Iteration 8, the plan will be amended to include suppression of the amygdala and the hypothalamus, in an effort to stem their impulses.

"OH, HELL NO," I yelled.

The door was locked. I heard the mechanical click. I felt electricity in the air.

But I still held the knob, had never allowed it to turn to closed. They were too fast in their trap. The door pushed open as easily as it had moments earlier.

The scene before me was chaotic. Naked, partially dead girls swarmed around Lucy. There had to be two dozen of them, and I wondered from where they all came. Behind them walked three large, masked men in protective suits, carrying sticks that crackled and sparked at one end. I couldn't tell if they were trying to clear a path to Lucy to save her, or if they were simply prodding the girls forward. It didn't matter—they weren't going to get to Lucy either way.

Lucy backed herself against the wall, about twenty feet from the door. She wielded a pair of scissors taken from the desk, slashing and stabbing at any of the girls who got too close. She stabbed one in the arm; the girl didn't flinch.

"No!" I shouted.

Lucy looked up at the sound of my voice. "Jo?" she said.

The girls turned, too, and I got my first good look at them. Their eyes were vacant and their jaws hung slack. *They were all born today*, I thought, feeling heartbroken and wanting to protect them. I shoved the thought back. They were all…fresher…than me, more meaty, less sinewy, but their wounds poured forth the same greenish-brown ooze I knew filled my own veins.

Lucy had done some damage in those brief first seconds. The girls closest to her were marred with slices across their chests and abdomens, arms and legs. The jaw of one girl barely hung by a thread. She didn't notice, pushing forward despite her injury. She looked broken, inhuman.

But not altogether unlike me.

It doesn't matter what they are or I am, I thought. *I need to save Lucy.*

The shouts of men filled the room.

"Move!"

"Now!"

"Get her!"

Prodded by the men, the girls charged me, too. But I was ready for them. I reached out and grabbed the desk chair beside me. As the girls began to charge, I threw it, hard, into the parade of monsters. They fell back, crashing into each other and the men behind them.

Like dominos again, I thought. *They have issues with balance. I wonder if it's an inner ear problem.*

As the men fell, too, the girls turned on them, crawling over their prone bodies. The men were stronger, and well-armed, but not entirely invulnerable. Sparks filled the air from their electric sticks, and the girls turned, as one, to face their own captors.

"Lucy! Now!" I shouted. While the girls were distracted, Lucy darted away from the wall, heavily favoring her hurt ankle. She stumbled, she weaved. When a girl got too close, Lucy stabbed her in the eye, leaving the scissors there. The girl fell.

Go for the brain, I thought. I felt like I was in a zombie movie. But these girls weren't fiction—they were real, man-made monsters.

Lucy arrived at my side and we turned to the door. The voice over the speakers screeched. "No! They're getting away! Girls, boys! Get them! Lovelies, my lovelies, don't turn on each other! Get them!"

Lucky for us, no one was free to get us.

Lucy and I crossed the threshold, together this time, and I let the door slam behind us. I only hoped it would stay locked.

TOGETHER, WE COLLAPSED ON THE floor. She was panting, breathing so heavily I thought her lungs might explode.

"I thought," she said, gasping for air. "I thought you left me. I thought you left me to *die.*"

I pulled her to me. "I'm so sorry, Luce. So sorry. I just thought… it doesn't matter what I thought. I'll never leave you again, I promise."

She pulled me to her in a bear hug, and held me there, until she started to gag.

"I'm sorry," she said. "I can't be that close to you right now."

"I know," I said

I stood, and pulled Lucy to her feet. She wheezed, still out of breath, her hand over her mouth and nose, but we began to run, searching for a way out.

AT THE FAR END OF the room stood a man, pressed flat against the wall. I skidded to a stop when I saw him, and Lucy crashed into me from behind. We faced each other, the man and I, staring, gauging, thinking.

The man was small and bald. His eyes were tiny behind thick-rimmed glasses. *Horn-rimmed glasses*, I thought, remembering a pair my father wore when I was very small. He wore a long white coat, splattered with blood and other fluids. In his hand, he held a scalpel, pointed at Lucy and me.

I started to speak, but the words caught in my throat. Behind me, Lucy's hand balled into a fist and pressed into my back. She was ready to come out swinging, but I pressed her arm back to her side.

I stepped closer to the man and reached out my hand. Something about his face was familiar to me. I'd seen it before, staring down over me with a loving smile, brushing hair back from my forehead, caressing my cheek. Like a parent, or…a creator.

"You," I said. "You did this to me." It wasn't a question.

His eyes burned white, glowing in the strange, underground light. He froze, a rabbit in a hunter's sights, knowing he was about to die. But this man was no rabbit. He dropped the scalpel and turned. With a flick of his wrist, he pressed an unseen button. A panel slid back and he disappeared through a hole in the wall. *Down the rabbit hole,* I thought.

In an instant, he was gone, as if he'd never been there in the first place. I wondered if I'd dreamed him.

The voice from above pressed in on us again. "You shouldn't have done that, Jolene, *dear*. Any of that. I hope you realize how much trouble you are in."

I raised my hand, all my fingers clenched into a fist but for my middle.

Sadly, the middle finger on that hand was long since gone, so the effect was ruined.

But Lucy helped. She flipped off any and all cameras that watched us, and then she nodded. "Let's get the hell out of here," she said. Pushing herself from the wall, she hobbled across the room.

"Oh, *dears*, you don't really think there's a way out down here. There's not. The only way out is up." The voice sounded agitated, though. A little uncertain, perhaps.

"I think we pissed them off," I whispered.

Lucy's jaw was set. "Don't care." Her forehead creased in pain and concentration. "Keep moving."

We reached a new door and opened it, passing into yet another strange and mysterious room. This one was darker than the one we'd just left, and the door slammed shut behind us.

"Ladies, I think you'll like this room," the voice hissed. We couldn't escape the voice. It followed us everywhere we went. "You should turn on your light, take a moment to look around."

Lucy pulled out her phone, and then bent over and retched.

We stood in a surgical room. On two tables lay two naked girls, each cut open from neck to pelvis. Their organs lay atop trays on several rolling tables. While Lucy backed away, I stood and stared with a clinical curiosity. I counted four lungs, two hearts, two livers, and various other organs that I didn't remember from high school biology.

The floor and walls were a Jackson Pollock painting, splattered with red and black blood and other brightly colored fluids. Over each girl hung bags of green and clear solutions that dripped into IVs placed throughout her body. I imagined the stench was terrible, over and above anything to which I'd already subjected my poor, battered roommate.

Sure enough, Lucy stopped heaving and lifted her head from between her knees. "What the hell," she gasped. "I can't breathe in here."

The voice answered, cold and seething. "You see," it said, "you interrupted our dear friend, the scientist, mid-procedure, when there was no one else around to handle you two troublemakers. But now that you're here, we'll have to destroy you both. I'm not sure he'll get these two closed back up in time. We will add them to the list of girls you destroyed tonight, including yourselves. Just four more *mistakes*. Four more X's on the wall."

I looked past the horror show on the tables before us. There was a door at the other end of the room.

"Come on, Luce," I said, taking her arm in mine. "Keep moving."

"We can't just leave them," Lucy said, still gasping. "They're desecrating the dead."

"Good point," I said. I stared at the bodies. "Got a light? My guess is those chemicals are flammable."

A lifelong pyromaniac, Lucy always carried matches. She tossed me a half-full pack. "Do it."

"We don't know if there's a way out," I said.

"I don't care. Destroy it all. End this."

"What about all the evidence on your phone? The photos?"

Lucy's mouth was set in a grim line, her jaw clenched and hard. "What's more important? Notifying those parents, or stopping these people from ever doing this again?"

"You're right." We spoke quietly, our voices heavy with grief.

Above and around us, the voice roared. "What are you talking about? I can't hear you. What are you saying?"

I struck a match and I smiled. This was right. This was what we had to do. I was only sorry I wouldn't be able to save Lucy. Or to say goodbye to my parents and Eli.

The match's flame was small, but sometimes, big things come from small beginnings. I touched the flame to a girl's toe. She sputtered to light immediately, and then she burned bright green. I knocked an IV pole to the ground, allowing the chemicals to spill and ignite around the room.

"No! Stop it! Don't burn my beautiful girls!" The voice howled as if in pain.

The other girl caught fire, and Lucy pulled me away. "Come on, come on! You have to come now! We have to try to keep going."

A little piece of me wanted to stay, to end things there, on my terms. A spark alighted on my parka, and I watched with detached amazement as it began to smolder, working its way down toward my brittle, paper skin. Once it reached there, I knew, it would all be over in an instant.

From another room, pops sounded, like fireworks. The flames had spread rapidly as burning chemicals leaked beneath the door.

Meanwhile, the spark on my arm continued to burn, and I let it.

But then I turned and saw Lucy's face, flushed and sweating in the light. She was so alive, so vibrant. I couldn't let things end there. Not if there was any chance of saving her. And not while she still wanted to live.

I held out my arm and she patted out the tiny flame on the parka sleeve. We turned and ran for it.

We ran through door after door, room after room, but the fire kept coming. It roared as it consumed everything in its path. The voice over the speakers continued to yell things at us, but we couldn't hear over the constant thunder of the flames and small explosions. We passed through more surgical rooms, rooms filled with jarred organs, a room dedicated to brains. Whoever ran this outfit had been doing it for years. It was massive, it was organized, and it was all burning.

And still we ran, down, down, down.

Beside me, Lucy began to cough. Thick smoke surrounded us, and I knew it had to be burning her lungs.

I ripped the scarf from my neck and shoved it into her hands. "Breathe through this!"

She did, but her footsteps became more erratic. She leaned on me even more for support, until I was all but carrying her.

We're not going to make it, I thought, staring at Lucy while I pulled her forward. *This is the end.*

Her eyes pleaded with me to keep going. I tugged and pulled, holding her up by the back of the pants. I didn't stop. We came to another door. It looked exactly like all the others.

I ran into it, full force, yanking Lucy along beside me. It burst open, and my nonexistent heart soared with relief. We tumbled back into the outside world, our bodies spilling out to a shallow path on the side of a mountain, surrounded by a raging blizzard. We were free, but the flames followed us through the door, so I kept on running until my feet found ice and slipped, and we began to fall.

Lucy and I flew off the path and slid down through the snow, down the side of the mountain like children on a sled in the winter's first snowfall. We rolled and tumbled, and when we finally came to a stop, I didn't think we'd gone any less than two hundred feet. Up above, I could barely make out the flames and smoke pouring from the open door.

Relieved laughter bubbled out of me as I lay back in the billowy snow. I turned to Lucy, smiling, but then I saw her lying there, motionless. Face down in the snow.

I couldn't tell if she was alive.

Hi Jo,

Look, we need to talk. I'm sorry I yelled at you earlier; I just don't want you taking stupid chances at this point, you know? I don't want to see you get hurt.

I tried to call you and Lucy. Neither of you answered. I guess you're probably pretty pissed. I get it.

Just...don't do anything stupid, ok?

Love,

Eli

Baby,

Where are you? I tried calling you a few times this afternoon, but you didn't answer. You've seemed a little off lately. I know you have mid-terms and that you had that fight with your boyfriend, but please. My mom-alarm is ringing. Something's wrong. I know it.

If I don't hear back from you soon, I'm getting on the next plane to New Hampshire. Daddy too. We're concerned, and you know how he feels about your safety. AND you know how I feel about the dry New England winters. Please, call me. Email me. I'm here.

Love,
Mom

Chapter 13

"Lucy? Lucy? Are you dead? Oh my God, Lucy! Luce! Wake up!"

She lay in the snow, immobile. I leaned in close to her mouth to try to feel her breath on my face, but with my own diminished nerve endings and the blizzard raging around us, it was impossible. We'd fallen so far, and I was terrified of hurting her neck, but since she was unresponsive, I took a chance. I rolled her over and shook her. Hard.

"Are you alive?" I shouted over the noise of the wind.

Nothing. She was still. So I shook again.

Her eyes fluttered, then flew open. "Ow, ow, Jo, stop!" I could barely hear her.

"Are you alive?" I asked.

"Yes," she said as she struggled to sit up. "I think so." She looked around her and shuddered. "I'm so cold."

We were in the middle of nowhere, far from the car, far from any place we recognized. There was no going up, back to the laboratory, where fire and death awaited us. But I didn't think we were safe where we were, either. In the middle of the blizzard, in the middle of winter in the mountains, wearing only a coat, her only hat blown away into the abyss, Lucy was a sure goner. If we sat there and waited for someone to find us, she'd freeze to death in a matter of hours.

"We need to walk," I said. "Down, I guess."

"But my car?" Lucy looked up, where the flames from the lab were the only real source of light in the snowstorm.

"Later. We need to get you safe first. Can you walk?"

I pulled myself to my feet, struggling with every movement. Balance, coordination—they were no longer my strong suits. Then I leaned over and offered Lucy a hand. She groaned as she put weight on her bad foot. "I don't know how far I can go."

"Do you have service on your phone?"

She pulled it out. "No, and my battery's almost dead. I need to turn it off. Where's yours?"

"In the car."

"Oh."

We were still shouting to be heard over the wail of the wind, and I looked down the mountain. Thin trees were blown nearly in half, flinging massive gobs of snow through the air. "Damn. Should we build a little snow fort? Isn't that what you do in a survival situation like this?"

"We can't! We can't stay here! Someone might come for us!" Panic filled her eyes as I fought to quash my own.

I shook her again. "Luce! I'm not gonna let anything happen to you! I'm here!"

Her eyes were wild, terrified. "You're not going to leave me again?"

"No! I'll never leave you again! I told you!" I took my hand and wiped the frozen tears from her cheeks. "I'm so sorry I left you before. I thought it would save you."

Lucy nodded, and stood. "Okay," she said, back in control. "Then let's go. I can walk. My foot's numb anyway, and the snow should help the swelling."

"I'm sorry, Luce, but did you just silver-line *this*?" I waved a hand, indicating the forest, the snow, the fire. Lucy was known for her positivity around the dorm, but she'd just carried it to a whole new level. Lucy only smiled.

We started out slowly, carefully picking our way between trees and rocks, hanging on for dear life when wind gusts threatened to blow us both off the mountainside. The thick trees through which we walked provided a bit of shelter and probably saved Lucy's life. I don't think she could have survived had she been fully exposed to the vicious winds.

Still, we weren't getting very far. We stumbled. We fell. Our clothes were soaked and Lucy shook uncontrollably. I tried to distract her by talking.

"So, Officer Strong, huh?"

Through chattering teeth, she smiled for a brief second. "He called me today. I didn't even know he had my number. Asked me out for coffee." Her face was already red, but I thought she blushed.

"What? When?"

"That's where I went when you were resting. I knew you were okay, so I met him at the café on campus. I needed some caffeine anyway."

"You're joking!" The conversation seemed to distract her from her pain. She stopped shaking quite so badly, and we covered more distance than we had before. "I can't believe you didn't tell me till now."

"Stop. It wasn't a big deal. And he was sweet! Such a gentleman. Not like the other guys around here."

"What do you mean?"

"I don't know," she said. "He was all worried about me walking in the snow. Wanted to pick me up, take me home, didn't want me out there on my own."

Lucy stumbled again, and I grabbed her arm. Of course, then I tripped, and she had to catch me. We were quite the team, on the side of the mountain in the middle of a blizzard, but the near-fall ripped something in my hip, and I groaned. "Wonder why he was so worried," I said as we limped onward. "It's not like there's a chance you could, oh, get kidnapped!"

But we paid more attention to our path again, and moved more slowly lest we tumble over the edge.

Still, I thought about Adam Strong. He was definitely handsome. He looked to be in his mid-twenties, and even there, in the driving snow, it was easy to remember his smile. A brief flash of envy lit within me when I realized I'd never again have the excitement of going on a first date. I tried not to let that color my thoughts as I wondered about a policeman taking too much interest in a girl about whom he was a little suspicious. *What did they talk about*, I wondered. *Did they talk about me?*

I was lost in thought, still trying my best to support Lucy as my own body threatened to give out with every step, when she called out. "A road!"

"Get out your…" I started to say cell phone, hoping that since we'd made it to a road, Lucy's service would be restored. I froze when I saw the van, the same one from Primrose Path. Its engine ran, its lights were off, and it looked neither warm nor welcoming.

"Get back," I hissed, yanking on Lucy's arm. She tripped and fell backwards, landing hard on the uneven ground. She cried out in pain. Behind us, the lights of the van turned on and flashed in our direction. "Stay down! They've seen us."

A door slammed. "Jolene, Lucille, I know you're out there. It's just a matter of time until we find you." The voice was masculine, threatening us with an unsavory end to our tale. We trembled and clutched each other, shrinking further back into the bushes.

Another door slammed. This time, a woman spoke. "Come out, come out, wherever you are, girls. We love you, and we'll forgive you for the damage you caused up there. Don't worry. We have a backup plan." Her voice had an edge, sharp as a knife. I didn't believe a word she said.

I yanked on Lucy's arm and we began to crawl through the snow, away from our pursuers.

We made better progress this way, on our knees instead of Lucy's bad ankle, and were quieter. Footsteps and shouts hung in the air but soon faded into the distance. They couldn't track us in the blowing snow. A gunshot rang out, and I realized how close to the end we'd come. I collapsed to my stomach, dropped my battered face in the snow, and felt myself fill with a cold, solid panic. Lucy reached an arm underneath me and pulled me along with her.

After crawling for what felt like an eternity, we found a small cave, its opening partially blocked by a snow bank. Inside the cave was inky black, but it would do. I pushed my hands through the snow, carving out a bigger path for us, and we crawled inside. Outside, the wind kept howling, whistling, and crying like a deranged banshee across the opening, but inside we were finally still.

Not like our problems were about to let up, though. The temperature was still well below freezing inside the cave, and Lucy's soaking, partially frozen clothes weren't doing her any favors. I took her cell phone from her trembling hands, hit the power button, and said a silent prayer.

It took a few minutes to power up, but when it came back to life, it was with a whopping three bars of service. We cheered, and then Lucy started to cry. "I'm so cold, Jo. I've never been this cold."

I put my arm around her, silently cursing the fact that I had no body heat to share, and I pressed a button.

Officer Strong's voice came through loud and clear after the first ring. It was deep and powerful, like Superman. "Lucy! I've been trying to call you. Where have you been?"

"Officer Strong?" My voice sounded worse than ever, more like a frog than human girl. I tried to clear my throat, but it didn't help. Lucy was snuggled up against me, shaking and sniffling, and I kissed the top of her head before I continued. "It's Jo. I'm with Lucy. We're in trouble."

"What? Where are you? I'll come right away. Does anyone know where you are?"

"We don't know where we are, not really. Eli knew where we were going, though. I have a lot to explain."

His voice was steady, even. Comforting. "Okay. Right. I'm at the station. Stay on the line. We'll find you."

"Thank you," I said. "But can you come alone?"

OFFICER STRONG APPEARED WITHIN TEN minutes, a small miracle considering the storm. We heard his voice echoing through our cave as he approached.

"Lucy? Lucy?" He sounded bigger than life.

Lucy huddled against the wall of the cave, shaking, draped in the old parka I'd removed from my own body to try to shelter hers. Outside, the wind and snow had finally slowed, and it looked brighter, more like late afternoon than the deepest night. Since it didn't look like Lucy was able to get up and go to Strong, I did instead. Being impervious to cold and pain came in handy, though I'd lost another finger during our Primrose Path adventure.

"Here," I croaked when I neared the opening of the cave. "We're here."

"Jo," he called. "Thank God. How's Lucy? What's wrong with your voice?"

"There's something you should know," I said. "You might want to sit down."

"What are you talking about? There's nowhere to si..."

Officer Strong stood in the thigh-deep snow, wearing a long, thick wool coat and knee-high rubber boots, looking like he'd just stepped out of an old World War II movie. I shuddered when I realized he looked like the bad guys, the SS men with their powerful Aryan features. He tromped toward my voice, lifting his legs high to clear the snow bank. I stepped into the light.

He froze, and then began backing away. Crashing into a tree, Strong stumbled, and a clump of snow from a tree branch fell and crashed on his police hat.

I couldn't help it. I laughed.

"You look hideous," he said, after he stared at me for a moment, brushing snow from his face and gaping like a fish out of water. "What the hell happened to your face? It looks like it's caving in and falling off, all at the same time."

"Oh, is it?" I said, as deadpan as I could muster. "Eh, it's fine. I'll just stitch it up later."

"You're messing with me. Right? You're got on Halloween makeup for some reason. What the hell is going on, Jo? And how are you not freezing? Where's your coat?"

I snapped back to reality at the reminder of the cold I couldn't feel. "Lucy! She has my coat. We need to get her warmed up, fast! Come on!" Forgetting my face, I ran into the cave, slipping and sliding on the ice and snow on lumbering, stick-like legs.

Strong passed me quickly. "Lucy!" he shouted as soon as she came into view. She raised her head, weak but conscious, and stretched her arms out to him like a child to a parent. He ran to her and scooped her up in his arms. "You're frozen."

"Yes," she whispered. "But not all the way. I think I can still be thawed."

"We need to get you out of here," he said. He glanced back at me, and his voice grew more stern. "You, too. You're coming with us."

I scowled as he rushed toward the entrance of the cave, Lucy wrapped in his arms. It had been a long day, and I hated being ordered around. "Okay, *Dad*," I mumbled. And then I chided myself. *Very mature, Jo. Very mature.*

Officer Strong buckled Lucy into the front seat of his squad car after removing her wet clothes. In her underwear, wrapped in a thick blanket from the trunk, she looked lost and forlorn, almost like she was already dead. Strong turned the heat on as high as it went in the front seat before coming around to my side of the car and opening the back door. I climbed in.

"Sorry about the bars on the windows," he said, before tossing the thick, wet parka on top of me. If he meant it to keep me warm, well, I didn't need to worry about that, now did I? Not that it would've worked. The thing was dense with barely thawing frost.

I shrugged out from beneath its weight. "It's okay," I said. "Sorry for…all this." I waved my hand around, indicating myself, Lucy, the snowstorm. As I waved, the tip of my pinkie finger tumbled to the floor, pieces of me crumbling like the powdery, frozen snow blowing around us.

Strong turned white, and I watched him gag, and swallow it back. I appreciated that; I never did like vomit.

"Okay," he said, his voice suddenly weaker. "Time to fix this. Try not to drop any more body parts on the way to the hospital."

"No!" Lucy said, suddenly acutely awake and aware. She sat up and knocked the blanket from her body. Her nakedness, her body, was chilling to me, its smooth skin and curving lines such a stark contrast to my own rotting flesh. I couldn't take my eyes off her. Neither could Strong, until he reached over and tucked her back in like a child in a bed.

"Why not?" he said.

"I don't want her to die." Lucy barely choked out the words, she was so weak. Then she fainted, falling against the seat back.

Strong jumped, his shoulders jerking beneath the thick, dark coat. He took a moment to feel for a pulse on her neck, his face awash in unadulterated panic. At least minimally satisfied with her heartbeat, he slammed his foot down on the accelerator, jerking the steering wheel, and the police car fishtailed its way onto the road. We sped down the mountain, toward University Hospital. As he drove, keeping one hand on Lucy's bare wrist, he looked at me through the rearview mirror.

"You. Talk. Now."

"Yes, sir," I said, all tiny and meek. Physically, I didn't feel tired or sore or cold; emotionally, I was a wreck. I wished I could cry, so hard I'd choke on my own fluids and never breathe again. But the tears wouldn't come.

So instead of giving in to hysteria, I slowly, carefully, told him my story. How I woke up dead but not, powered by electricity and a battery I couldn't see. I told him how I ran. How Lucy was only trying to help me when she lied to him. How I was afraid to die.

About halfway through my tale, his cell phone buzzed. He picked it up. "Strong here."

There was a pause, while he listened.

"Yes, I'm in the car…"

"No, not yet. He's not…"

"Right, I'm on it." He hung up.

"What was that?" I asked.

"Don't worry about it," he said. "Keep talking."

I finished with our day's field trip, and was just warming up to my account of the monster girls when he pulled his car into the emergency room ambulance bay.

He turned to face me as he shut down the car. "I need to get her inside," he said. "You'll be safe in here, and I'll come out to get you soon as I can."

"You'll let me know how Lucy is? Right away?" My voice shook.

He nodded. "Yes. Just sit tight. Stay out of trouble. And seriously, you look like hell. You'll scare anyone who looks through the window. You better cover up."

With that, he yanked open his car door, pulled Lucy across the front seat, then hurried her inside, cradled in his arms. *His name really works for him*, I thought, after the ER door closed behind them. *Strong indeed.*

I WAITED FIVE MINUTES BEFORE I decided to leave. In the car, I was a sitting duck. Outside, I could run, I could hide, and I could hopefully make it back to the dorm. Unfortunately, I had no way of getting out of the police car's back seat. The back doors had no internal handles, and the divider between the front and back seat kept me from crawling through the front.

As did my stiff, battered, drying out body.

I'd pay for some full-body ChapStick, I thought, then brushed my hair back from where it hung in tangles before my face.

A clump of hair came away with my hand. My hair, which had once been long, blonde, and quite thick, was falling out *en masse. Salt in the open wound of my vanity.*

I brushed the hair to the floor of the police car, and then went back to plotting my escape. My next step was to kick the window. I hated to get Strong in trouble by damaging his car, but the way I saw it, circumstances had me beyond apologies. I braced myself against the driver's side door and gripped the armrest in my hands. I stared at the glass, wondering if the shattering glass would do even more damage to my poor body, but it probably didn't matter.

I spoke out loud, taking comfort in my own voice. "Unless they have a really great mud bath that will rehydrate me, and restore all my skin cells, I'll never win another beauty pageant." Then I laughed. "Not like I ever won one to begin with. But I could've! I swear!"

Outside the window, a winter bird flew across the orange-streaked sky. The wind blew through the trees, and the bird rode it, rising and falling at the whim of the breeze. It was free, utterly and uncontrollably free, while I sat trapped in a police car like a common thug.

I screamed and thrust my feet out across the car with all my strength. They hit the window with a tremendous crash, but I heard only the crunch of my own bones. The glass vibrated, but stayed intact.

After a few more kicks, the results were no better, and my foot hung on my ankle at a nauseating angle. I didn't doubt that something inside was broken or detached. It was quite possible that if I kept kicking, my foot would fall off entirely, and I wasn't quite ready to be an amputee at age nineteen, so I accepted the inevitable: I was completely stuck.

Crossing my arms across my chest, cringing at the snap-crackle-pop sound from my shoulders and elbows, I sat in the car and watched the world outside. The bird was gone from sight, and in the darkening evening sky, the lights of the emergency room bay spotlighted the emergent chaos.

A father walked by, carrying a little girl who held a towel to her lip. Her face was flushed with tears, but she looked safe, riding in her daddy's arms. Despite the terror in her eyes, I longed to be her for the fleeting moment. To be safe in my father's arms. It sounded like heaven.

An ambulance pulled beside the squad car, and technicians unloaded a gurney. On it lay a person, covered entirely by a white sheet. *Dead. Blissfully dead,* I thought. *It must be so nice. So much better than this.* Then I cursed at myself for being weak. Outside, there were shouts and cries as the gurney slid on some ice. A smallish woman dove after it, quicker than the massive men around her. She saved it before it toppled on its side, but it tipped just enough to dump the white blankets into the filthy snow. The body lay, still strapped to the gurney, silent because it wasn't a half-dead freak like me. The medics were paralyzed for a moment, but then, sheepish, they picked up the soggy blankets and covered the body's face. I tried not to care that the dead body looked far more alive than I.

Others came and left as the sky around the hospital darkened completely. They faded into a time-lapsed blur, and as they did I thought about Lucy. Lucy, who was inside the hospital, possibly dying from exposure and hypothermia. Lucy, who stood by my side while I literally fell to pieces. Lucy. My best friend.

Please be okay, Lucy. Please be okay. Don't be dead. I can't handle it if you're dead. Please be okay, Lucy. Please be okay, Lucy. It was my mantra as I stared out into the night.

Please be okay, Lucy. Please be okay. Lucy. Please be okay, Lucy.

It felt like hours passed while I sat there in the darkening back seat of Officer Strong's police car. With no watch on my wrist and no clock in the car, I had no way of knowing exactly what time it was. Out of nowhere, a dark body appeared outside my window. I jumped back from it, banging my head on the opposite side of the car as I tumbled to the floor.

"Officer Strong!" I said. "Finally! Is Lucy okay?"

But instead of Strong's long, dark coat, I saw a different pair of dark pants and dark jacket backlit by the flashing lights of an ambulance. Someone crouched down and looked at me through the window. But it wasn't Officer Strong.

From the OoA Files, dated February 15

Memorandum

Subject 632G-J remains at large. Removal from her current location has proven impossible, thanks to the crowds of students always surrounding her.
However, during the search, a new subject has been identified and apprehended. Subject's companion has too much knowledge and must be eliminated.
The search continues.

Hi Mom,

I think I need you and Dad to come.

I love you.

Your Jolene

Daddy and I are on our way. We'll be there by tomorrow evening. Hang tight, and call me when you can talk. My heart's in my throat. I'll see you soon. Baby, I know you don't have your own phone, but please, call me. As soon as you can. From any phone. I'll answer. I'm waiting to hear from you.

Love you.

Mommy

PART 2:
SACRIFICE

CHAPTER 14

I SHOUTED, AS BEST as a frog-voice could shout, first in fear and then in anger.

"Eli, you scared the crap out of me!"

He stood outside the police car, one arm against the roof, staring through the window at me. His face was pinched in a furious scowl, one that my haggard face would have mirrored if it could have. *As if he's the one who was abandoned, sent out to die, and then locked in the back of a police car like a criminal. As if he's the one who was falling apart.*

His anger only made mine snowball. I glared at him with my white-out eyes.

He yanked the door handle, jerked it open, and pulled me out.

"Come on," he said. "We're leaving."

I tried to pull away. "Quit! You might pull my arm off! Asshole!"

"Asshole? Me?" he hissed. "I'm the asshole who went running off and almost got Lucy killed? *I'm* the asshole? Come on. Get out."

Still I struggled. "I'm not going anywhere with you. I'm staying here, and waiting for Lucy!"

He spoke through a clenched jaw. "People are starting to stare, and attention is the last thing you need right now." He was right, but I wasn't about to admit it. "Besides, if you want to wait for Lucy, you're going to be waiting a long time."

My stomach dropped. I stopped fighting and followed him out of the car. "What do you mean? Do you know what's going on with Lucy?" Eyes followed us as we left the emergency bay and walked toward the darkened parking lot.

"Quiet!" he said, his voice sharp as a tack. "You sound like a monster and look even worse. Keep your mouth shut until we're in the car!"

I muttered one more "asshole" under my nonexistent breath, but followed in silence, dragging my bum ankle through the snow like a zombie-girl, until we reached his car. Even in the dark, I saw Eli shake his head in annoyance at me more than once. Fury radiated off of him like steam from a street after a storm on a hot summer day.

Eli opened the door for me, a gentleman even in moments of duress, and I half-fell into the car, pulling my bad leg in behind me. He closed my door and climbed into the driver's seat.

Finally safe in the solitude of a locked car, I felt like I could speak again. "Please, Eli! Tell me, I need to know. Have you heard from Lucy?"

Eli stared out the windshield and cracked open his window as he pulled out of the parking space, the tires slipping on black ice before finding traction and moving in the right direction. I reached over and touched his arm. "Please. Talk to me."

He jerked away from my touch and cracked his head on his window. He cursed, loudly. But when he spoke again a moment later, his voice was low and in control. "Don't. Touch. Me. Don't ever touch me again."

A memory flashed—Eli pulling off my shirt, kissing the tender spot just above my clavicle, as if he'd never be able to stop—and I almost cried out at its intensity. My hand fell silently to the center console of the car. I felt like I'd been slapped. "Please," I said in a voice barely audible. "Please. Just tell me what you know about Lucy. I won't touch you again. I promise."

Eli pulled the car into a spot in the far corner of the parking lot. He turned it off, but still wouldn't look at me as he spoke. "Lucy's going to live, but she's really sick, Jo." He was quiet and measured.

"Does she have hypothermia? Is she okay?"

"No," he snapped. "No, Jo. She has *arsenic* poisoning. *Arsenic!* Like it's a hundred years ago, and someone tried to poison her. But no one *tried* to poison her, Jo. Someone just did."

"Who?" I was confused. It had been a long day, and I never cared for riddles. "Just tell me!"

"*You* did, Jo! Who the hell else could it have been? You! You're filled with all that chemical crap. She's been breathing it in for forty-eight hours. And it's poisoning her. By trying to help you, she got sick. And then, oh, should we even *mention* again you two moron twins going out to try to find the bad guys on your own. You're *both* lucky you're still alive, or at least as alive as you are. What the hell were you two thinking?"

Crap, I thought. I needed comfort, support in this evil time, so I reached for his hand.

Of course he jerked it away again. "Stop trying to touch me! What, do you want to kill me, too?"

Shaking my head, I sagged against the passenger's side door. "I'm sorry," I whispered.

And I was.

IT WAS OUR THIRD DATE, *Eli's and mine. He made me dinner at his apartment and then we headed out to see a late movie. It was already past dark and the night had turned cold fast. I reached forward and turned up the heater. Eli caught my hand.*

"No, don't," he said, pulling my hand onto his thigh, wrapping his fingers around mine.

I yanked it away. I was cold. *"Why not?" I said, teasing. "Too cheap to pay for heat?"*

The car wound down a twisting, turning mountain lane, passing under occasional streetlights that let off hazy, foggy circles of light. As we passed through one, Eli glanced at me, then pulled the car to the side of the road with a jerk. The streetlight shone down on the car, filtering in through the windshield like the dying embers of a fire.

He reached across the car and took my cheeks in his hands. They were warm, and remarkably soft and gentle. He brushed a stray lock of hair from my lashes. "It's just…" he said, and then he looked away. I couldn't tell if he was embarrassed, or confused. Maybe he was both.

"What?" I said. My own voice was quiet, subdued. Soft. "What's wrong?"

He turned back to me, a sheepish grin on his face, his cheek dimpling slightly. "It's just that you're so pretty when you're cold. Your cheeks get so pink. It makes me want to hold you close to me forever, you know?"

I slid across the car, pulling myself over the center console until I was seated partially on his lap, the steering wheel pressing deep into my hip. I leaned forward and kissed the smile from his lips, wrapping my hands around his neck. His mouth opened, and his tongue found mine. His hands wandered beneath my coat in search of warm, supple flesh. They found it, and he pulled me closer.

I CAUGHT SIGHT OF MY reflection in the window as Eli drove us back to the dorm, each of us sticking to our separate sides of the front seat.

Saying I looked ill would have been the understatement of the century. My eyes sank so far into my cheeks they looked like hollows in my face. The flap on my cheek, which I'd so carefully sewn the day before, was no longer attached and fluttered in the breeze that blew in through the open windows. Much of my nose was gone, leaving a hole in the center of my face, and what little remained was mottled black and gray. My lips were also gray, and when I opened my mouth, I saw receding gums and massive, chalky teeth. *Skeletal* teeth.

I was a monster. Uglier and more terrifying than ever before.

No wonder Eli couldn't bear for me to touch him.

I pulled off a glove, and as I did a fingernail dropped to the floor. Eli shuddered. "You're *not* leaving that in here. Pick it up. Throw it out the window."

There was nothing I could do but comply. He deserved more than detached fingernails on the floor of his car. We drove the rest of the way to the dorm in silence.

When we pulled up to Calvin Hall, Eli gave me a critical glance. "Well, we can't take you past the front desk looking like that, that's for sure. Don't want another death by heart attack on our consciences. I'll have to slip you in the fire door."

"Won't you set off the alarm?"

"Nope. We used to sneak beer in all the time that way freshman year. There's a trick to the latch." For the first time, I saw a shadow of a smile cross his lips, but he quashed it before it could grow.

"Are you coming up?"

He nodded. "Let's go."

We wrapped my head in a scarf, my ski mask long since disappeared, and pulled a hoodie up over it. Eli kept a hand on my back as he pushed me through the open fire door and into the elevator, which was good since I was starting to feel my battery run low. Any help in propulsion was appreciated.

The elevator was empty, and I said a silent thank-you to whatever god was watching out for me. Eli covered his mouth with his sleeve, a cheap barrier against my stench and chemical emissions. I tried not to feel bad about it. It was better that he protect himself. I didn't want *him* being sick on my conscience, either.

As we walked down the hall, I noticed my door stood open. "That's weird," I said, but it was also lucky. I didn't have my keys with me anymore; they were back in Lucy's Honda on Primrose Path. A place to which I never wanted to return.

"Since when do you leave your door open?" Eli said.

"Um, I don't know that I did."

He gripped my arm and froze. "Do you think someone's been in there?"

My head swooned; it had been a long time since I'd left the cozy warmth of the car charger. "Not…sure…" I managed, before I collapsed.

I WASN'T OUT LONG THIS time. Eli carried me past the prying eyes peeking out from other dorms. We reached my bed, and he plugged me into the wall. My eyes fluttered open almost immediately, and, out of sheer habit and shock, I gasped.

My room was a disaster. Ransacked, searched, whatever you wanted to call it, it had been done to my room. Clothes were strewn about, hanging on furniture and across my mirror. My laptop lay in the middle of the floor, the screen-saver flickering. Books, notebooks, pens and pencils. The mess was everywhere.

"What…" I said, as soon as I took it all in.

Eli sat at my desk, looking confused. "No idea," he said. "But if you and Lucy didn't leave it this way, apparently someone's looking for something."

I was still woozy, but I sat up in the bed. "Will you bring me my computer please?" I said. "I can't get up quite yet."

Eli nodded, did as I asked, and then retreated to the other side of the room.

The laptop came to life as soon as I touched the space bar. A browser was open, set to my email, and an email from my mother was highlighted. I shrugged. I didn't feel like talking to her right then, so I left the email unread.

"Whatever," I said. "I'll just clean it up later."

Eli shrugged again. "Shouldn't we call someone?"

"Who?" I said. "Who would I call? The police? Campus security? The President? We already know someone's after me, and I doubt anyone can help. Besides, I'm sure Officer Strong will come by at some point anyway. Seriously." I thought for a moment. "Look, Lucy's safe now. She's in a hospital, far away from me, and safe from whoever's doing this stuff. That's what matters most. And you...you should leave too, Eli. Just go, far away from me. So I know you're safe, too. The rest of it? It doesn't matter. They can have whatever they want from this room."

Eli nodded. He still looked so angry with me, I couldn't bear to look at him. He stood up and headed toward the bathroom.

"You're not leaving, are you," I said. It wasn't actually a question.

"No. Strong made me promise to stay with you when he called me. To keep you safe. He actually told me to wait with you in his car, but that sounded stupid. I can keep you safe here. But I'm staying in Lucy's room. With the door closed." He sighed, and suddenly he looked less angry, more sad. "You know, Jo? All this stuff going down? It's dangerous. Someone's going to get hurt. And I almost wonder, well, maybe it would've been better if you'd just died, like a normal person would have."

He left my room and closed the door behind him.

Alone, I used all my strength to walk across my cluttered room, pulling my cord behind me. I sat down at my desk and stared into the mirror at my monster face. I replayed his words in my head, over and over and over. They hurt, like a knife to the throat, and as much as it pained me, I knew he was right.

As I stared, to my surprise, a single, green-tinted tear rolled down my cheek.

I brushed it away with an angry swipe—*too little, too late*—and turned back to my computer.

Jo1995: Did you know #arsenic poisoning can cause severe abdominal pain, nausea and vomiting? Me, either.

Jo1995: Holy crap, it also causes cancer. You hear that? #Arsenic causes cancer.

Jo1995: Ew, the rashes caused by #arsenic poisoning are disgusting!

Jo1995: Why isn't #arsenic trending yet, people? This is serious stuff!

Jo1995: I am the worst friend ever. Stupid #arsenic.

EliPete21: @Jo1995 Go to bed, Jo.

Jo1995: @EliPete21 I can't! Come talk to me?

EliPete21: @Jo1995 Hush

THE SOUND OF infomercials from Lucy's room was about to put me over the edge.

Ladies, are your thighs not what they were when you were twenty? Well, this ThighBuster machine will slim them right down so you can fit into your sexy skinny jeans again.

Check out what the MasterSham will do for you! Watch as I pour this gallon of liquid on my carpet. One touch with the MasterSham and the carpet is dry as a bone!

MasterSham, I thought. *My life IS a MasterSham. I AM a MasterSham.* I looked down to my legs, on which the skin was starting to crackle. *And if I lose any more of my thighs I'm in even more trouble.*

I stood up from my desk, unplugged, and headed to the bathroom. Chances were Eli was sound asleep over there. I always gave him a hard time for falling asleep with the TV on full blast, and I figured I could sneak in, turn it off, and at least have some quiet in my room. On the way, I stopped at my open window and took a peek outside. The snowy squall of the afternoon was finally over. The moon shone brightly on the fresh snow, and the smoking bench was surrounded by other students from my dorm, smoking and talking and laughing like they hadn't a care in the world. I used to hang out there sometimes, never smoking, telling lewd jokes like I was cooler than I actually was, trying to out-gross the boys as a way of fitting in. Those days seemed distant, and I missed them desperately. Longingly. I rested my battered hand against the glass of my window, pressed against it, reaching out for a life that was no longer my own.

As I stared, a black-hooded figure caught my eyes. He stood slightly behind the smoking group, set back within the trees beside my building, not far from my window. The smokers didn't seem to notice his presence. I couldn't see the figure's face, but he saw me, and raised a hand in greeting. I jumped back.

"Eli!" I shouted. "Eli, get in here! Quick!"

I may have sounded like a deranged bullfrog, but at least I was loud enough that within three seconds Eli stood beside me. He was bedraggled, confused, startled. "What? What happened?" He'd not yet rubbed the sleep from his eyes.

"There's a man outside my window!" I said, pointing. "Look!"

Eli ran to the window. "The smokers? Jo, what are you talking about?"

I looked, and he was gone. The smokers, however, gazed upward at my room, their eyes drawn by the noise I'd made and the light in my window.

"No, a man! Right behind the smokers!" I was frustrated. He'd been there. I saw him. I thought.

"Well, he's gone now. I'm sure he heard you. There's no way he *didn't* hear you. I'll look for footprints in the morning." He was shivering, even though he wore pants, shoes, socks, and his fleece.

I closed the window, using my full body weight for leverage. I didn't think I could rely on muscle strength anymore. "Right. Fine.

Someone's out there, *right now*, Eli! I swear! It's probably one of the guys who chased us today!"

He sighed. "Maybe. Possibly. But what would you like me to do about it? I'm just one guy."

"Should we call Strong?"

"He's busy with Lucy. I spoke with him earlier, before I came to get you. He's not leaving her side." Eli actually smiled, then turned back to the window. "About time that girl found a good guy. She's sweet. I like Lucy. Always did. Thought you and she made a good little team."

I resisted the urge to go to Eli by repeating the word "arsenic" to myself like a mantra. I wanted to run to him, let him fold me up in his arms, let him pull me down onto the bed beside him. It was a childish need, I realized, to feel safe and protected, a damsel in distress with her knight in shining armor.

But I couldn't endanger Eli the way I had Lucy. And it wasn't exactly like he was dying to hold me anyway. "Go back to your apartment," I said. "I can take care of myself."

He shook his head no. Then, for the first time since I'd showed up at his apartment two days earlier, he reached out and brushed his fingertips gently across my cheek. He didn't wince.

I only wished I could have felt it. Really, truly felt his touch, apart from the vague pressure that washed across my face.

From the hallway came a shout, and then a knock on my door, shattering the moment of kindnesses and regrets. "Jo! Eli! Open up!"

It was Strong. Eli reached the door in two strides and threw it open.

"Officer Strong!" I said. "What is it? Is Lucy okay? Oh, God, is she…" I couldn't say the word.

He stepped in and let his coat drop to the floor. "No, no, she's fine. Lucy's fine. But we need to talk." He kicked off his tall, wet boots, and left them in the center of the floor, where melting snow collected in a soggy puddle. Strong sat in my desk chair, straddling the back and ramrod straight. "In the first place, why are you two here? Didn't I instruct you to wait at my squad car?"

"It was cold," said Eli. He shrugged. "Besides, I don't remember you being in charge of me. I don't have to listen to you."

Anger flashed, dark and heady, across Strong's face. His hands balled into fists. But then, as quickly as it appeared, it was gone, replaced by something calm and tranquil. *Like the eye of a hurricane,* I thought.

"This badge says otherwise," he said, mildly reaching into his pocket and pulling it out like a cop in an old TV show. "Next time I tell you something, you better listen."

Eli only shrugged again.

Adam made a yuck-face. "It stinks in here. Open the window, would you?"

As Eli stalked to the window, I propped myself against my desk, trying to keep weight off my bent and broken ankle. I crossed my arms in front of my body, preparing to hold myself together through whatever news Strong was about to deliver. "Please," I said, barely able to get the words out. An image of Lucy, dead beneath a white sheet on a gurney, sliding across black ice, flashed in my mind. I couldn't take it. "How's Lucy? Is she all right?"

They stopped facing off, alpha males staking a claim on my room, and as one, they turned to me. It hurt to see them both wince.

His attention fully on me, Adam nodded, but his face stayed grave. "I told you, she's fine. They're pretty sure she's out of the woods. The doctors warmed her up first thing, and now they've got her on fluids. That will help with the arsenic. I guess Eli told you?" I looked down at the floor instead of responding. "Okay. He did. So she should be fine pretty soon. When I left, she was sound asleep in her hospital bed."

Eli nodded. "Great news," he said, although he, too, was still solemn.

Adam continued. "I've come to tell you, though. You're not safe here anymore. You need to come with me now. You *both* need to come with me. As soon as you've, um, cleaned yourself up a little more. Can't have you in the car smelling like you do. I'll wait here." He settled into the chair, chin on his arms.

"No!"

I jumped. Adam jumped. We both turned to Eli, confused.

"What?" I said.

Eli took a deep breath before he spoke to me, as though it was just the two of us in the room. "I said no. We're not leaving here. We're not going with Adam. We're not going anywhere. It's the middle of the night, and this has been the worst couple days in my little stupid life." He turned to Strong. "I haven't heard or seen you do anything that makes me think Jo is any safer with you than she is with me, and I can take care of the both of us. Plus, you're the only cop we've spoken to. Where the hell are your friends? Why the hell haven't you ever called for, oh, I don't know, reinforcements or something? There's no one outside our building, no one offering us any explanation about what the hell happened to my girlfriend! Or all those other girls, either. Yeah, Jo told me about the others. There are people *dying* out there, and we have only you to deal with, and frankly, I don't trust you. So until you can tell me why you felt the need to come here at two o'clock in the damn morning, then no. We are absolutely, one hundred percent, *not* going with you."

I sat down on the bed, hard. Something in my back crunched like a bag of potato chips. Even though I knew it meant nothing in the grand scheme of things, I couldn't help but think, *He called me his girlfriend. Maybe that happy ending….* Even the thought trailed off. I wasn't blind.

The storm of Strong's anger flashed, but once again he forced that eerie calm over his face and body. Tranquility in a sea of calamity was certainly a skill I'd never mastered. *Maybe something they teach in the police academy,* I wondered, watching with an almost detached curiosity. Lucy was going to live; that was all I cared to know.

"Calm down, buddy," Strong said to Eli. "I don't think she's safe anywhere. And I've been purposely *not* calling this in until Jo tells me she's ready. Look, I like Lucy, I do. And Jo? I'm sure I'd have liked her if I met her before, you know? That's kept me quiet so far. But I *am* a cop. And it's my duty to do my best to help solve this case. When my colleagues get involved, well, Jo's right. She'll be at a hospital within minutes, and probably dead within the hour. So I'm trying to help you in a less orthodox way. I can't do that here, though. Not anymore. There are too many people."

"This is a public place," said Eli. "They can't exactly come grab Jo from the dorms, at least not without causing a ruckus. This is the safest place for her!"

Eli and Adam faced off, standing nose to nose like two cocks in a henhouse. If I didn't do something, someone was going to throw the first punch, and, from the look of things, Eli would wind up in the hospital beside Lucy.

I had an idea. I walked to my desk chair, sat down, and plugged myself back in. I looked at Lucy's phone in my hand and flipped through the pictures of the girls who, moments after getting photographed, had awoken and tried to kill me. I thought about the email from "my creator." *Screw that*, I thought. *And screw you. My parents created me. You destroyed me. You bastard.*

I slammed my fist down on the desk.

Microscopic pieces of me sprayed up, creating a cloud of toxic dust that wafted quickly through the breezy room.

Eli sneezed.

"What?" said Adam, staring at me.

"You two need to knock this off. You're being ridiculous," I said. "My safety doesn't matter anymore. What matters is catching these bastards, keeping them from hurting anyone else. I want to do anything

I can to make it happen. So use me as bait. Leave me here, or put me somewhere else, I don't care. Let them take me, and then you can catch them."

"No way, Jo. Are you crazy?" Eli's face turned purple.

Adam sighed. "Forget it."

"Are you crazy?" I said. "It's the only way."

Adam shook his head. *No.*

I shrugged. Frankly, it didn't matter to me what they said. It was my decision. "Look, it's my body. My life. I'm dead no matter what I do. There's no coming back from…from *this*." I paused, looked in the mirror, and shuddered. I was hideous. "I'm a monster," I said. "And there's no changing that now. So let me use what will probably be my last few days on this earth to do something good. Let me help you catch these bastards."

Adam nodded silently and placed a hand on my shoulder. I pushed it away. "Arsenic."

"Yeah," he said, and he stepped away again. "We need masks. Gloves." He looked out the window. "The thing is," he said, speaking to the darkness. "The thing is, that's the most unethical thing I as a police officer can do. But it's also probably the best plan we have. At least, it's the *only* plan we have. We can get you out of here, contact them. Let them come to you."

"You can't be serious." Eli looked furious. "You'll kill her. She can't fight back. She can barely walk. She doesn't even have a nose anymore, for God's sake. This will kill her. You will kill her." His voice sounded choked, but his eyes were dry. "I won't take part in this."

"Yes, you will. Because you know Jo's right."

"No. She's not going to die. Someone can fix this."

They'd started shouting somewhere in the argument, and I rushed to the window and slammed it shut. *Might as well keep the neighborhood noise pollution to a minimum*, I thought. I felt detached from them, as though I watched a play or TV show playing especially for my benefit, about some other girl in some other place with some other monstrous event. Though I knew they argued over me, I no longer felt like me, so it was easy to sit back and watch.

Eli once again pushed his face into Adam's, puffing out his chest and trying to look tough. I'd only ever seen him do that once, at a bar, with a ton of alcohol in his belly, and moments later he'd thrown a punch. A knock sounded at the door. "Everything okay in there, Jo?" It was my RA.

"Yeah," I called out, not opening the door. I shoved my way between the two guys to separate them, and they jumped away as though they'd been shocked. "Sorry, I'll turn the TV down."

"You sure? Can I come in?"

"No, I'm fine, I promise. And…um…I'm naked. Yeah. So no, you can't come in. Thanks for checking." I paused, and whispered, "Now please go away, thanks."

We held our collective breath. Well, I tried, anyway, and was remarkably successful. No surprise there, of course. Finally, the sound of footsteps leaving my door echoed down the hallway.

I didn't give them a chance to start fighting again. "Now you two listen to me," I hissed. "Either we are in this together, or I give up. Adam, you can call your friends. I'm done. But if we're in this together, we're doing it my way. You two assholes, about to start a fight in my room, get out. Now. I'm done with being guarded. Let me be. I want one more night in this room. You two just…watch. Wait. Someone's coming for me. I know it. Even here, they're not going to leave me alone much longer. So when they get me, catch them. It's really that simple. And now, it's the middle of the night. It's time. You two….get out." I walked to my door and opened it.

"Are you…" Eli started to protest.

"Out," I said.

"But…" It was Adam's turn to object.

"No. Get out. Leave me alone. Now."

They looked at each other and shrugged, on the same team for a moment. Adam picked up his coat on the way out. Then he looked back over his shoulder at me as he walked out the door. "Thank you," he said. "This is a very brave thing you're doing. My number's in Lucy's phone, if you need it. Tomorrow, we put your plan in action. I'll be here early. Be ready."

Bravery, I thought as I closed the door behind them. I listened to the murmur of their voices in the hall, planning and scheming. Then I heard Lucy's door open and close, very quietly. I walked to my bathroom door and locked it from my side. *Bravery. That's when you have a choice, and you take the harder road. I have no choice. I'm dead already. My only choice is how to die. And I choose to get the bastards.*

I sat at my desk and plugged in again, then flipped open my laptop.

Dear "Creator,"

Please notice I used quotes around the word "creator," because I think we both know that calling you a creator is the joke of the century. You don't create; you destroy. You destroyed the lives of all those girls. Their lives, and the lives of their families.

But what you didn't take into account, what you didn't realize, is that with me you really did create something special. You don't know yet how strong I am. How tough. How impenetrable is my will to survive.

Do you know why you don't know this? Because you don't know ME.

I was strong before you. Now that we've met, I'm the strongest person on this earth. I feel no pain, no fear. I am nothing but strength.

And I am coming for you.

So you better run.

But don't think you can outrun me. You may be fast, but I promise you. I am faster. And I am coming. Those eyes you feel on the back of your neck? The ones making the little hairs there stand on end? Yeah, those are me. I'm right behind you.

And I say screw you, and your idea of creation.

Yours truly,
Dead Girl Jo

Jo1995: And THAT, my friends, is how you stir up some shit. Stir stir stir.

EliPete21: @Jo1995 Double bubble toil and trouble… extra helping of trouble…

Jo1995: @EliPete21 Aren't you supposed to be resting somewhere else?

EliPete21: @Jo1995 Yeah, I'm not leaving you. Not for a million bucks.

Jo1995: @EliPete21 Le sigh.

Jolene,

You dare defy me? After all I've done for you? You threaten my very existence? I am shocked and appalled. I am only trying to SAVE you.

Know that I am not afraid of you. You are ours for the creating, and ours for the destroying. We will never stop, until the end has passed. Each iteration of girls has been better than the last. You will not be the last of our girls to awaken, but you will be the last to cause such trouble.

And you will not be around much longer.

Your battery? It has a half-life of less than a week. I planned to switch it out next week.

So go ahead and threaten. I only laugh. From you, we are learning much, much more than you know.

Your parents will bow down before us. They will beg for our help, when the end comes.

So think about that while you write up your empty threats, dear Jolene, and know we are not afraid. And we won't rest until I succeed beyond your wildest expectations.
Your creator

P.S. Don't mock me. You won't like what happens.

I SNAPPED MY LAPTOP SHUT with a bang. Then I smiled my gruesome, skeletal smile. *My work here is done. Hell, they're even threatening my family now. Screw them. My parents are in Colorado. They're fine.*

I reached for Lucy's phone, which sat on the desk beside me. I was finally ready to call my parents. I needed them to know what was going on, and I needed to hear my mother's voice.

My fingers were barely a centimeter away when it started to vibrate. A picture of Officer Strong flashed on the screen.

I hit the green button. "Hello? Officer Strong?"

The sun was just beginning to rise, and the windows in my room were brightening. Strong panted into the phone for a second, like a lewd prankster, before clearing his throat.

"Jo?" he said. He was hoarse, and I wondered if he'd slept.

"Yeah, it's me."

"I'm on my way to your dorm. I don't know how to tell you… they…they got her. They took Lucy."

It was early September. We'd only been on campus a few weeks, Lucy and I continued to feel each other out, circling one another like boxers before a fight. We wanted desperately to be friends, but the dynamic of sharing a bathroom with a complete stranger was difficult to negotiate. We tiptoed, knocked gently on doors, played music quietly, took short showers, and only went to the bathroom if we were sure the other room was unoccupied.

Then one night, Joe-from-down-the-hall showed up at my door with a bottle of Southern Comfort he'd sneaked past the front desk of Calvin Hall. He held it up like a peace offering, or his ticket to a private party with a couple of girls. "Do you and Lucy want to get drunk?" he asked.

I played it cool. "Don't know," I said. "Let me check with Lucy."

I closed the door in his face.

I ran to the bathroom and burst in, not bothering to knock. It was empty. My heart raced; I'd not done much drinking in high school, had never had Southern Comfort, and didn't want to look like an ass by myself in front of a cute boy.

I banged on Lucy's door. "Lucy? Luce? Can I come in?"

She pulled her door open. She wore tattered sweat shorts and an old tank top. No bra. For a fleeting second I felt like a prude in my ever-present underwire, but I quashed the thought as I searched for the right words. Cute boy...brown liquor...

She eyed me with confusion. "What's up? Are you okay?"

I grinned, all discomfort vanished in the face of my roommate. My friend. "Joe's outside my door. He has some...whiskey? Bourbon? I don't know, but it's brown. He wants to drink it with us. You in?" Please be in, please be in, please be in, *I thought.*

Her lips curled up at the corners. Her eyebrows dropped to a crease in the center, and the beginnings of a flush blossomed in her cheeks. It was a face I'd come to love in the following months. Mischief and mayhem, all rolled up in a Cheshire smile, camouflaged by the most innocent looking freckles you'd ever imagine.

"Sure," she said. "I'll try anything once."

We took the first shot together, Lucy and I, from little white Dixie cups with blue and white daisies. The liquor burned as it went down, and we breathed simultaneous fire as Joe doubled over in laughter, and we doubled over in shared agony.

We took the second shot together from the same cups. And then the third.

The following morning, Joe was long gone. The Southern Comfort bottle lay empty on its side. Lucy and I had slept, side by side, tangled up in a heap, and when we awoke, we shared headaches and violently ill stomachs. Our cell phone photo galleries were littered with pictures of us together. Two girls, so different, and yet so beautiful and alive. And ridiculous. Jo sits on Lucy's lap, drunk. Lucy grabs Jo's butt, drunk. Lucy and Jo hug while simultaneously flipping off the anonymous photographer, drunk.

After that, we had no choice but to be best friends. Once you share a night like that, you're attached for life.

Attached for life. Lucy and I were attached for life. We were supposed to grow old together, the old college friends, showing up for weddings and births, parties and divorces. That was how it was *supposed* to be.

But suddenly I was (mostly) dead, and Lucy was missing. And life had turned upside down and backwards, inside out and topsy-turvy.

I wanted to hyperventilate. I tried to *make* myself hyperventilate. I wanted to feel something physical. But I couldn't. So instead, I just said to Adam, as calmly as if he *hadn't* just signed my best friend's death certificate, "So what do we do next?"

"We find them. And we get Lucy back. Go wake up Eli. I'll pick you guys up in ten minutes. Meet me out front."

Eli helped me dress. There was no need for modesty anymore. He pulled a clean shirt over my head, clean pants up around my hips, a coat over my stiff shoulders. Then he wrapped my whole face in one of the beautiful silk scarves I had no further energy or desire to protect.

Eli smuggled me back down the stairs and out the fire door. He shivered beside me in semi-hostile silence while we waited for Adam's squad car to appear. In Lucy's absence, Eli was really stepping up to help me, and while he froze in the early morning wind, I whispered, "Thank you."

I might as well have remained silent. He ignored my gratitude, the single tender moment from earlier in the night blown to bits by the news that Lucy was gone.

Strong's squad car appeared exactly ten minutes later. Eli mumbled something under his breath.

"What?" I said.

"Military precision," he said. "Cop drives me nuts."

I nodded, and ducked my head to get into the back seat when Eli opened the door. He walked around to the front seat, climbed in, and we were off. Adam never bothered to say good morning.

The sky brightened as we headed down the mountain in silence. As soon as the sun peeked over the jagged horizon, it bounced off the stark white snow and the sky exploded in a kaleidoscope of colors and textures and light. I loved living in these mountains much more than I ever expected to, and I stared out the window at the rainbow sky and tried not to worry about Lucy. It was hard, though, in the pressure-cooker silence surrounding me. I needed someone to do something, to say something, but I felt paralyzed with fear, as if nothing *I* could do or say could possibly help.

After fifteen minutes of driving away from campus, up and down winding mountain roads, Adam pulled into a parking lot designated a "national lookout spot of the White Mountains." I had to admit, the view was amazing, but I had no clue why we stopped.

Eli and I sat still, expectant and silent, while Adam looked out at the snow-covered valley below. It was dotted with picturesque farmhouses and log cabins, picket fences and barns, like a Currier and Ives puzzle I'd put together with my grandfather when I was a child. We waited, Eli and I, for something to happen.

Finally, after checking his watch three times, Adam spoke. "You know," he said, making me jump, "I've gotten used to your smell, Jo. Either that, or you're so far gone even the stink has left you."

I didn't know what to say, so I stared at the bars between us and pretended my feelings weren't hurt.

"What happened, Adam?" Eli said. "You need to tell us what's going on."

"They took her." He shrugged.

"We know."

Strong turned back to look at me. His face was twisted with rage, a Halloween caricature mask of his normally handsome face. "So what I need to know from you is...what do you know that you haven't told me? Who else knows what's going on? You've hidden stuff from me all along." He raised his voice, a cruel mimicry of my own. *"Oh, I'm Jo, and I'm fine. Nothing's wrong. I'm just having a girls' weekend, it's not that my face is falling off."* Louder, and angrier still, he continued, "What are you still hiding?"

"I...I...I don't know anything else!" I said. "Don't your cop friends know more than me by now? Didn't they investigate the cabin? I have pictures of the other girls on Lucy's phone. Can we use them? I have it here. Did you send them to the station?"

"No more questions!" Adam roared, and this time even Eli jumped. "I want answers! What do you know? Who else have you talked to?"

"Jesus Christ! Officer *Strong*! How strong is it, to yell at a girl like Jo? She's trying to help!" Eli reached across the front seat and shoved Adam into his door, then opened his own and got out into the thin morning air.

He opened my door. "Come on," he said. "We can find her ourselves."

Eli spoke like a petulant child, but I preferred his petulance to Adam's fury. I walked with him to the fence at the edge of the overlook, afraid that Adam would follow, but equally terrified he'd leave us there on the mountaintop. I tried to tell myself it was going to be fine, that his fury was that of a Romeo who'd lost his Juliet, but this felt different. Off, somehow. I shook off my confusion and turned my attention to Eli.

He wouldn't look at me, but I didn't blame him. I was barely a shadow of the girl he'd once maybe, possibly, cared for. I was an ugly, wretched, pitiful beast. We stood beside each other, shoulders almost-but-not touching, and I felt the fury emanating from his body. *Fury at me?* I wondered. *Does it matter?*

After a moment, Eli took my mangled, broken, gloved hand into his, pulled it to his lips, and kissed it gently. "What I said before? Yesterday? About you, you know, dying?" He gulped, and closed his eyes.

I nodded. "I know. You don't have to…"

"Yes, I do. I didn't mean it. I'm sorry. You're a victim in this, just like all those other girls. Just a victim."

I stepped away, pulling my hand from his. "I'm different, though. I'm a dangerous victim. I *poison* people. You shouldn't touch me."

"You're not dangerous. Not really. Not on purpose, anyway." He shrugged, and reached out and pulled me back to him. "Besides, you have gloves on. I can hold your hand."

"Yeah, but I don't know why you'd want to."

"Because I love you."

"What? Are you crazy?" The butterflies in my absent stomach may not have been real, but I felt them as though I was a normal girl and this was a normal conversation. Eli had never told me he loved me.

He smiled and kissed my hand again. "I mean, I know we broke up the other night. I don't know if we'd have gotten back together. I don't know if, if we did, we'd have made it dating another week. Maybe it's just regret, but I'd like to think we'd have made it, as a couple. Who knows. But no matter what, Jo, I do. Love you, I mean. As a friend, as a girlfriend, and as Jo. I just thought it was time for you to know that. I should have said it a long time ago."

"I love you, too," I said, my voice almost failing.

"Good," he said, smiling. "Now that's settled, we should get back to finding Lucy."

"Yes, let's," said a deep voice from right behind us. Strong's voice.

"Jesus, dude! Don't sneak up on us like that." Eli dropped my hand

and stepped away, almost stumbling over the knee-high fence that protected visitors from the steep drop-off beyond it. I grabbed his coat and held on, but made a face when I heard something rip from inside me. *Just another body part to try to repair later.* I knew full well I was lying to myself.

Strong looked down at the ground and shuffled his boots through the snow. "Sorry. For scaring you, here and back there. I know better than to lose my cool like that. But, this is too much. We need to find her."

I walked to him, then past him, patting him on the shoulder. "The phone's in the car. That's the best place to start looking. We need your friends to look at the pictures, figure out what other girls are missing. Maybe that'll give us a clue for where to go next."

I SHOWED STRONG THE PHOTOS on Lucy's phone. He studied each one carefully, and then emailed the complete album to a detective at the station. His cell phone rang thirty seconds after he hit the send button, and Eli and I waited in the car while Adam paced around it, holding the phone slightly away from his ear, looking more and more frustrated, and talking back into it.

"No, it has to be now…This has taken too long already!…Yes, safe with me…No! Now!"

The words filtered through the windows, over gusts of wind that rocked the car like the baby in the treetop. Adam's voice grew louder until he shouted, and the conversation pulsed onward, a dissertation about my entire case. But finally, he was done. He shoved his phone deep into his coat pocket and climbed back into the car. I was busy flipping through the pictures again, one at a time. *Flip, flip, flip.* I stopped and toggled between two of them, pictures of the desk and the tackboard from the room below the lab.

"Blonde, brunette, blonde," I mumbled quietly to myself. It all seemed like nonsense, and the pictures were so small it was hard to see anything. "Brunette, blonde, redhead, brunette. Crap! What the hell do all these people have in common, and how do we find Lucy?" I threw the phone at the door, and it crashed to the ground. The battery popped out and landed beside it.

Both Eli and Adam jumped, and turned to stare at me. The car idled in the parking lot, waiting, like the rest of us, for the next move.

"What?" Eli said. He sounded exasperated, exhausted. I understood.

"I'm just trying to figure this out," I said. "And I'm getting nowhere. The cabin, the papers I saw, it was nonsense and I hate it! I just want my life back! I want Lucy back!" The world suddenly felt like it was closing in on me. My brain slowed down and I felt myself shutting down. "Guys, I need to recharge."

"We're not going back to the dorm," Adam said. "We've got to start looking for Lucy."

"I need my car charger then. It's in Lucy's car. Can we go get it?"

"Where's Lucy's car?"

"2959 Primrose Path." My words were slurred, slow. "The cabin. Go now."

The darkness closed in, but I felt the car peel out of the parking lot and speed away. I hoped we were headed toward the cabin, but Strong's and Eli's words, coming from the front seat, sounded like they traveled through mud to get near my ears.

A minute later, I blacked out.

The next thing I knew was warmth, cozy like a hot tub on a cold winter's day. I was in the front seat of the squad car, hooked up to my charger. Eli stood outside, but Strong was beside me.

"Morning," he said in a sandpaper voice. I wondered if he'd been yelling again while I was out. "Feel better?"

I tried to nod, but only succeeded in rocking my head back and forth. "It takes a few minutes," I slurred.

"We're at the cabin," he said. "Or what's left of it. Since we're here, when you're up for it, have a look around what's left. See if it sparks a memory that could help find Lucy. We've got some time while my guys at the station look into a few things."

"Have we looked inside?" I tried to say. There was no way the whole underground fortress was burned out. But no actual words came through my numb mouth.

So we sat in silence, Strong and I, while my strength came back and Eli's head floated past my window again and again as he paced around the car. Finally, I felt my strength return, and I pulled myself up to look out the window.

I promptly fell back against the seat, because the cabin? It was gone. *Poof,* I thought. *Gone like magic.* Only police tape marked the area where it had once stood, indicating that the root of my new existence ever stood at all. Police tape, and the black ash and soot that flurried over the melting snow.

The view of the mountains and valleys beyond the empty expanse in the ground was spectacular, though. Breathtaking, if only I'd had breath to take. Snow-covered fir trees in the distance, blue sky, the storm of the day before only a distant memory. The place which had caused so much pain had been replaced by a place of overwhelming beauty.

It was cathartic, in a way. There was no *inside* in which to look for Lucy. There was just a big, gaping scar in the earth, and I wondered how deep it ran. Regardless, the memory of the flames consuming everything in our wake was fresh. There'd be nothing left, even deep underground. Lucy wasn't here. She was gone.

But it was also a death sentence to me. Through all the hours I'd spent since waking up on the table in the cabin, I'd still maintained a slight kernel of hope. *Maybe they're not all bad guys. Maybe someone there will take pity on me. Maybe, even though it looks like I'm so far gone there's no returning, they can still fix me. Maybe, maybe, maybe.*

With the end of Primrose Path came the end of all my hope. That tiny kernel withered. It shriveled up. It died.

I am nothing but a pile of dust.

I bit my lip to hold my mouth closed and to stop myself from screaming. It wouldn't do any good anyway. I was nothing.

But Lucy? Lucy was something, and I had to do everything I could to save her.

Unaware of the tempest raging in my silent, decrepit head, Strong rolled down the window and waved Eli over to the car. "Come on, get in. She's awake again. We need to start canvassing neighborhoods."

"Wait, what?" I slurred. "I thought you wanted me to look around?"

Adam groaned as Eli climbed in. "Can you walk yet? No? I didn't think so. And I'm tired of sitting here, stewing in your stink." He paused and then started the car, blasting the heat on so high his blond hair blew back from his forehead. "I waited, though, because if I didn't make you see that this goddamn place was burned to the ground, you'd keep asking to come back, to look for Lucy at a place which *no longer exists*!"

I jerked away as I fought the urge to cover my ears with hands that didn't cooperate with my instructions anyway. Something about his tone frightened me, made me feel like a little girl staring down a man offering me candy from the open door of a large, gray van. I didn't like the feeling.

The car flew down the steep driveway, Strong's foot heavy on the gas pedal. We drove away from Lucy's little Honda and the pile of ash that destroyed my life. I froze in my seat, by choice this time, afraid to move lest I set off Strong again. I tried to see Eli's face through the rearview mirror, to gauge his thoughts, but the mirror pointed toward the ceiling. Then Eli punched Strong's seat, shaking the whole car.

"Hey, stop the car and let me out! Stop!"

I figured he had decided to go get Lucy's car and search on his own, but when Adam let him out, he went only to the mailbox standing at the bottom of the driveway and opened it.

"My team has already been through that, I'm sure," Strong said. "You won't find anything worthwhile."

But Eli's hand came away from the mailbox full of envelopes. "Sure, maybe yesterday, but not today." He opened my door and tossed me a handful of mail. He sounded more cheerful than he had in days. "Strong, you drive. Jo and I can investigate."

THEY GOT A LOT OF mail at the cabin. My pile was mostly catalogs, a strange mix of electronics, home improvement, and women's clothing, all addressed to "Resident." Somehow that felt like the right mix for Primrose Path, though. Just bizarre enough to make sense. I flipped briefly through a Gap catalog, eyed a red dress that would have looked fabulous on me two weeks earlier, but then snapped the catalog shut. *No dresses for you*. The girls in the catalog seemed to have it all: beauty, nice clothes, cute boys by their sides. I remembered how I used to feel like one of those girls, as my wasted hand rose to my nose-less face, and I cringed. I had none of that anymore. I had nothing. I *was* nothing.

I dropped the catalog to the floor. As it fell, a postcard fluttered out and landed beside on my lap. On the front was a tropical beach scene, all blue skies, teal water, and white sand. I flipped it over.

It was addressed to Sandy. Just Sandy. The original address was crossed off, and was forwarded to Primrose Path. I jumped when I realized the original address was a campus address.

Dearest Sandy, it said. *Remember going to the Bahamas when we were little? This picture reminds me of being all sandy with my Sandy. Why won't you write me back? I miss you, little sister.*

There was no signature. I guessed, though, that a sister wouldn't need one.

Sandy. Sandy with my Sandy. Something tickled my brain over the name Sandy. Sandy wasn't just the bobby-soxer from *Grease;* she was a clue, a name, a name that sounded familiar, like déjà vu. It was on the tip of my tongue but nowhere closer, and I couldn't come up with a face for the name Sandy.

I looked backward. "Eli, do you know anyone named Sandy?"

Strong sneezed violently. "Excuse me. Did you just say you found a name on the mail?"

"Well, no, I didn't quite say that, but yes, I did. Sandy. It was addressed to a Sandy. I almost feel like I know a Sandy, but I don't guess I do."

"Me either," said Eli. "And all I have are bills. There's a name on them, but I somehow doubt Michael Smith is going to be helpful."

"Eli, shut up a minute. Jo, repeat: we have a suspect name? Sandy?" He was straining to drive down the winding, icy roads while turning to look over my shoulder at the postcard I held. "What *is* that?"

I read them both the message on the postcard. Then I said, "And it was forwarded. There's an older address here. It's a campus address."

Adam slammed on the brakes, and the car skidded to the side of the street. "Campus? Are you serious? That can't be right."

"It is," I insisted, and I thrust the postcard toward Eli, who pulled it from my hand and scanned the back. "See?"

Eli nodded. "Yeah, she's right. We should go check it out."

"We're wasting time," Adam said. "We should be out walking the streets."

"That's stupid," said Eli. "This is our first real clue, *Officer*. Shouldn't we follow it? Don't they teach you to follow leads in the police academy?"

"Yes." Adam turned scarlet again. "But on campus? That makes no sense. We won't find anything."

"Please," I said. "Please. We have to try everything. We have to find Lucy."

Adam slammed on the brakes. The car skidded across the road. I yelped and grabbed the door handle. "Fine," he said. "I can tell you now it's a waste of time." He jerked out his phone. "I'll do this now to placate you two. But I need to call it in first."

WE SPED TOWARD CAMPUS IN silence.

In the front seat I continued to charge, the warmth of electricity a welcome feeling. But it was impossible to ignore: I was drying out. Whatever embalming fluids had been used to preserve me, they were wearing out. My body was stiffening, even getting crumbly in spots like the tips of my remaining fingers and my chin. I flaked off in clumps, leaving pieces of me on the car seat, dandruff of the damned, ashes that would eventually wind up in a vacuum bag.

Beside me, Adam's eyes never left the road, and his jaw never unclenched. His fingers gripped the steering wheel so fiercely that his entire hands turned white. The driver's side window was cracked, and his hair flew about in the breeze.

I was a little touched by his obvious concern for Lucy. I felt like a secondary character in a romance novel, watching the hero race away to rescue a damsel in distress. The thought made me grin that hideous smile, but it didn't matter that I was a bystander, a red-shirt. Lucy deserved a good guy, especially after all I'd put her through, and considering the fact that she'd been kidnapped. I wouldn't allow the idea of her being dead or, worse, like me, to enter my head. Somewhere, she was alive and well, and we were going to find her. No problem.

Then she could help Adam learn to control his temper, and they'd find Eli a new girlfriend after he'd had time to adequately mourn his last one, and they'd all live happily ever after. It was a cozy little fantasy, something straight out of my Sixteenth-Century Lit class, if I ignored the fact that I wasn't in it.

It was getting on toward noon, and the sun was high in the sky, making the ice on the roads slick. We passed several salt-spreaders out doing their jobs, but still Strong had to work hard to keep the car on the road. In the back seat, Eli flipped through one of the electronics catalogs I'd passed to him through the bars of the squad car divider. "Huh," he said, when we were still about twenty minutes away from campus. "I wonder if this is how they're powering you." He pressed the open catalog up to the divider, and I turned to look, ignoring the way my neck sounded like a ripping piece of paper when I moved.

It was a picture of a large pump with wires coming out of all sides. It looked almost like a heart, and I shrugged. "Maybe? Who the hell knows what I've got going on inside. Maybe I'm running on bananas!"

For the first time in ages, Eli laughed a little, a sound that made me feel better, like this really would work out okay in the end. At least for my friends. "You're a freak," he said.

But Eli's laugh had the opposite effect on Strong. He slammed on the brakes again, and Eli pitched forward into the back of my seat, knocking me forward as well. "What the hell," Eli said, rubbing his shoulder from the floor of the back seat.

Strong turned to glare at us. "You're laughing. I'm sorry, but do you two think this is a *joke*?"

"Hey..." I started to interrupt, but one look from Strong shushed me.

"We have a clue. We're on our way to investigate, even though I know it's a dead end. Now please shut the hell up so I can focus on not getting us killed on this stupid ice-covered road? I'd rather stay alive long enough to actually find your friend."

"Calm down, man," said Eli. "I'm sorry. I didn't mean anything by it. I want to save her too." His voice was velvet. He'd used it many times on me in the midst of an argument.

Strong shot him a dirty look, then started to drive again. "Just keep your mouths shut. We're almost there and I swear to God, Jo's about to make me puke."

THE ADDRESS ON the postcard led us to a cluster of on-campus faculty housing. Strong parked the squad car in front of a tiny, boxy, bright yellow house with deep green shutters. Unlike those around it, no one had shoveled this home's front walk or the tiny porch. There were no footprints in the snow. It was vacant.

I looked up and down the street; classes were in session, with people walking here and there by the classroom buildings. No one walked nearby, but I wrapped my scarf around my mutilated face. Just in case.

Strong got out of the car first, then opened the door for Eli. Eli opened my door, and together we walked up the front stoop, tracking through the knee-deep snow. Eli shivered in front of me, and I patted his shoulder as we walked. He didn't flinch.

When we reached the front door, I looked at Strong. "You're the cop. Do we knock first?"

He shook his head, and then reached for the knob. It turned easily in his hand and swung inward, revealing a small living room. Dust had settled on most surfaces, and Eli sneezed as a cloud of dust flew up in the cold breeze that stayed with us as we stepped inside. "Should we take our shoes off?" I whispered. I didn't want to track in snow and mud.

Eli just shot me a look and walked inside, tracking gray snow on the cream-colored carpets.

The room was dark once Adam closed the door behind us, so I walked to a set of heavy drapes and pushed them aside, letting light flood in through the grimy windows. They made visible a space furnished with a mix of antiques and Goodwill pieces, but devoid of any piece of the person who last lived there. No photos, no pictures on the walls, no shoes on the floor by the front door.

"It doesn't look like anyone's lived here in a while," said Strong. "We should take a quick look around, and then get back to looking for Lucy. We won't find anything useful here." He used the very tip of his finger to nudge the lone pillow on a nearby couch. A cloud of dust puffed around it when it flopped over onto the couch cushions.

"How do you know no one's been here?" said Eli. "Jo, you look around the kitchen. Strong, you take the bedroom. I'll look in here and the bathroom. Let's see if we can't find *something.* Whoever lived here knew something. They moved to the cabin in the woods. So let's find out…who's Sandy?"

I found the kitchen small, and mostly clean. Cabinets were polished, floors were swept, but everything was covered in that thin sheen of dust that settles on every surface of an empty house.

While the living room had been furnished, the kitchen was barren. Neither spoon nor knife, cup nor plate, graced its cabinets or drawers. The microwave stood empty. The refrigerator was empty, though it hummed quietly, standing guard, ready to do its job and make things cold as soon as someone moved back in. It seemed to long for a cheery souvenir magnet or even a cold bottle of beer.

I headed back to the living room with nothing new to share, into the room where bookshelves stood empty and closet doors hid absolutely nothing. Eli grew frustrated, shoving aside couch cushions and curtains hoping to find something, anything, that could lead us to Lucy. Finally, he flopped onto the couch, and Adam soon joined him.

"Nothing," he said as he slid down beside Eli. "Absolutely nothing. Like I told you." He looked satisfied.

"Ditto." Eli leaned his forehead onto his hand, a gesture of defeat.

I'd just seen something, though. In a dark corner, hidden mostly behind the brick mantel that jutted out into the living room, stood a coat rack. At first glimpse it looked empty, but when I looked again, I saw something hanging from a hook, tucked away beside the bricks.

I walked over to it.

It was a cardigan, big and cable-knit. It was the brightest shade of orange I had ever seen.

Except, I had seen it before. I knew the cardigan. It happened to be the favorite cardigan of my favorite professor.

"Sondra," I whispered, mostly to myself. "Sondra, Sandy." I turned to Eli. "Holy crap, Eli, it's Sondra Lewis!"

The men jumped to their feet.

"What did you say?" said Strong, walking to me. His face was white, his eyes were wide. He looked as though he'd seen a ghost.

"What do you mean?" echoed Eli, following.

I held out the sweater in front of me. "It all makes sense now!" I said. I was excited. "No professors ever go visit their students just for something stupid like the flu! She was checking up on me! Sondra Lewis, English Department! It's how she knew my email, it's how she knew where to find Lucy! Sondra is Sandy, and she's my professor, and she's the freaking bad guy!"

Strong's face grew very red in the sunlight that poured in deceptively cheerful buckets through the open blinds. Eli smacked his forehead with the heel of his hand. "Why didn't we see it sooner? Jesus, Jo, teachers *don't* make dorm calls. She was spying!"

"And nobody wears a sweater this bright and garish except for Sondra Lewis! She even talked about it the first time she wore it. Her sister, her *sister*, knitted it for her, but she said they'd had a falling out and hadn't spoken in years. She sounded sad about it. This is her awful sweater!"

"Come on, guys." Where Eli and I were excited, anxious and turning for the door, Strong was calm, cool behind that reddened face. "Look, I'm a cop, and my life is about evidence. An ugly sweater doesn't make an innocent person a villain. What if you're wrong? You're standing here accusing someone just because you found an ugly sweater. The world is full of ugly sweaters. That doesn't mean this one implicates your teacher!"

"Look," I said. "I know you're scared. I know you have rules to follow, and I know you want to find Lucy as bad as Eli and I do. But still, I *know* this. I *know* I'm right. Look at this sweater! No tag. Handmade. Sondra Lewis *is* our bad guy. Or at least, she's one of them."

I didn't need further evidence. I'd been in the lab when the weird, disjointed voices spoke to us through the sound system. Now that I knew, I realized, one of those voices was her speaking. I could close my eyes and go back in time to the terror of those minutes, and the voice, though distorted, was hers. Her syntax. Her diction. Hers.

I knew.

And I had led her straight to Lucy.

Strong shrugged, unconvinced, but Eli stood strong by my side. "We have to find her," he said. "Even if Jo's wrong, and I don't think she is, it won't hurt anyone to talk to her, right? So can't we go to her office? Like, now?"

"Yeah, let's go!" I said. "Find her, and I bet we can find Lucy. Eli, what time is it?"

"One thirty. Tuesday."

"Great!" I stepped up to Strong and looked up into his eyes. "She has office hours Tuesday from noon to four. I used to meet with her every week almost, just to chat and talk books and such. She'll be there now. She's always there. I can take you to her."

Strong's face cleared, the internal doubt storm past. He took a step back, looking apologetically at my lack of nose and crumbly face, and said, "I can even do you one better, if you're sure. Are you sure?" I nodded. He took out his phone and dialed. "Williams, it's Strong. Go ahead and put out an APB. We have a suspect in the missing girls case. Are you ready?" He turned and walked toward the front door, gesturing us to follow. "Okay. Sondra, s-o-n-d-r-a, Lewis, l-e-w-i-s. She's an English professor at Smytheville. Look her up on the web site. Yep, we're headed to her office now. Yes, I doubt we'll need it but you better send some backup, just in case. Right. Yes. Okay, yeah. Out." He turned back to us as we headed out into the snow. "You kids better be right, and this better lead us to Lucy. I'm done with red herrings."

We reached Shepherd Hall in less than five minutes. I was positive Sondra Lewis, aka Sandy, would be waiting for us, heavily armed. I glanced around nervously, eyeing each student and professor who passed, before allowing myself to be pulled inside the building.

"But where's your backup?" I asked Strong as he led the way through the automatic glass doors that parted, inviting us into the bustling classroom building.

"They're on their way," he responded, then tugged on my arm. I stumbled. Of course I stumbled. "Come on, let's go. We're wasting time."

Wrapped in winter clothes from head to toe and flanked by Strong and Eli, my legs barely held me up. I wanted to crawl under the floor and hide. Around me, the building vibrated with energy and life as students walked the halls in between classes, chatting and debating in corners, the air humming with constant voices. Through the scarf, which I wore like a veil, I saw friends and classmates, and I struggled against the instinct to call out to them. Everyone gave us wide berth, from either the presence of a uniformed police officer, or the stench I emitted. I wasn't sure I cared either way.

"This way," I mumbled, forcing myself to take the lead. It was the best way to make sure I wouldn't run. Not like I *could* run. My gait was zombie-like, lurching, and Eli kept a fistful of my coat in his hand at all times, rescuing me when I stumbled. Beside us Strong was stoic, silent.

I headed to the elevator, since Sondra Lewis's office was on the fifth floor and my legs couldn't handle the stairs. Like the Red Sea did for Moses, the sea of students parted for us as we pushed forward toward the shining metal door.

When the elevator arrived, we three climbed in. I pressed 5. Before the doors shut, a handful of giggling girls walked toward us. The first one stepped in, but made a terrible, ugly face. She turned away, pushing her friends back, as if they'd hit a force field. They left, but not before eyeing me with green-tinged, nauseated faces.

The doors closed.

"Do I really smell that bad?" I asked.

"Yeah, you do," said Eli. "Positively ripe. Right now I'm just praying the elevator doesn't get stuck. That would suck."

The stars aligned in our direction for once; we didn't get stuck. I heaved an unnecessary sigh of relief. Strong and Eli stared at me, and I'd have blushed, if I'd had blood with which to do it.

"What?" I said, opening my arms wise. "A girl's gotta breathe sometimes."

Then we rushed to Sondra's office, the one with the vase of fresh flowers hanging on the wall outside. Normally they were fresh and sweet-smelling; now they were dried and withered. Like me.

Also, the door was closed.

"I don't understand," I said. "It's never closed during office hours. Even when someone's in there. She's an open-door kind of professor." I tried to knock, but my dried, gloved hands only succeeded in a muffled thud. "Professor Lewis? Are you in there? It's Jo Hall." But my voice was so quiet, so raw, I doubted she could hear me through the thick wooden door.

"Allow me," said Strong. He nudged me aside and took hold of the doorknob. "Police, open up!"

This door, like the door at her old house, opened easily, but her office looked much more chaotic than the house. Student papers lay half-graded on her desk. Books sat piled in corners, topsy-turvy. A purse lay open on the ground.

Eli looked around and shrugged. "Looks like somebody left in a hurry."

Strong stepped out to make yet another phone call, but Eli and I looked around.

I rifled through a few papers on her desk, where I found a memo matching the ones I'd seen back in the house. Same font, same paper. I thought of the folder of papers I'd left unread at the dorm and wondered what clues they held, if only I'd taken the time to read them. *This time*, I thought. *This time, I'll read it right now.*

From the Office of the OoA Advisory:
Re: The Search for Subject 632G-J

The search for Subject 632G-J has been successful in location. Subject is no longer at large, and is in custody, awaiting the arrival of our new founders. Agent AS keeping close tabs on Subject, simply awaiting the signal now to bring her into the facility.

Subject 645-L has been apprehended and awaits new equipment readiness to begin transfer. Subject is held at facility under lock, key, and constant guard.

Subject 651-S still thrives.

New founders are expected at 16:00 hours. Arranged pickup by Agent SL.

Cleanup efforts to begin at old facility as soon as police reports are properly filed.

Until then, continue to report to facility every three hours for check-ins. We need constant manpower on the streets to avoid any other untimely scenes.

All hands must be on deck at all times right now.

"OH, YOU HAVE GOT TO be kidding me. What the hell *is* this? Some kind of bad sci-fi flick? Who *are* these assholes, anyway? And why the hell are they handing out paper memos? This is the twenty-first century!"

"What did you find?" Strong stood in the doorway, his face once again red and inflamed. For someone who'd just met her, he was definitely taking Lucy's disappearance hard. It seemed every piece of news, each new discovery, was a salt in a raw, open wound. "Hand it over."

I bristled, but did, and then watched his face get redder and his eyes grow wider as he stared at it, and Eli read over his shoulder. Both were silent, and then Eli looked at me, a smile *almost* appearing on the corners of his lips.

"I know, right?" I said. "Ridiculous. Don't you just want to punch someone?"

Eli laughed. "Right now, I can't remember the last time I *didn't* want to punch someone. Actually, yes, I can. Last Wednesday, around midnight. That was probably the last time."

I grinned at him, my face cracking and flaking. "I have that effect on people sometimes. You know, making them want to punch someone."

He reached out and rubbed my shoulder. "Well, at least now we know we're on the right track. Let's get out of here. I can't handle your stench in this little room." He still smiled, though, and I knew why. It was a bit of a thrill, getting closer to finding our friend.

Everything's going to be okay.

Outside the office, Strong remained red, but his voice sounded calm. "I'll call this in on the way out." He reached out and took my arm and jerked me out of the office.

"Where are we going?" I said.

"To find Lucy. My buddies have a lead."

THE INITIAL EXCITEMENT I felt at finding a lead withered as Strong drove the car further and further away from school, from Primrose Path, and from everywhere we already knew was connected with finding Lucy. The day was passing by too fast. Lucy had already been gone for at least eight hours, and all the TV shows I'd ever seen said you only had forty-eight hours to find a kidnapping victim. After that, their survival rates plummeted.

We were wasting time, driving through New Hampshire mountain country, further and further away from civilization.

But Strong pushed away any questions from Eli or me. "It's where they said to go," he said over and over, and remained vague about who "they" were. His partners on the police force? FBI? CIA? Other sources not yet identified? I didn't know, and he wouldn't say.

After an hour of driving in pensive silence, during which time we drove deeper and deeper into the White Mountains, further from our home and school and hope, Eli spoke up. "Strong?" he began tentatively, as if unwilling to rock the boat. "I know you seem to have a plan, but could you let Jo and me in on your secret? Like, say, *where* we're going?"

Strong shot a dangerous look over his shoulder. "I told you. We're going after Lucy. I have a lead. It's gonna take a while. You just have to wait."

"Then can we pull over somewhere? I have to take a piss, and I'm starving. I know worrying about my friend should suppress my appetite, but what can I say? I'm a stress-eater." In the rearview I caught the tail end of his most winning smile.

It was the night before a major bio-chem exam. I sat in Eli's apartment, there for moral support, and watching in disbelief as Eli cleaned out the fridge, eating everything he could get his hands on. Macaroni and cheese, pizza, and some hot dogs went down first. Later he made Ramen noodles. It was gross, but also kind of impressive.

When the fridge was empty and the cabinet bare, Eli decided he needed a cheeseburger. "Will you get me one?" he asked. "I need to get these formulas memorized."

"No way! You've eaten more than your body weight already!"

He flashed a smile, then, charming, adorable, highlighting the dimple in his left cheek. Soon after, I drove to the diner to pick up a deluxe cheeseburger platter.

Eli's best smile never failed to work on me, but it didn't work on Strong, who made no sign of stopping the car.

It was time to intervene. I reached for Strong's arm, but he recoiled from my touch. "He's not lying," I said, as gently as my shattered voice allowed. "I want to find Lucy as soon as we can, but we've been going non-stop since seven this morning. It's almost four now. Not everyone's as lucky as me, to run on battery power. Eli needs a break."

Strong eyed the gas gauge on the dashboard. "We need gas." His voice was flat, holding nothing like the kind concern I'd heard earlier in the day. He glanced back at Eli. "We can stop at the next gas station we see. You can piss and get some food."

It took another ten miles of driving on the slick, steep roads and curving byways before we found an ancient, lonely gas station. Strong pulled the squad car up to the solitary, rusted out pump. There was a small store attached, with an Open sign hanging cockeyed by a single chain in the propped open door. Eli eyed it with concern. "Fresh blueberries," a sign screamed in bold white letters in the window, despite the fact blueberry season had ended six months earlier. "Jams, jellies, apple butter!" said another.

"You," Strong said, looking at Eli. "Get food, do your business, then back here. Five minutes or less." He opened his door to get out, but then looked back at me. "You. Sit there. If you get out, you'll garner unwanted attention. You need to stay quiet under the radar, if you want to save Lucy."

I nodded, swallowing back a snarky comment about the lack of people around us, and having no one from whom to *garner* any unwanted attention. Strong didn't appear in the mood for humor. Besides, I'd been sitting so long, I didn't want to get up anyway. I didn't trust my legs to support me.

Eli stood outside the car and leaned his head back into the opened door. "You gonna be okay out here?" he whispered as Strong fumbled with the gas tank. "He seems…tense."

"Yeah," I said, waving him off. "Go, um, find something yummy… in that…abandoned shack. Maybe some blueberries?"

He chuckled. "My thoughts exactly. Wish me luck." Eli turned and was gone, swallowed whole by the dilapidated country store.

Alone in the car I did a movement test run, bending and flexing my knees and elbows. Sure enough, it was harder than ever to move, as if all my muscles were dried up pieces of beef jerky like my father used to buy for me from a local farm. I groaned, and then pulled down the passenger seat mirror.

I saw my face. I closed my eyes and pushed the mirror away.

No use crying over spilled milk, I thought. Then, out loud, to no one but myself, I said, "All that matters is finding Lucy. I swear."

I believed it.

Outside, Strong finished pumping gas into the squad car. I expected him to get back in, to prepare to drive away. Instead, he pulled out his phone again, stepped away from the car, and began to talk.

I tried to listen, but he was too far away and his voice was too muffled by the upturned collar of his heavy coat. By the looks of it, though, he wasn't happy. He paced restlessly, raised his arms to the air, and shook his finger at me.

While I watched Strong, the back door opened and Eli slid in, grunting loudly. "God, Jo. I keep thinking you can't smell any worse, but then I leave you for a minute, and when I come back, I realize. It's worse."

I flipped him off, taking care to use the hand that didn't have a middle finger anymore.

"Very funny," he said.

"I'm sorry," I said, looking down at my hands, wondering for a brief moment how many of my other fingers were still attached beneath my gloves. "I could ask Strong to strap me to the roof if you'd like."

"Nah." He patted my shoulder through the bar. "You might blow away, and I've gotten used to having you around. And we need to talk anyway, now, here, while Strong's out of the car." I heard the fizz and pop of a can of soda opening, then the sound of Eli taking a long pull from the can. He belched. "Sorry. Mmm, that's a lot better. There were a few people inside. Really nice for a little hick store. Anyway, question for you. Do you think this is a little weird, this whole 'driving to nowhere' thing? I mean, I don't feel like we're any closer to finding Lucy than we were first thing this morning. Not really, anyway."

"We've learned some stuff, right? I mean, we know who's behind it now."

"Correction. We know *one* person behind it. Probably not the only person. And I'm starting to wonder what Strong has up his sleeve."

I nodded. "I know. I'm worried. If he's so worried for her, why are we just driving around?"

"Right? I mean, I know we're also trying to protect you, but at some point don't you think that we could be giving statements down at the station? And I'd like to know what Strong's buddies are doing to get our friend back."

"Yeah," I said again, and I stared out the window at Strong. He grew increasingly agitated with whomever he was talking to on the phone. "Maybe we should ask him to take us back? To your apartment, where this all began? Maybe we missed something there? Or maybe we should try on our own again?"

"Yeah. Or maybe we ask to be taken down to the station. Even though…well…even though I know what it'll mean for you."

I did my best to turn to face him, wincing at the sound my back made as I rotated my spine. But I needed to see his eyes when I spoke. "Look, Eli, I'm done. I know that. I'm scared as hell about it, but there's nothing I can do. So if you think going to the police all the way will help Lucy, I want to do it. I've…I've done enough damage, don't you think?"

His eyes filled with tears. It took him a second to speak. "No. No. Don't forget none of this is your fault. I hope you can remember that. Hold onto that thought, you have to remember." He ran a fleece-armed sleeve across his nose as he sniffed. "Okay, though. That's what we'll do. Now we just need Officer Chatty Kathy to get off the damn phone and get back in here."

It didn't look like Strong's conversation was going to end anytime soon, though. I turned back around and stared out the window.

"What time is it, anyway?"

"A little after four. Why?"

"Nothing really. It's just that we've been on the road for a while, and I've been out of touch. My parents have already been freaking out a little since I've been acting a little weird. Mind if I hit my email from your phone? Strong's got Lucy's."

I felt the pressure of the phone poking into my shoulder a moment later, and I reached up for it. He had two bars of service, more than enough. I pulled off the glove on my right hand and slid my finger across the screen to unlock it. But nothing happened.

"Ah, dammit," I said. "I don't think your touchscreen works for dead fingers."

"Here," he said. "Hand it back. I'll do it. What's your password?"

A minute later, he flipped through my emails in the back seat. "Okay, it doesn't look like…oh, now….wait a sec. Jo? Did you tell your parents to come here?"

If only my heart had been beating in that moment. If only I'd been able to feel the physical pain of it skipping a beat in my chest. If only I'd been able to feel my blood pressure drop and my head begin to spin. If only I'd been normal, in that moment. It would have felt so much better than it did to have absolutely no physical reaction to the *new* scariest news I'd heard in the prior forty-eight hours.

"What did you say?" My voice was low and filled with fear and fury.

"I said…well, here." He thrust the phone back up and it dropped into my lap. I fumbled with it, almost relieved to discover that my hands at least could still shake. But not relieved enough to forgive them for doing it right then when I needed them most. While I fumbled, though, the phone went back to sleep.

"Dammit," I said. "Can you unlock it please?"

We had to try a couple times more before I could actually read the emails. Someone, someone who was not me, had hacked into my email account multiple times, emailed my mother, and asked her to come. I read her email over and over.

Dad and I are on our way...tomorrow evening...hang tight...

"Oh dammit..." I said, panic rising in my head but not my belly, where I would have been able to handle it. "Dammit dammit *dammit!* Eli! Do you know what this means?"

"Yes," he said, his voice flat.

"My parents! They're on their way here!"

"Yes."

"Someone, someone who is *not me,* told them to come, and they're coming! They could be waiting for me at the dorm right now! My parents! They're in danger!"

"Yes."

"God!" I shouted, my voice like shards of glass under a heavy boot. "Can't you say anything other than yes?"

"Yes," he said. "Once I figure out what else to say. But for now, holy Jesus, we need to get back! Now!"

"But why? Why would they do this? Why do they want my parents? My parents didn't do anything to them! It's me they're after! Why?"

He reached through the bar and touched the back of my head. "Who knows? Money, I'm guessing. They're loaded, right? And if they can't use you anymore, if they've given up on you....well, maybe now they want your parents." He paused, and thought a moment. When he continued, his voice was grave, heavy with meaning. "Your parents are in danger!"

"You think?"

"You better call them," he said, his voice still so flat I could barely hear it. Or maybe he was whispering. I wasn't sure. "Maybe you can stop them. Tell them to take the next plane back west?"

"Yes!" I tossed the phone back over my shoulder, through the bars. "Will you dial this number for me?"

He misdialed twice before we finally got the phone to ring through to my mother's cell phone. But the phone rang, and rang, and rang some more. Outside, Strong yelled into his phone, his own voice muffled by the thick glass of the squad car. Around him, the few people from inside the store had gathered to stare.

Finally, as I was about to hang up because I couldn't handle the dismal idea of attempting to say anything useful via voicemail, I heard my mother's voice on the other end of the line.

"Jo?" she whispered. "Jo, is that you?"

"Mom," I said, and relief at the sound of her voice made my own falter. "Mama, where are you?" Then I glanced at the phone in my hand and remembered. "How'd you know it was me at this number? Why are you whispering?"

"Shh. Stay calm now, baby. Daddy and I are together. Lucy said it was Eli's number, so I assumed it was you. Lucy's here too."

I didn't need her to spell it out any further. I could take it from there.

Holy crap, they have them, my parents are captured, they're with Lucy, Lucy's alive, but my parents are in danger and I have to save them and I don't know how to do it. Luckily, I didn't have to fight to keep my breath even or steady; I stopped pretending to breathe while I forced myself to think. *Stay calm, don't panic.*

"You're with Lucy?" I said.

In the back seat Eli popped to attention, momentum carrying him forward to crash into the front seat. His fingers shot through the bars and he pulled himself upright.

I ignored him and kept talking. "Where? How? We've been looking for her. Are you at the dorms? Where *are* you?"

I wasn't staying calm. Not at all. Her next words didn't help.

"Baby, we're in trouble. There are people here, bad people. They told me they did terrible things to you. Is it true?"

"I wanted to tell you, I never thought they…Mom, are you okay?"

"Jolene Elizabeth Hall, *is it true?* I need to know if what they say is true! Tell me *now*." Her voice, always so fluid, so soothing, was tight like a rubber band stretched to the brink of breaking. The tightness rendered it shrill, too, and beside me Eli flinched.

I didn't want to answer. The interior of the car closed in around me. Eli went fuzzy, the afternoon light went dark. I closed my eyes. "Yes," I whispered. "Yes, it's true. Everything they said, it's probably true."

"So you're…" She trailed off, and the sound of her sobbing threatened to kill me, to finish me right then and there with no further interactions with my bloody creator.

But I wasn't dead yet.

I opened my eyes. "No," I shouted. "No. I'm not dead. I'm not dead yet." I'd never been so sure of my own words. "Where are you? Tell me!"

Suddenly it was my father's voice at the other end of the line. He had a man's voice. It belonged on football fields, or at fancy martini bars, wheeling and dealing. At various times in my life, he'd use his voice to terrify me, and to delight me. But now he sounded old. Exhausted. Pushed to the limit. "Jolene?"

"Yes, Daddy, I'm here."

"Oh, thank God. Whatever you just said to your mother, it doesn't matter. It can be fixed. They told me, the people holding us. They told me they can reverse it. We can save you."

"No, Daddy."

"Yes. We have to do a few things, help them out, and we will.

They're right here next to us, Jolene. There's three of them. They had your mother's phone, and only gave it to us when Lucy said it was Eli's number. Jolene, listen to me. Do not call the police. They need you here, as soon as possible. They say you're running out of time. But they can still fix you, as soon as I wire them the money and get them the connections they need."

I shook my head violently, almost dropping the phone. "But Daddy, they're lying. And you can't negotiate with them! They're killers! They've killed dozens of girls already, it won't matter to them if I die, too!"

"Stop it, Jolene. Don't say that! It'll upset your mother, and it's not true. I have their word." He sounded desperate, like he was grasping at straws, and he knew it. But he didn't want me to know it. And he hadn't even seen me yet.

"Daddy, they just want your money. Don't give them anything." I paused, glanced back at Eli. "How's Lucy? How are you and Mom? Have they hurt you?"

"We're fine. Your mother is shaken, but we're unharmed. Wait, no, stop…"

There was a crackle on the phone, and then once again I heard my mother's sobs filling the air, so much more clearly than they'd been moments ago.

"What happened?" I cried.

Then it was Sondra Lewis's voice taking over the airwaves. "You're on speaker, dear Jo. Your parents and Lucy are with me. I heard you blew my cover this afternoon, that you figured it all out. Good detective work, dear. I'm rather proud of you."

"Let them go," I said, trying hard to block out the sound of my mother's hysterics from my ears. "Let my parents and Lucy *go*!"

"Oh yes, but dear, we need your parents' connections. Lucy's connections. The funding your families can provide. You do remember burning down our entire facility, don't you? We need to rebuild, resupply. Of course, lucky for you, we have a backup location where, believe it or not, we can still fix you. That way, you won't be a complete waste. And if not, when you die, we can at least use you for spare parts." She giggled, a high-pitched sound that used to wake students from their mid-class slumber, but now made me half-crazed with anger.

"You're a psychopathic bitch."

"Oh no, dear. I'm not. Come back to us and I'll prove to you exactly how not crazy I am. How not crazy my friends are, *dear.* You've caused us enough headaches this week. It's time to come home."

"No," I said. I turned to Eli and frantically mimed at him: *Get Strong,* I tried to say, but he just stared at me in silence, a look of horror on his face. Outside, Strong shouted into his phone. I decided to stall, to keep them talking until he could come in and use his fancy phone tracker to find out where they all were. "Let me talk to Lucy. Let me hear her voice."

In the background I heard a crash, then I heard Lucy. "Ouch, okay, okay, *quit it!*" Lucy sounded pissed as hell, not at all dead, and I was thrilled. "Jo, I'm here. They're assholes, but they haven't done anything to us yet. Your parents have been here for about an hour. But look, don't come. It won't end well if you…*ow! I said quit!*" There was another crash, and then Lucy was silent.

"Lucy?" I called. "Luce? Mom, Daddy, is everything okay?"

There were more sounds of struggle, and then once again Sondra Lewis's voice was the loudest. "Jo. Dear, sweet Jo. All this will be over soon. Just come home. Now."

"No! Never! Not on your terms!"

My mother cried out, and it sounded like she was in pain.

"Well, then, dear, we'll just have to do this the hard way."

"Let them go, you bitch!"

And then the phone went dead.

"Mom? Mom? *Mommy?*"

My mother didn't answer, and when I tried to call back, my call went straight to voicemail. "Hi, you've reached Vera Hall. I'm sorry I missed your call, but if you leave a message…"

I hung up.

"Dammit," I said, before I doubled over, folding down upon myself, my shoulders shaking and heaving in a cruel mockery of true crying. I stayed that way until the driver's side door opened and Strong loomed over me, red-faced and angry.

"What's going on?" he said.

"They have my parents."

"I know," he said.

STRONG REACHED IN AND GRABBED my arm. He yanked me hard so that I tumbled out of the car. My charger burst from the dashboard and the cord dangled in the snow. I flew through the air, across Strong's broad shoulders.

I yelped. "What the hell?"

From the back seat, Eli yelled and tried to open the door. His fingers squeaked against the glass as he tried to reach through to help me, but I was well beyond his reach.

"You know what, Jo?" he said, his voice cold. "I'm so tired of smelling you. You can ride the rest of the way in the trunk."

"What? No! No, stop!"

I kicked and yelled and even bit, but the mouthful of Strong's uniform coat knocked two teeth from my mouth. I spat them in the snow. Profanity poured from my mouth as he carried me to the trunk of the squad car and dumped me in. I landed in a heap in the small, carpeted space, where I lay in sudden, stunned silence as he slammed the trunk closed. I was enveloped in complete darkness.

Through the back seat I heard more struggling, and then silence. I didn't know if Eli was still in the car or not, but it soon began to move.

For once I was grateful for my lack of human senses. The motion didn't bother me, not immediately anyway. I couldn't smell musty carpet or exhaust. I knew carbon monoxide wouldn't kill me.

But. In the darkness, I was scared. More scared than I'd ever been before.

CHAPTER 19

TIME PASSED, BUT I had no idea how much. The car moved forward, left, right, up and down, and I learned I wasn't entirely immune to motion sickness. My head spun, a vortex in a car trunk. It was a strange sensation, the spinning without the stomach-churning nausea, and yet it wasn't a new feeling to me.

I WAS TEN YEARS OLD, on a trip to Miami for one of my father's annual lawyer conferences. My mother and I tagged along, looking forward to our annual week of beach and pool and shopping. My parents sat on either side of me in our first class seats, and I enjoyed the doting attention of a handsome flight attendant who brought me chocolates and a shiny metal pilot pin.

But the flight was turbulent. Extremely turbulent. The type where the pilot says, in an oppressively calm voice, to stay in your seats except in an emergency, and you somehow know the emergency is now. Where the flight attendants tour the cabin with empty smiles, securing any loose belongings before belting themselves into their own fold-down chairs.

At first, it felt like a roller coaster ride. We went up. We went down. We hit bumps. We dropped for hundreds of feet at a time. I grinned at my parents and raised my hands over my head. "Look, Mom!" I said, laughing. "No hands!"

But then the plane banked, turning to try to get out of the chop. As one wing dipped, my stomach dropped. I felt like the seat had dropped out from underneath me, like I was free-falling without a parachute.

We banked the other direction, and then the other. Each time, I felt more and more out of control. The free-fall in my stomach headed toward Mach speeds. After a minute, my head began to spin, whirling with a tornado's ferocity.

The smile melted from my face. My arms sank to my lap. I looked at my mother, away from the window through which I had stared at the cotton ball cloudbanks. "I don't feel so good," I said, bile rising in the back of my throat.

She was like lightning. Before I could blink, she'd reached into the pocket on the back of the seat in front of her. She pulled out the barf bag and held it open in front of me.

It wasn't a second too soon. The entire contents of my stomach spewed into the bag. Out came the chocolates, the sodas, the tiny airline pretzels. It was all gone. And still the plane kept banking, so I kept vomiting.

My father turned away, disgusted, but my mother never missed a beat. When the first bag filled, she somehow had a second one waiting. Within moments, with a free hand I never saw, she plastered a Dramamine patch behind my left ear. Soon, I felt woozy and weak, but the vomiting stopped as suddenly as it came.

But my head didn't stop spinning for a long time. Not until after the airplane landed and we drove away in a chauffeured limousine. Not until after we reached our resort hotel with a lagoon-shaped pool that called out to me even while I wobbled. Not until after I slept the afternoon away on the overstuffed couch in our penthouse hotel suite.

My head spun like that as I rattled around in the trunk of Adam's police car. I wanted so badly to throw up, even though I knew it wouldn't stop the spins.

Throwing up would have at least felt productive.

But my body couldn't do that anymore.

My body couldn't do anything anymore, other than wait. And wait. And wait some more.

So that's what I did, in the trunk, while I continued to spin.

Eventually, my internal battery ran low. Thoughts grew thicker, harder to maintain. Even the spins slowed down. I longed, thickly, for the warm buzz of the car charger, even more for the electrical socket in my dorm room. We become so quickly addicted to the few things in life that feel good. It hurt that I'd never feel that again.

And then, I shut down.

I'd love to say that shutting down felt good, a relief, like how a good nap can seem such an amazing escape from a rough day.

But instead, shutting down felt final. My eyelids fell shut, locking me into darkness more complete than the blackest night.

I will not shut down. I will not shut down.

As though I was a computer accessing a file, I found deep in the recesses of my mind a memory of a photograph of my mother and father when they were very young. As a little girl I'd carried the photo with me in a small, glittery-covered purse everywhere I went. It hung from a braided cord across my chest and back, sitting low on my hip. If I was apart from my parents, I'd pull it out and look at it. My small fingers would trace the curls in my mother's hair, the slope of my father's shoulder. They held each other in the photo, their faces close together, foreheads touching. My mother's lips parted in a wide, laughing smile, and my father's eyes crinkled at the corners in the way they did when he was happy. Really and truly happy.

The photograph in my mind faded.

With an effort worthy of Hercules, I found another. This one was much more recent. Lucy, at our winter formal, wearing a slinky black dress with her hair in a pile of red curls falling over one shoulder. Her skin pale, her eyes wide. She grinned, a devilish, curling grin, a dimple barely playing on her right cheek. The background of the photo was faded and dark, but there, clear and bright, the focal point of the photo, was Lucy's hand, fisted but for that one, tall, manicured middle finger. She was flipping off the photographer. *I was the photographer.*

Had my body listened to my brain, I'd have smiled.

The photograph in my mind faded, faster this time.

I will not shut down. I will not shut down.

In the waning power I pulled up one last image. It wasn't a photograph this time, culled from the file cabinets of my brain. This was a feeling, a smell. Cheeseburgers and ketchup, aftershave and laundry detergent. This was Eli's bed. This was Eli. This was the feel of his arm around my shoulders, our skin bare and warm. This was what my life had been. This was what it no longer was. This was what it would never be again.

I will not shut down. I will not shut down. I will…

The feeling faded. The black came and took me away.

THE NEXT THING I KNEW, after the black, was white. Bright-ass, burn-your-eyes-out-because-they've-been-closed-for-an-eternity kind of white. I knew my eyes were open when I saw the white, but I also knew almost immediately: I couldn't move them. I couldn't move anything.

I was awake, but I was paralyzed.

Again.

For a moment, though, in the initial surge of wakefulness, I could actually *feel.*

The cold steel of the table on which I lay.

The warm hum of the electrical current flowing through the cord in my back.

The soft breeze blown by a fan twenty feet away.

The cool air all around me.

I even smelled the cold, chemical smell of bleach and formaldehyde. The warm, burning smell of decay.

Oh, so that's what I smell like, I thought. *I'm disgusting.*

I was naked, I could tell, and back in the laboratory. Only it had to be a different laboratory, since Lucy and I had burned down the first one. The thoughts that clouded my head were muddy, murky, and I fought to forget the image of the fire chasing us down the staircase, but didn't have the power to do it. I relived that moment over and over again, the flames cutting through the mud and making me wish I could scream.

As that thought finally began to fade, I wondered if it had all been a dream. Maybe we had never found the lab. Maybe I'd made it all up. Maybe this was my first awakening and everything before had been a terrible nightmare.

Maybe I wasn't a monster after all.

Then I heard the voices.

"I still don't understand why you brought the boy. You should have left him there on the side of the road. He's nothing to us, a nobody from a nobody family. And even if you were too weak to kill him outright, exposure to the elements would have finished the job for you." I recognized the voice, but through the haze of my barely-there brain it was going to take a while to put a name to it.

"Yeah, and then we'd have had even *more* cops around here than we did after your misguided attempt at a *peaceful* capture. I brought a stupid little frat boy here; you got the whole stupid lab blown up."

The second voice I knew. I mean, I knew I knew it, but the words coming through that voice weren't making sense.

"Besides," the second voice growled. "I *want* to kill him. Later. When the others can watch. I want to feel their fear as I take his life." He caressed the last words, his voice soft like velvet. I thought I heard him sigh.

Strong. The second voice is Strong. And he's been helping us. Or at least, he said he was.

A third voice, another female, cackled with sharp laughter. Over it soared the sound of flesh hitting flesh, a slap across the face that I could not see. "You sound like a cliché," she said. "Need I remind you that we have a mission here? That we are working on something bigger, more important than your own sorry need to inspire fear? We are trying to change the *world* here. We're close to unlimited access to all the money we need, and a soldier with an ambassador parent. You know what a gold mine that'll be? And every step you take to endanger the mission is a step for which you will have to answer when the Master returns. And he is coming. He is coming *soon*, and he is not pleased with either of you."

I still couldn't see anything beyond the white light of a fluorescent bulb. I couldn't even move my eyes.

"Is he really coming?" It was the first voice again. The first woman. She sounded scared, terrified even, and I heard a catch in her throat that I'd heard dozens of times before while I sat through countless discussions of archaic British literature.

Her name is Sondra Lewis. She was my professor at Smytheville, and she's one of the bad guys. She hurt me. I tried to move my eyes, to confirm what I already knew, and I failed. *Flow, electricity, flow!*

"Yes," snapped the third voice. The one I didn't recognize. "He's coming soon, and he's not happy."

The voice was feminine, but hoarse. Throaty. Like the woman had smoked at least a pack a day for a dozen years. She paused, but then continued at a much more crisp pace. "But so much of the damage can still be undone. We can use this one for parts. Her battery, her pump—they're still in good shape. And we have so much more research to share. Look at what the doctor's done in his time with us. He had one lab up and running; he'll have the new one ready soon, as long as we don't mess things up again." She sounded hopeful, but I could also sense fear.

"But why are we doing this to her, if we're just using her for parts? Why the restoration? Why won't you let the doctor dissect her now?"

There was another slap, a louder one, and Strong groaned in pain. "You know I won't take that forever," he growled.

"Yes, you will," the third voice said. "And you will remember who is in charge here, and who will take the biggest fall when the Master gets here and sees this mess."

"He wouldn't…"

"Hush. Yes, he would. The agent whose oversight caused this dilemma has been terminated. You know that. Now, would you like to save your own worthless lives?" She paused, and then continued even though there was no verbal response. "Yes, I thought so. So. We're clear. And let's be clear on this, too. We are restoring this girl simply because if her parents see her in the shape she was in prior to her arrival here, there's no way they'll think we can reverse the process."

"Why do we care?" said Sondra. "We're just going to…"

"Hush," said the other woman. "We've said too much already. There are too many unknowns."

A chill went down my spine, and something inside me shuddered.

They're going to kill me.

I'd known it, on some level, for so long, but hearing it loud and clear while trapped and paralyzed on a surgical table? That was the icing on the cake.

I had to get out of there. Deep inside me, deep within the pit of a stomach I no longer knew for sure I possessed, a seed of fury sprouted roots. As I listened to my captors, it began to grow. And with it, I grew thirsty for revenge.

"Now," the angry voice continued. "Will one of you please check on her and confirm she's still functional? We need her awake soon if we're going to get anywhere with the parents."

Strong's face appeared below the white light, close to my own. I lay still, silent, because I had to. I willed my eyes not to move, not to give away the fact that I was awake and aware. It worked.

There was cold pressure on my bare chest. A stethoscope. I wondered what he was listening for, since I knew there was no heart beating in my chest.

"She's humming," he said after a moment. "It's faint, but it's there. The heart pump is still operational. She looks a lot better, and smells better, too." He smiled over me. "Good job, Jo," he said. He patted my cheek. The touch of his hand on my face caused my skin to crawl as though with maggots.

Kiss my ass, scumbag, I thought. *If I could move, I would hurt you. Doesn't matter how big you are.*

"Good," said the unknown woman. "Let her charge a bit more. We want her awake, but not too strong."

"I don't think she's discovered yet how strong she actually can be."

"Then let's keep it that way, Adam. We're almost done with Jo. She has nothing left to offer us, except that one crucial connection."

"And the boy? What shall we do with him?" Strong's voice rose with excitement, and I wondered if that was the only part of him that rose.

My face twitched as I almost let it smile. Luckily I stopped myself in time. The paralysis neared its end. It was time to amp up my willpower and self-control.

The woman snorted. "You'll have your fun with him. Don't worry. He won't leave this place alive."

"Yes, Martha," said Sondra and Strong in unison, and somehow I didn't think they were having any fun.

That was fine with me, though. I wasn't, either. But I was starting to feel like maybe, just maybe, I could.

Design Docs, Iteration 4

Hydration is key to maintenance. To keep subjects fresh and functional, we need to keep fluid flowing into them at all times they are not in use. Removal from hydration source causes rot-like effects as cells dry out and wither away. Dehydration can, to some extent, be reversed, but some damage is irreparable. Therefore, subjects should not be away from hydrating fluids for more than three hours at a time. Anything longer than that and they will begin to smell, attracting undue attention, and losing their glow of life.

"BRING THEM OVER here," the woman called Martha said.

An hour had passed, judging by the ticking of the clock that hung somewhere in the room. I had, for a while, been able to wiggle my toes, imperceptibly I hoped, though I was somewhat sure I heard the crinkle of dry leaves every time I moved. I could no longer feel anything but the flow of electricity into my body; I was back in sensory deprivation.

"Here," she said, from close beside me. "Their voices will help her wake up."

I heard the squeak of a door opening on rusty hinges, then the clickity-clack of high heels against a hard, tile floor.

"No. That can't be my Jo." That was my father. I heard him stifle a gasp, and my nonexistent heart began to break.

"Let me go. I have to see her." That was my mother. She sounded calmer than my father.

More shuffling steps. Then slowly, cautiously, my mother's face floated into my field of view. It took every ounce of self-control not to reach out to her. I wanted her so badly I could taste her perfume in my barren mouth. But I knew I had to play it cool, to keep my cards close to the chest while our captors were nearby.

My mother's eyes trailed across my withered body. Her hand hovered above my cheek, my forehead. She turned and looked away, I assumed at my father. "I'm afraid to touch her," she said. "She looks so fragile. Like she could blow away."

"It's not her," my father said. I couldn't see him, but I could picture him, standing with his legs spread and his arms crossed on his chest. It was how he always stood when stubbornly opposing an argument. Even when he knew he was beaten. "You've got a girl here who maybe once looked a bit like Jo, but it's not her. Look at her! No hair, gray skin! How can you expect me to believe..."

My mother turned back to me. This time, she focused on my eyes. She moved her face closer to mine, wrinkling her nose only once against the smell I knew must have burned inside her nostrils. Soon, she was almost nose-to-nose (had I still had a nose, that is), forehead-to-forehead with me. I lay still, battling against every impulse to move that sparked within my body.

She stared into my eyes. Her own eyes searched, pouring deep inside me, looking for a hint of her little girl.

She found me.

Her eyes filled with tears. Her mouth fell open and her hand dropped to the table beside me. Her knees buckled. She stumbled, and my father's face appeared beside hers. He caught her, and they both disappeared from my field of view for a moment before they reappeared, together.

My mother inhaled, and it sounded like her throat had closed. And then she wailed. It was primal, and shrill. It was inhuman. I died in that moment, for at least the third time. No child should ever see her mother's grief over her own death. It should be against God's laws.

It was certainly against mine, and the seed of fury became as strong and as thick as a tree trunk, deep within my core.

My father had to see for himself, and even as he held her tight, he moved closer to me. He, too, searched, and he, too, found. He turned white.

But then something in his demeanor changed. He brushed a fingertip against my temple, and I heard him wipe his hand on his pants. While he stared, a corner of his mouth turned up, and he winked.

He knows. He knows I'm awake. I don't know how he knows, but he does.

But my mother didn't.

"What did you do to my baby?" my mother shrieked. "What did you do? You're all monsters! Monsters!"

My peripheral vision was improving. My parents stepped away from me as my father held my mother around the waist. She flailed and punched outward with her arms and legs, ripping through the air, trying to tear someone apart, someone who remained tantalizingly out of her reach, and out of my line of sight. Her arm hit the lamp that hung over my head, and it swung in a violent, dangerous arc on its thin chain, spotlighting my parents' struggle with a slowed down strobe effect.

"Knock it off," Strong said, his voice sharp and cold. He stood nearby, just outside the boundaries of their dance. "Listen. This can all be a bad dream. All you need to do is give us what we need, and we'll send you all on your merry way. "

Don't believe him! He's lying! I screamed silently. The light above me continued to swing. Left, right…left, right… I wanted it to stop. It made my head spin again.

Beside me, my parents were suddenly still. My father panted, his breathing ragged and labored. But my mother was calm.

"I don't believe you," she said. Her voice was dangerous, like the time she caught me writing dates on my hand the morning before a history exam.

"But it's allowed," I said. "The exam's open book."

"I don't believe you," she said.

And for the next two weeks, I'd spent two hours every day bent over my thick history textbook, my mother watching carefully as I committed full chapters to memory. I never cheated on a history test again. My mother hated liars.

She stood, suddenly statuesque and graceful, beside my father. Her hand pressed against his stomach, holding him still beside her. "I don't believe any of you are capable of reversing this…this…this *this!* My Jo is gone. There's nothing in there, behind her eyes. She is *gone.* And we will give you nothing."

And she, my elegant, well-mannered, well-groomed mother, reared her head back and spat a wad of phlegm across the room. I heard it splatter. I heard Strong shout, a choked, gagging sound that turned the remnants of my stomach.

A strong, massive hand reached into my line of sight and grabbed my mother's arm. Strong. He yanked her from my father's grip.

He shouted, "Vera! No! Stop!"

I heard grunts, the dull thuds of punches landing, and the crunch of bones breaking. Inside, I cheered for my father, and hoped he came out on top.

"You'll pay for that," Strong cried out, spitting what I hoped was blood onto the floor. From somewhere nearby, Martha cackled. She was enjoying this.

"Don't you *ever* lay a hand on my wife again," my father responded.

"Or you'll get even worse than that."

My father came back into view, shaking his bloodied hand right above my face.

That's just like him, taking credit when it's due. My head shook, almost of its own volition, in near-amusement, until he pulled my mother close beside him.

An angry handprint raised red and ugly across her cheek. Her typically immaculate makeup ran in dark smudges beneath her tear-reddened eyes. Her hair was disheveled, pulled out in clumps from her signature up-do. My father wanted me to see her.

He wanted me good and angry. He knew how much stronger I was when I was angry. Always had been, always would be.

I WAS SEVEN, IN THE first grade at Hawthorne Elementary, and my mother was out of town for the week. My father had been called in to see the principal after a playground fight landed Nicky R. in the nurse's office with a broken nose.

We sat in a booth at a Friendly's restaurant. I expected a punishment, not ice cream, but was smart enough to eat my sundae in fearful silence while my father apprised me.

Finally, he spoke. "What happened?"

There was no sense in beating around the bush. Even at seven, I could see that.

I sighed. "He looked up my skirt. Pulled it up in front of all the other kids. They all saw my underwear."

"So you punched him?"

I took a bite of Rocky Road, chewing thoughtfully on a piece of frozen marshmallow before I spoke.

"Uh-huh. I didn't think I'd actually hit him, but I guess I was stronger than I thought."

"Huh," he said, and he took a long pull from his root beer float. "Well, I don't want to fault you for being stronger than you thought." Sip. "Actually, I'd rather like to encourage you to stand up for yourself, especially against boys." Sip. "I won't tell your mother about this. Not this time. Don't let your fighting become a habit, Rocky, but don't let anyone push you around either, okay?"

We finished eating our ice cream with the camaraderie of co-conspirators. I always felt like I gained his respect that afternoon.

IT WAS GROWING HARDER TO remain still, but I needed to. I knew that. If I could be still for long enough, amass enough strength from the electrical current flowing into me, I'd be able to fight.

The rage within me took root, and continued to grow. At the sight of my mother's battered face, I clenched my fists. I didn't mean to, and tried to stop myself, but it happened. I moved.

Strong saw.

"She's awake!" he said. "She moved!"

With that, he yanked out the cord from the ground, and the hum of electricity that gave me strength was cut off. It felt weird to be without it; within a heartbeat, I felt its absence like a knife in the gut.

I doubted that I had much more than an hour's worth of power, but no one needed to know that. Nor did anyone need to know I somehow felt stronger than a circus muscle man.

Not, at least, until I was sure of it.

THEY MOVED ME TO A chair, propping me up like a quadriplegic. Sondra and Martha both wore surgical masks as they carried me between them. I played weak, lifting neither head nor foot nor remaining pinkie finger.

In part, it was to try to dupe them into believing I *was* still weak, that I couldn't put up a fight even if I wanted to.

Another part of me, though? It just wanted to be a pain in the ass. I wanted to make them work for their paychecks.

The paycheck I planned to ensure would never come. At least, not from *my* family's bank accounts.

Once I was seated, my parents knelt in front of me.

"Hey, Champ," my father said. It was an old nickname, given to me when I was eight years old and won the championship race in the backstroke at summer camp. "You've certainly gotten yourself into a pickle this time, haven't you?" He looked around. Strong and Sondra were engaged in some deep conversation, each whispering and flailing about dramatically. They weren't paying any attention to us. Martha was nowhere to be seen.

My father lowered his voice a few decibels. "Can you speak?"

I didn't move.

"I understand if you don't want to right now." He was whispering by then. "Blink once for yes, twice for no. I mean, if you can blink at all."

Instead, I winked. He smiled, and raised his fist in a silent cheer.

My mother gasped, and Strong and Sondra turned abruptly toward us. "What?" said Sondra. "What is it?"

"It's…it's just…" my mother stammered, searching for the right words. She found them. "I touched her. I touched her knee. And her skin, it's like powder. It flaked away where my fingers hit, and it startled me."

"Yes, dear," said Sondra, all sweetness and honey. "That's because your daughter *ran away*. Had she behaved herself, she'd be in much better shape still. She'd be *finished* and beautiful and complete. Instead, she's what you see before you: a tragic work in progress. Now if you'll excuse us…"

Sondra and Strong turned back to their conversation, but my father had other plans.

"If you'll excuse *me*," he said, sarcasm ruining his attempt at politeness, "I have a request you may wish to consider if you expect any future cooperation from my wife and me. You don't have children, I can tell. But this is my child, and I think I'm within my rights, whatever they may be within this dungeon, to request a blanket. I have no desire to be forced to view my teenage daughter without clothes. I don't care that the circumstances here are a bit…" He trailed off, and then gestured toward the electrodes and scars across my chest and stomach, that stood out like homing beacons against the shriveled, sinewy gray of my skin. "…gruesome."

Strong shrugged. "She still out?"

My father nodded. "Like a light, from what I can tell."

"Then I guess it wouldn't hurt. Sondra, go get them a blanket. Tell Martha she's still unresponsive. And, oh, yeah, I guess, bring in the others. It's probably time we all have a little chat."

Annoyance flashed across Sondra's face, but a furtive smile from Strong restored her obvious adoration for him. "Shall I include Eli? Is it time?"

"Yes. I want them all here." A slow, careful grin spread across his face. His nose was crooked, and smeared under with blood, but somehow that only added to his handsomeness. His evil, maniacal handsomeness.

"I'll need your help with him. He's feisty, and you're so much stronger than me." She batted her eyelashes, a professorial damsel in distress.

"Fine." He turned to my parents and me. "You two, come here first. I can't have you wandering off."

My father shrugged, then he and my mother stood and walked over to Strong, playing the part of ideal prisoners. They allowed him to bind their wrists behind their backs with duct tape, though my mother winced when he wrapped hers.

"Not so tight," she said, trying to pull away.

Based on the look on my father's face, Strong had been smart to bind him up first. For some reason, though, my mother looked slightly victorious as Strong and Sondra left the room.

My parents turned and pounced.

"Jo, is that really you in there?" my mother said, sprinting in her high-heeled pumps to kneel in front of me.

"Can you talk?" My father spoke over her, his voice booming in the cavernous room.

"Yes," I said. "But I don't know how much time I have. Can one of you drag me to the wall and plug me in? I don't want them to know I can move."

My father moved easily, with a fluidity that belied his bindings. He pressed his back to my chair and slid me easily toward the wall, and then, with his hands still bound, found the cord that we'd rigged up days before, and plugged it into a normal wall socket.

I was glad to have the hum of electricity flowing through me again, although it was much fainter than it had been when I was recharging on the table.

With that settled, I turned to my mother. I had so much to tell her, it all bubbled out in one vacant breath. "I'm so sorry. So sorry. This is all my fault. I was stupid. I tried to walk home in the middle of the night and they got me. I was mad at Eli, and he'll tell you he made me go, but I could have stayed. Whatever you do, don't blame Eli, okay? He feels bad enough as it is. But I'm so sorry. This is all my fault, I promise you."

Tears filled my mother's eyes, but her jaw was resolute. She elbowed my knee, her attempt at a comforting pat while her hands were bound. "No, sweetheart. This isn't the time for that. This isn't your fault, and it isn't Eli's. These are terrible people, and they've done something terrible to you. Why didn't you go to the police when you escaped? Or call us right away? We could have helped."

My voice was broken, and it came out as little more than a sandpaper-whisper. "I know. But by the time I woke up, this was already done. I was already embalmed. There wasn't an easy way to turn back. So Lucy and I, we tried to fix it ourselves. To fix me." I shrugged, and happily noticed my shoulders didn't crackle quite like they had before. My skin was less flaky, too, more supple. They really *had* fixed me while I slept. But that didn't matter. I continued. "Besides, we thought Strong *was* a cop, that we had the police on our side."

"Oh. Him," my father cut in, furious. "He got us, too. Met us at the front door of your dorm a couple hours ago. Don't know how he knew it was us, but he did. He told us he had news about you, and we believed him." He frowned and rubbed his chin, five o'clock shadow bristling beneath his fingers. "He dumped us here, in a cell. That's where we found Lucy. She filled us in on the rest."

"But how did he…" I started to say. Strong had been with *me* all day.

My mother interrupted. "I knew we shouldn't trust him," she said. "Didn't I tell you we shouldn't trust him?"

"Actually, you never said anything of the sort, dear."

I smiled. I couldn't help it then. I always loved when they bickered. And when I smiled, my face didn't crack. But there wasn't time to think about that.

"You guys! Stop arguing. Please! There's more!"

"Apart from the obvious?" asked my father.

"Yeah," I said. "First, Strong was with me all day. I don't know how he was with you, too. And second, it's good I didn't call you. They want your money!" As I spoke, my mother leaned her head against my knee. I jerked away. "Mom! Don't!"

"What, baby?" She lifted her head but didn't leave my side.

"Toxic. I'm toxic. When they did this, they must've used arsenic. When they took Lucy, they took her from the hospital. They were treating her for arsenic poisoning."

My father looked confused. "But she's fine. Well, except for her pinkie. Frostbite. She thinks she's going to lose it. And possibly a broken ankle. She'll need a doctor to take a look at it."

"What?" I said, embracing only for a split second the relief that followed the news that Lucy was going to be all right. Because I knew her current health didn't matter if we didn't all get out of this alive. "She was at death's door when I left her. I can't believe she's not dying." I sighed, and thought. "But that brings me to my next point. What I need you guys to know is, they *cannot* reverse this. The damage is done to me. I'm done for."

"Don't say that, Jolene! Don't ever say that!" My mother sounded on the verge of breaking down. My father stepped closer to her so the front of his legs pressed firmly against her back. He leaned forward, squeezing up against her body, trying to hold her together.

"It's true. I promise. Even before, I knew. I didn't email you to come, they hacked my account. I would have told you to stay away. I knew it was dangerous. But I'm glad you're here, so I can say goodbye." I paused, and then stared down at the cord that trailed out from behind me. It was my umbilical cord, the only way I could cling to life. "And then I heard them say, when they thought I was asleep, that they can't save me. They just want your and Daddy's money, your access. Lucy's, too. They want her mother, the ambassador. Mama, I'm afraid they're going to want to make you all like me. And I can't let that happen to you. I can't. I can't let you end up like me."

I stopped speaking. My parents wept.

And when you're frightened, and you feel alone, there's nothing more shattering than seeing your parents cry.

My resolve faltered. I wanted nothing more in that moment than to be five years old again, sleeping in the bed in between my parents after a nightmare. I longed for them to fold me up between them, to protect me from the darkness. I couldn't keep on fighting alone.

But then my father stood again. "I love you, Jo. You're my sunshine. My light. My rainbow. Everything good in my life? It comes from you and your mother. And now that I'm here, you're not doing this alone. I'm with you, until…" His voice cracked. "Until the end. Every step of the way."

My mother nodded. "My baby," she said, and she sniffed. "I'm here with you, too. We're all in this together." She heaved a deep, tremulous sigh, and fresh tears flowed from her eyes.

"Okay," said my father, shaking himself as though he were a dog casting water from his coat. Tears leapt from his cheeks, dotting the ground around him like dew. "That's enough of that. We don't have much time. Jo, do you know what their ultimate goal is?"

"No," I said. "Not yet. I have a stack of their files back at my dorm, but I haven't read them yet. I figured I could do that after… But no matter what, we can't help them."

"Shh," my mother said, standing up suddenly and eyeing the door. "They're coming. I can hear their voices." I heard them, too. Loud and clear.

"Okay," I whispered. "Look, just let me keep charging here. I need to get as strong as I can for now, to see how far we can carry things. Block me. Don't let them see. They'll unplug me. They want me weak."

My father nodded, then stepped aside so he stood in front of the outlet. "Right. Go back to being comatose," he said. "We'll get them talking, see what we can learn, see how long we can stall. But when I give the signal, pull the tape off my hands, okay? I need my hands back. Then we can…"

But I never learned his plan. He stopped talking as the door burst open and Strong and Sondra walked in, dragging Eli and Lucy behind them. I leaned back in my chair, mouth slack and eyes half-open. Strong wore a blanket draped around his shoulders.

Eli looked like he'd been through hell and back again. His face was bruised and bloodied, and I remembered the sounds of the fight in the car when I lay in the trunk. Dark, heavy eyelids, head drooping down, Eli looked as though all the fight had long since been taken from him. My heart sank.

But then I looked at Lucy.

And Lucy looked angrier than I'd ever seen her, and she looked whole. Not sick. Not broken, save her significant limp. But her fury was palpable, and I flashed back for a second to a memory of Lucy slugging a football player whose hands were a little too grabby while they danced one night at a club. I knew from that point on never to get Lucy good and angry—she had a fiery redhead temper, and she could kick some ass when inspired.

She looked inspired right then. Really, truly inspired.

This might work out after all, I thought. But then I looked at my father, looming over me, and wondered. *But what's the signal? What's the plan?*

CHAPTER 21

"GET YOUR EYES off her." My father, once again painfully aware of my nakedness while doing his best to block my electrical cord snaking its way to the wall, scowled at Strong. "You there, give me that blanket."

Strong held it out, but stared at me and flicked his tongue in and out of his mouth while my father reached out for the blanket with his tied-up hands, then attempted to spread it over me while he faced the other direction. My mother stepped forward, and together they covered me up to my neck.

"You bastards," my mother said, and I started at my mother's choice of words. She *hated* bad language. "You bastards killed my only child. Look at her. She's comatose."

I played dead as best I could. It wouldn't do to let the bad guys know I was ready to fight.

Lucy side-stepped Strong and Sondra. Her pale skin neared purple with rage. She ran to me, knelt before my feet, and tried to look into my eyes. "Jo? Are you even still in there? You look terrible, even worse than before."

I love you too, bitch, I thought.

"Actually," said Eli from across the room where he slumped against the wall. A huge swollen lump glowed red on his temple. "Actually, I think Jo looks a hell of a lot better. Of course, you didn't see her yesterday, or earlier today. She was…a disaster. But this is better. How'd they fix you?" He sounded honestly curious, ever the pre-med student.

I, of course, didn't answer. Not that anyone expected me to.

"Oh, right. You can't move yet, can you? They let you shut down. Assholes." He glared at Strong and Sondra, but then groaned, holding a hand to his side. "You assholes better be able to bring her back to us." He sounded only half-hearted, though. He groaned again, his face flushing with pain.

"Eli!" my mother said, old habits dying hard. "Language!"

"Sorry, Mrs. Hall." He slid down the wall until he sat, barely holding his upper half upright.

I clenched my jaw tighter, willing myself to stay quiet. I didn't know what sound to make—a laugh and a scream both trembled just below the surface of my self-control, waiting for me to slip up and let them out. Either would be my downfall.

Lucy looked at my dad. "I think he's got some broken ribs."

He nodded and glared at Strong. His jaw clenched, and he worked hard to loosen it. I'd seen that jaw muscle clenched many times in high school. *Drinking with friends until dawn? Tight jaw face. Sneaking a boyfriend in through a window? Tight jaw face.* Always followed by thunderous shouting.

But not this time. He heaved a great sigh instead. "Look," he said, pleading with Strong. "Man-to-man, *mano-a-mano*, please, tell me, why did you do this to my girl? Who are you working for?"

Strong puffed up and looked pleased. "I thought you'd never ask." He turned to Sondra. "Your turn, Miss Recruiter. Wouldn't it make more sense to recruit them than to take their money and run? Teach a man to fish, right? Go on. Teach fishing."

Sondra giggled like a schoolgirl and pushed him playfully. It was then I noticed the gun in her waistband, which flashed when the light hit it as her shirt pulled up. "Adam! That's not exactly an enticing way to present information to them." She spoke in her syrupy voice again, and walked to my parents and patted my mother on the arm. "Here, you poor dears. You've been through so much. Why don't you have a seat?"

They didn't move.

She continued as though they had, as though she was just having a chat with some friends on a quiet Sunday afternoon. "The answer to your question is simple, Mr. Hall. We are the Order of the Adversaries. Sounds intimidating, right? But we're nothing of the sort." She laughed, a playful sound that belied her age.

My mother nodded encouragingly, like she was interested, the same way she always responded to Jehovah's Witnesses who came to spread the good news at our door. My mother was a champion at being pleasant in unpleasant situations. Sondra ate it up, and continued in a singsong voice. She had her script memorized.

"Have you ever felt like the world is going to fall apart, my dears? Our country is divided. It's ruled either by heathens, or by a religious right that believes only in filling its own pockets. There are murders in the streets, mass shootings by the dozens, and no one lifts a finger. That's where we come in. We're ready and willing to lift our not-insignificant fingers to do the job no one else wants. We are preparing for the Great Upheaval.

"We believe in a complete absence of religion, of government, of anyone telling anyone else what to do, how to live, or what to buy. We support survival of the fittest. And to that end, we feel our country *requires* the Great Upheaval."

"But how?" my father said. "How can we fix things?" He sounded honest, earnest. I was impressed. But beside him, Lucy stewed, glowing red. I wondered how long this could last, and what plan my father was formulating while he let Sondra blather on. Lucy wasn't going to remain silent much longer.

Nearby, Strong's eyes glazed over with pure, unadulterated pride, as if he were listening to a prophet speak. His hand floated up to cover his heart. Clearly, they'd both drunk the Kool-Aid.

"Well, that's where our girls come in. They are our spies, our soldiers. With them, we can achieve infiltration and penetration. Penetration into churches that corrupt, government organizations that neglect. Penetration into fledgling governments with access to nuclear capabilities." Here, she nodded at Lucy, who responded by sticking out her tongue.

Sondra ignored her. "And penetration into industries with the chemicals and technologies we require to grow our army, extend our reach ever further. With our girls, we'll have the most loyal, most dedicated soldiers in the history of the world, because we've created them! We can control them utterly."

"But what will they do once they achieve…penetration?" My father covered a disbelieving laugh with a wet, sticky cough. "And why can't you just recruit normal soldiers? Why all girls?"

"Oh, dear sir, who doesn't trust a lovely girl? We'll have beautiful soldiers, ready to perform any duty, and it's the lust of our leaders that will allow them to succeed. Our process has been less than reliable thus far, but now we feel we've perfected it enough to share our methods around the world." She blushed, and cast her eyes down with shameful pride. "We have offices around the country, you know. And laboratories as well. We're growing, and soon, when we've shared our research and created more and more girls, we'll be the biggest organization of our kind in the world."

Suddenly, over against the wall, Eli snorted, and then doubled over, clutching his stomach. I jerked inadvertently, ready to leap to his aid, but my mother pressed herself against me, reminding me to stay put. I was afraid he was dying.

But then he took a deep breath, and with his head between his knees, he let out a giant peal of laughter. We all stared at him, me included, unable to control myself any longer. As everyone stared, consumed by the sight of Eli's hysteria, he laughed until he cried, and finally, Sondra had enough.

"When you've quite finished, *dear*," she said, fury palpable in her voice.

"I'm sorry," Eli said, gasping for air. "It's just…you're anarchists creating *femme-bots*! You're a giant freaking parody of yourselves." And then he lost control again.

"Femme-bots?" repeated Sondra. "I'm sorry, I don't understand."

Strong appeared at Eli's side and let loose a kick that landed directly on Eli's already-battered rib cage. Eli howled and flopped to the ground, writhing like a dying fish on the shore. My mother pressed herself against me again, holding me down with a hip, while Lucy launched herself across the room, knocking into Strong.

Without the use of her arms and her sharp fingernails, though, she was ineffective at best. She bounced off Strong's brawny shoulder and landed on the ground beside Eli, silent, seething. Her face betrayed no pain, though she'd whacked her head against the wall. She leaned in front of Eli, protecting him from any further action by Strong.

But Strong was done, for the moment. He shrugged, and then spoke to Sondra. "Femme-bots. *Austin Powers*. It was a movie that came out in the nineties. I'd never thought of the association…but… suffice to say, he's mocking us. We can't have that now, can we?"

"Oh, dear," she said, and she reached out and took Strong's arm. All trace of persuasion was gone from her face, like she'd been shut off and was no longer the Order's star recruiter. Eli had destroyed that moment of respite for all of us with his outburst, and for that he had paid. "That surely won't do. Maybe it is better that the Master's headed here. Maybe he can talk some sense into this boy." The sticky-sweet side of her voice was gone, replaced by something flatter and more threatening.

"I don't expect the Master will have much to say to him," Strong said. "He probably won't be here by the time the Master arrives."

Who is the Master? I wondered. *And when will Dad give the signal? What if I miss it?*

Urge after urge to *attack* surged through my body. I was going to lose control soon.

FROM SOMEWHERE DEEP WITHIN THE underground lair, an alarm sounded, and everyone in the room jumped.

"What's that?" my mother said.

"None of your business," Strong snapped. He looked startled, though. Concerned. "Be right back."

He left without another word, leaving Sondra standing awkwardly alone. She looked nervous, and suddenly pulled the gun from the back of her ill-fitting pants. She trailed it around the room, pointing at everyone in turn. "I don't want any funny business," she said.

"We don't, either," my father said. "All we want is to fix our daughter. Let's get this done. I want our baby back."

My father stepped in front of me. It looked like a protective gesture, but his hands were suddenly enticingly close to mine. The tape that bound them had a loosened corner, where he'd obviously been working with his fingers to get it started. I could just reach out and pull the tape off, if I wanted. It might pull some of his skin off, I realized, but that would heal. And then we could get out of there.

But I had to wait for the signal.

"We already told you," she said. "We need money. Lots of it. Any business connections you have that will help us in our quest. Give us what we want and we'll reverse the process on Jolene."

"You're such a damn…" Lucy exploded with anger, but my mother shook her head at her, so slightly I was surprised Lucy even saw it. But she must have, because she stopped shouting and risked a glance at me.

I winked.

"Liar," she whispered.

My father thought for a moment, then said, "You know, Sondra, the problem I'm having, though, is this: I agree with Lucy. I think you're a liar. I think your organization is garbage. And I can't wait to see the rest of this goddamn place burn. Jolene, *now*."

The signal!

I reached out and ripped the tape from my father's wrists. He cried out in pain, but his hands were free within a heartbeat. He ran forward, surging like a locomotive, toward Sondra Lewis.

Sondra's mouth fell open, but her eyes narrowed. She was ready for him. She pointed the gun at my father's chest, but before she squeezed the trigger, Eli's glazed-over eyes lit up and he pushed himself to his feet and launched into Sondra. She flew through the air, and the gun fell from her hands. My father was unable to stop and crashed instead into Eli, who stood where Sondra had been. They tumbled to the ground, and Eli yowled in pain.

Sondra landed on the ground beside Lucy, flat on her back. Lucy jumped to her feet, then pinned Sondra to the ground with a foot against her throat. "Don't move," Lucy said. "If you do, I'll crush your windpipe. One stomp is all it'd take. Try me. Please." Then she turned and grinned at me. "I *knew* you'd charged long enough! Welcome back to the land of the living!"

Sondra didn't move. She whimpered, a baby animal trapped by a predator. With no gun and no Officer Strong to protect her, she was reduced once more to just a lowly adjunct professor.

I grinned, my cheeks able to handle it. "Thanks," I said to Lucy. "What should we do with her?"

As I spoke, I reached to pull the tape from my mother's hands, but found she'd already done most of the work. "I kept that awful man from taping them too tightly when I struggled. I think he underestimated me," she said, and then offered me a hand to pull me to my feet.

Against the wall, Eli hadn't moved since my father had body-slammed him. My father leaned over him, concern etched into his tanned features. I walked over to them, my mother beside me.

"I'm so sorry," I heard my father whisper.

As I approached, Eli's face calmed. He managed a pitiful imitation of a smile. "Jo," he said, his voice thick. "You smell a lot better."

"You look like crap."

"Yeah. Thanks. Feel like it too. Where's the professor?"

"Over there, on the ground with Lucy."

"Yeah, I have her," called Lucy. "But could someone come untape my hands?"

"Mom, could you go help Lucy please?"

I knelt down beside my father and Eli. "Eli, can you get up? We need to get you guys out of here."

"Jolene, where's your blanket?" My father's voice was gentle.

I looked down at myself, and then shrugged. "Daddy, does it really matter anymore? You've all seen me. And look, I'm so messed up, I look like the Mummy, or some crazy villain from a movie. Please don't freak out. I need you."

"I'm not *freaking out*, dear. I just can't look at you like this. Please cover up. For me?"

"Daddy, my modesty went out the window the minute I woke up naked on one of these stupid tables. Besides, my only concern right now is getting you guys *out*. Now, Eli, can you get up?" My voice was firm. *I* wouldn't have argued with me. I watched my father think about debating, and then decide against it.

Eli nodded and tried to push himself up. "I think so. Oh, ouch. Okay, something's broken, but I can walk." With my father's help, he was soon on his feet, his wrists were free, and the white-hot pain had left his face.

And then, as the adrenaline of a sudden escape left the living people in the room, we all looked at each other, the door through which Strong had exited, and then down at Sondra, pinned beneath Lucy's booted foot.

"Well," Eli said. "What now?"

"Who has a cell phone?" I asked.

"Nada."

"Nope."

"They took them. After you called."

I tried to come up with a backup plan, and as I considered I stared at Lucy. She looked so strong and tough. "Weren't *you* on death's door last time I saw you? What happened to your arsenic poisoning?"

Lucy snorted. "Arsenic poisoning? What are you talking about? Eli, what is she talking about?"

He groaned and leaned against the wall again. "That's what Strong told us was wrong with you when you were in the hospital."

She laughed. "Ridiculous. I never got past the waiting room. Sondra and that other woman were there waiting for me. Sondra said she was going to take me somewhere to get more help. I was halfway frozen, delirious, so I didn't ask questions. As soon as they had me away from the public eye, they drugged me. Probably the same way they drugged you last week. I guess Adam carried me to their car, but I was never even seen by a doctor. He probably made it all up to make you feel bad."

"Um, kids? I hate to break up the sharing session," said my father. "But I really think we should be going."

I raised my hand, loving the flexibility of my semi-healed body, even as I could feel the power from the cord cease when I unplugged. “Where, though? That way leads to Strong. And to who knows what else. And for all we know, they could be watching us.”

The voice came from above, below, around. It was Martha. “Don’t worry, dearies. We *are* watching. And we are *not* pleased.”

In the background, I heard Strong’s voice. “Bastards. Let Sandy go.”

"OH, HELL NO."

We all turned to Lucy. She'd pressed her foot even harder against Sondra's throat, and Sondra began to thrash about on the ground, struggling to break free. Lucy didn't budge, though. She was statuesque, regal, her chin tilted toward the ceiling, where, somewhere, a video camera was trained down on her. Her body language screamed defiance, and she slowly raised a hand and extended her middle finger.

I laughed. I couldn't help it. Beside me, my parents laughed too. All we could *do* was laugh.

On the ground, Sondra started to turn blue.

After a second, when we hadn't heard a response from Strong and Martha, I looked around. "We need to go," I repeated. "They're coming. And I don't know how many people are here, but I have a feeling it's not just them. At least, not for long. You heard them talking about the *Master*. I'd rather not be in this room when he gets here." I pointed at my prostrate professor. "Daddy, help Lucy. We're taking the professor with us. Wait a sec, are you really even a teacher?"

My father and Lucy yanked Sondra to her feet, each with a tight grip on her arm. She coughed and sputtered, but nodded. "Yes," she said, her voice tortured and hoarse.

My father nodded. "Yes. So, *Professor*. What way's out?" He shook her arm, and she groaned.

"Easy!" she said. "I'll show you, but you have to promise not to hurt Adam! Take me to the police, do whatever you will with me, just promise you'll let him go."

Lucy shuddered. "Oh, God, are you guys? Really? That's disgusting." She froze there, clutching Sondra's arm and staring at her with a mix of horror and confusion. "I can't…I just can't…" Her mouth gaped.

"Knock it off," Eli said. "Stop standing there like that matters right now. You know it doesn't. We need to move." He left the wall and shoved Lucy roughly from behind. "Move!"

But as he shoved, even though it looked like he only meant to move us all forward, he knocked the normally graceful Lucy off her balance, and she stumbled, losing her grip on Sondra's arm. Sondra yanked her other arm free from my father, who was busy trying to catch Lucy. My mother yelped, as the sudden freedom from Sondra's burden sent my father back into her. They all went down, except Sondra, who slipped through the only doorway in the room, still coughing. She was gone before Eli or I, the only two still standing, could react.

"Crap!" Eli said.

"Crap!" my father shouted.

Lucy didn't yell because she was facedown on the concrete floor. Eli limped to her side and pulled her up from under her arms.

I ran into the hall, surprised at how springy my knees felt. I heard Sondra's coughs disappearing as heavy footsteps headed our way from the same direction. I called over my shoulder. "Everybody hush! We go this way." I pointed the opposite direction.

"How do you know?" My mother stood behind my right shoulder.

"Don't you hear that? They're down that way. Sondra's still coughing, and Strong is clomping."

"I don't hear anything, but I trust you. We go your way."

Everyone crowded around me. Lucy peered over my mother's head. "You hear something? Do you have bionic hearing?"

"It would make sense," my father said. "They're creating something new. Why not create something spectacular? With enhancements? Modifications?"

Eli breathed out. "Cool. I wonder what else you can do. How haven't we figured this out already?"

"I guess they fixed me." I paused. "Shh. Listen, they're getting closer. I think we should go."

Lucy looped an arm around Eli's waist, and my father took my mother's hand. I stood in front of them all, peering into the hallway that opened before us. Suddenly we heard a click, and the room and hallway plunged into darkness. It was total.

Behind me, the whole group gasped, and spoke over each other.

"Crap, I can't see anything!"

"Oh no! What next?"

But I was calm. "It's okay, you guys," I said. "I can see in the dark, too. That explains how I didn't kill myself that first night in the forest. I was just too scared to realize what I was doing."

Behind me, Eli coughed, and then groaned. "Great news. The blonde leading the blind. I guess we're all in your hands now, Jo."

"Eli, hush," I said, and Lucy giggled. It was odd to me, how quickly we adjusted to this strange new world in which we lived. We clung to our banter like a security blanket against the horrors around us. Our laughter was a balm, a salve, against the pain. Even in the midst of war, people fall in love, and they laugh, and they cry. That was us, in those first moments in the hallway.

I didn't have time to think about that right then, though. Right then, I had to save my family. I cocked my head like an inquisitive puppy and listened. The footsteps grew louder, the voices more insistent. They were coming.

I started to walk away from those noises, cutting a path through the inky black. My family, the people whose lives I held in my rehydrated hands, followed.

THE HALLWAY BECAME A TUNNEL, all stone walls and damp floors. We crept without speaking, afraid to give away our position. My mother removed her high heels and navigated her way barefoot, like me. Without the pain-free feet I enjoyed, though, she stumbled frequently, tensing in pain when her feet found something sharp. She tried so hard for silence I decided not to point out that our position was painfully obvious to our captors, as we'd not yet passed anywhere that *wasn't* this one long, straight shaft. There was no other position we could be in.

This tunnel was different from the one we'd traveled down in Primrose Path, and it became increasingly evident that the Order of the A-holes, or whatever they called themselves, had more than one secret lair in and around the Smytheville campus. I wondered where we were, but I kept my mouth shut, and kept my group moving forward, using my brand-new super-sight to navigate the way for all of us.

I turned around and glanced over the heads of my family. In the distance, I saw the faintest flicker of flashlights, bobbing through the darkness like drunken fireflies. "Shh," I said, and I listened. First I heard nothing but the faintest of whispers, but then, as if someone turned up the volume inside my ears, I heard their voices. All three of them. Only three of them. But they sounded pissed.

"They can't get out of here alive," Strong growled.

"They won't," said Martha. "The others will be here soon."

Sondra coughed. I pictured her for a second, back when she was my professor and I was her student, lecturing my classmates and me on the works of Ben Jonson and Christopher Marlowe, wearing her ill-fitting clothes with her librarian hair and glasses. She'd been so meek, so mild, so full of useful tidbits of information about iambic pentameter. In that second, I almost felt bad that Lucy had probably done real damage to her throat; she'd struggle to lecture again, at least for a while. And then I heard a click.

It was a distinctive sound, one I'd only ever heard in the movies, but it was unmistakable.

"They have the gun out, you guys!" I whispered frantically. "Someone just cocked it." I don't know why this surprised me, but it did.

"How do you…."

"Bionic ears! I heard it. Come on, we have to go faster. Grab onto each other. I'll lead you!"

Lucy grabbed onto Eli and my father. My father grabbed my mother. She smiled and reached out for my hand.

"Are you sure?" I whispered. "I still might be toxic."

"You're my daughter," she said. "The love of my life. I'll never let you go."

Like a group of first graders on a field trip to a museum, we became a train of people rushing down the tunnel. I led us down a long flight of steep stone steps, deeper into the mountain. Behind me my mother shivered, so I knew it grew colder and colder, the deeper we went.

"This may not be the way out," I said. "I still can't see anything other than more tunnel."

"Keep going, Jo," my father said. He was getting winded, they all were, but still we ran. "We have no choice. Can you still hear them?"

"Shh," I said, and everyone pressed against the cold walls. I heard footsteps in the distance, but I couldn't see the beams of the flashlights. We'd just turned a sharp corner, though, so it was impossible to know how far behind us they were.

"Yes, they're still there. I think there has to be something up ahead. Otherwise, why wouldn't they just wait for us to come back out. Eli, you doing all right?"

"Yeah, thanks. I'm the least of our worries right now."

But his voice was less than convincing, and I remembered how gray he looked, even before we started running the track meet through the tunnel. "Lucy, you got him?"

"I won't let him go," she said.

And so we ran further.

And we ran down.

And eventually, the tunnel ended at a wall.

I skidded to a stop right before it, and my blind followers crashed into one another. I fell into the wall, forehead first, and slapped a hand against it. Closing my eyes to ward off the ugly thoughts that flowed into my head, I squeezed my other hand into a fist.

"Shit. Shit. Shit."

"Jo!"

"I'm sorry," I said, turning to watch my father pick up my mother from the ground. "I'm sorry for everything. This is the end."

MY PARENTS, LUCY, AND ELI pressed against the wall, huddled together and whispering. I tried to ignore the sounds of their voices as I ran my hand along the wall, searching for a solution that I didn't believe was there. Not anymore. Not there, at the dark end of the dark tunnel deep in an underground labyrinth.

Even though it was dark, I could see quite clearly the outline of each brick and cinderblock. Water dripped down the walls, so my fingers glided easily over the rough stones, though I watched two fingernails fall to the floor, the magic fluids clearly pumped into me over the prior few hours not helping to keep them attached. Once, my nails were neatly manicured at all times. Now they rested beneath my bare, decaying feet. I stepped on them and ground them into the dusty, damp floor.

I silently thanked our pursuers for giving me some enhanced abilities in exchange for all they'd taken from me. I could hear their conversations easily as they bounced off the silent walls.

"The others are on their way, but they're not here yet!"

"Damn snow."

"The Master won't be happy if we have to kill the father."

They repeated themselves, filling the tunnel with worried chatter. They feared the Master. He would hurt them. Their end, if ours wasn't to his liking, would be no better than mine. But as they'd not yet said anything to indicate we were stuck, I kept going. They were still afraid we'd escape. There had to be a way out.

If only I could *find* it.

It was on my shoulders, I knew, to help my parents, Lucy, and Eli escape. Their eyes couldn't adjust to the thick, palpable dark; their ears couldn't hear our enemies' whispers. The burden was heavy, unbearable, and part of me wanted nothing more than to give up, to sit down and throw in the towel and admit I couldn't hack it. That I'd failed. Especially when I felt the charge start to drain out of my battery, and I knew I didn't have much time left.

But they stood so close to me, those people I loved. Lucy and Eli. They stood by my side through our unexpected journey. Beside them: my parents. The two who'd given me life, a short nineteen years earlier. They'd be devastated to go on without me, but I couldn't fail them. I couldn't let them *not* go on without me. They'd survive. They had to. Or else it would be like I'd never existed. Never mattered.

And I couldn't bear their deaths on my shoulders, however briefly my life would continue after theirs ceased.

"Daddy," I called. "I can't see a way out yet. I feel like there should be a door somewhere, but I just don't see one."

"It may be there's not one, baby. If not, that's okay. You've done your best." My mother responded instead of my father. She sounded serene. At peace. I wondered if she'd already accepted death, imminent as it felt for all of us. I wondered if she thought that for her, death might be preferable to survival without me.

It was a chilling, sobering thought.

As if I hadn't already been sober enough.

For lack of anything better to do, I accused. I got angry. "You guys still can't see? Why haven't your eyes adjusted?"

"The human eye can't see in a light vacuum," my father said, but I noticed he started moving down the wall, his arms outstretched.

Lucy, too, started walking, running her hands along the wall. "We can't see, but we can still help you look," she whispered. "We have eight more hands that can search the walls for something."

"There's nothing *there*! At least, not *here*," I said, frustrated. "We must have missed something back there. But they're still coming. They're getting closer!"

It was true. They *were* getting closer. In a matter of minutes, or even seconds, I'd see a change in the subtle light patterns, indicating their arrival. It was weird; now that I knew I could do some things, I was already good at controlling them. I could turn my hearing up, just by thinking about it. I could see further, just by trying. It was amazing. But still I couldn't quite force myself to see around curved walls.

I stumbled and crashed into a wall, stubbing the big toe on my left foot. It fell off and lay on the floor, mocking me, reminding me that the magic elixir hadn't healed me all the way. I was still very much a walking dead girl.

I cried out in frustration and threw my arms into the air, trying to look anywhere other than at my big toe, staring at me accusingly on the floor.

And then I cried out in excitement instead.

Because there, in the ceiling, right above my head, was a door, like the door to an attic long forgotten. It was possible it wouldn't lead anywhere useful, but it was better than nothing.

"Daddy, Lucy, come here and help me. I found something."

MY FATHER LIFTED Lucy to his shoulders, like children playing Chicken in a swimming pool. She wobbled there, and they almost tipped as she stretched to reach the chain to the trapdoor that hung, tantalizingly, *just* out of her reach. They grunted in tandem and moved in tandem, and suddenly, as the rest of us circled around, our arms reached up in an empty promise to catch Lucy if she fell, she reached the chain, and there came a creak and a squeak as the trapdoor fell open.

Lucy tumbled backwards, off my father's shoulders, and landed on Eli with a crash.

From the floor, Eli groaned. "Really? You had to fall on me? Ouch, Luce, just ouch." He sounded pitiful.

My father and I stood together and stared up into the opening in the ceiling. "Can you see anything?" he asked.

I smiled, my face cracking and popping. "I see another chain, going to a light bulb. Fingers crossed it lights!"

He nodded. "Does it look safe?"

I shrugged. "Safer than meeting the Order of the Idiots, armed and dangerous, while we stand here, undefended, in a pitch-black tunnel."

"Good point. Who's going up first?"

Lucy popped up, barely even fazed by her six foot fall to the floor. "Me!"

Without another word, my father pulled Eli to his feet, and together they boosted Lucy up into the ceiling. Eli winced from the exertion, and he almost fell, but Lucy pulled herself up and turned on the light. As the square of brightness burned their eyes, my parents and Eli all turned away. Seconds later, Lucy called, "You guys, get up here!"

They boosted my mother next, and then looked at me. "Oh, no," I said. "You guys next. Climb on."

"What?"

"I don't know, let me try something." I reached for my father, held out my hands for him to step into.

"I don't know, Jo. This isn't..." But I pushed as hard as I could, and he acted on instinct and vaulted himself up into the hole. He tumbled in, and I heard another grunt, and Lucy cried out in pain. "Sorry," he said. "Jolene, how did you do that?"

"Don't know," I said. "I just had a feeling I could...come on, Eli, let's go."

He gave me a look. "Be gentle."

A brief moment later he was safe up above.

I couldn't describe it to them, but ever since I'd heard Strong talk about how powerful I could be, I had been noticing things.

Things I'd been too terrified to notice before.

Like the fact that, since I felt no pain, I could push myself harder than I ever knew possible. I thought of my run through the woods on that first terrible night, and I realized I'd been doing it even then. I'd never stopped, never slowed, but it hadn't occurred to me until that moment just how powerful that made me.

"What's up there?" I whispered.

Lucy stuck her head down, her red ponytail falling down like a lava flow. "It's a huge vault or something. Solid walls. There's like, food and stuff. Get up here, you can see for yourself."

I shook my head. "No. Close the door. I have a plan."

"What? No!" Lucy scooted back. "Mr. Hall, get over here! Help me pull Jo up!"

My father's head appeared in the rectangle of light. "Here, sweetie," he said, reaching his hands down to me. "Come on, we'll get you up here."

"No," I said again. "I have a plan. Get back, get down, close the door. They're coming. Fast."

"Get up here," he said.

Instead, I reached up, used the hanging chain for leverage and slammed the door on him. I was bathed in darkness once again. I liked it, I won't lie. I felt safe in the dark, protected, like I held the secret advantage. I listened in my parents' direction and heard my mother whispering. "David, you have to go down there. Go get your daughter."

He was silent for a moment, and when he spoke his voice was strained. "No. She's a grown woman now, and she has nothing to lose. Nothing but us. We have to let her try."

I tried to cry for a split second, but failed. It didn't matter. I turned my hearing to the bad guys to distract myself from my roaring emotions. They were close.

"Turn off the flashlights now," Martha whispered. "If they didn't get out, they'll be stuck right up ahead. The Master and I explored this tunnel when we first moved in here. It ends soon. They don't need to see us coming."

Suddenly, I remembered: I didn't *actually* have a plan.

Each second took hours.

I was naked. I was mostly dead. I was short a toe, several fingers. My arm was broken, my nose gone.

How the hell was I going to help *anyone*? Let alone, all the people I loved most in the world.

I tried not to panic.

"This isn't going like we planned," Sondra whispered. They were close, less than a hundred feet away. The tunnel was bent, though. They couldn't see me yet. "I'm not supposed to be a part of these types of things. I just find you girls." She sounded terrified.

"Shut your mouth and hustle up." Sondra cried out as, I guessed, Strong shoved her forward as he spoke. Or maybe slapped her. I couldn't be sure.

I didn't care in the least.

"Psst, Jo," came a whisper from above my head. I looked up and saw the trapdoor was again cracked open. They'd turned off the light in the vault, and Lucy hung through the opening. This time, however, she was holding an ax.

"Here," she said. "We thought it might help with whatever you have planned."

I reached up and wrapped the remaining fingers of my right hand around the blade.

"Careful," she hissed. "Take the handle instead."

"Like it matters." I winked at her, but she didn't see. I didn't tell her another finger dropped to the ground. The ax was sharp. "Where'd you get it?"

"I told you this place was stocked. Looks like somebody planned to live down here for months or something. Your dad said maybe it's a leftover shelter from the Cold War or something…*hey!*" My father had pulled Lucy back into the vault. She was gone from sight and the trapdoor closed.

I slid down the hall, further away from the hunters. My plan settled. I could corner them, let them come. If I kept them hunting me, or if I corralled them in the corner with my new super-strength, my parents and friends could sneak away, back the way we all came. I tried to telegraph my idea directly into Lucy's head, but apparently the Order hadn't seen fit to give me the powers of telepathy. I'd just have to hope for the best.

I stopped walking when I reached the wall at the end of the tunnel. Crouching down, I gripped the handle of the ax and said a silent prayer.

Dear God, if you're there, please save my family and my friends. Please get them out of here. Please don't let this happen to them.

There was no response. No lightning came and struck Adam down. No flash flood washed Martha and Sondra away into another world. Not like I had expected that to happen, but a girl can dream, even in an impossible situation.

So I let the bad guys come while I waited in pensive silence. I had no choice.

I got my first view of Martha when they rounded the corner. She was tall and skinny, even taller than Lucy. Gorgeous. In the darkness I judged her hair to be a coppery auburn. Even in an area devoid of light, it seemed to sparkle and curl, all the way down to her waist.

She wore a long, flowing, robe-like garment and way too much makeup. Her lips glowed in the dark, they were such a bright red.

I wonder if there's any lipstick on her teeth.

I wanted there to be lipstick on her teeth. Perfection like Martha's had to be marred in some way. She looked just like a high priestess from any book I'd ever read that actually included some sort of Woman of Power. Like she *wanted* to be a cliché in a movie.

Or like she was hiding something under those robes. I wondered what it could be.

And with only a glance, I saw how much both Strong and Sondra worshipped her. How in charge of them she really was. They walked a step behind her, flanking her, each with a hand stretched out and touching her back. It could have been a safety thing, but in the way their hands rested so lightly, I read love. Adoration. Even…fear? In their opposite hand, they each held a gun.

I tried not to flinch when I saw them. I couldn't get used to the idea of all this danger. *I'll never really be a superhero, will I? But it doesn't matter. I can help.*

In front, Martha was unarmed.

Or so I thought, until I saw, nestled in her hand, a small black object. It took me a second to figure it out.

A Taser. Crap. Electricity is my Kryptonite. I'm sure of it. I couldn't let her reach me with that thing.

I was grateful for the silence in which I could exist, since I didn't have to breathe, and couldn't feel my arms or legs going numb as I crouched. In front of me, Martha glided and Sondra and Strong stumbled forward. I flattened myself even closer to the wall as they passed.

"Do you see them?" Strong whispered, and Martha shushed him.

They neared the wall, and me, but they didn't know it yet. The darkness was my friend, and I hoped to use it.

"They'll be close, and unarmed," whispered Martha, her impossibly shimmering mouth curling into a cruel smile. "Try not to kill Lucy. We need her. And do remember not to damage Jolene's heart pump. We can't waste materials, you know." She paused, took another step. They were less than a dozen feet from me. "And…*now!*"

Strong and Sondra let go of Martha, who allowed them to step in front of her. They each pulled out an economy-sized Maglite from behind their backs and turned them on. I flattened myself to the ground on top of the ax, so the light trained on nothing but blank, cinderblock walls.

"What the..." Strong said. "Where'd they go?"

Sondra's light cast down, and it shone on me. She screeched and jumped back.

I had no idea what I looked like under the harsh spotlight, but seeing her jump away in fear gave me an inkling. Keeping my body on top of the ax, I looked up, slowly. With the light in my eyes, I snarled. I growled. Letting my sparse hair fall before my eyes, I reached out my decimated hand toward them, channeling a ghost in a movie I'd seen as a child.

The threesome stepped back.

It was just a small step, but it was a step.

I began to crawl forward, jerking and twitching.

And Sondra Lewis began to cry.

The gun in her hand began to shake. She sniffled and sobbed. "No, Jo. Jolene. No. You were going to be our best soldier. The scientist assured me. You were strong, and I was so glad I found you. My favorite student. But now look. Look what we've done to you, Jolene. Such a beautiful girl. So far you've fallen." She dropped to her knees and dropped the gun.

Strong and Martha turned to Sondra. Behind the trio, I saw something move. With the light in my eyes it was hard to see what it was, but I took a leap of faith.

I leaped to my feet, pulling the ax up with me. Strong and Martha turned to me, but Sondra remained collapsed on the floor.

I stared into the black eyes of Martha, and pulled the ax over my shoulders like Casey at the bat.

Then I smiled, baring my teeth and licking my lips with my parched tongue. "Thanks for all you've done to me...*bitch*."

She wasn't fast enough with the Taser. I closed my eyes and swung. The ax landed with a dull, sick thud, and I tumbled to the ground. Someone screamed. A gunshot rang out. Rocks exploded behind me and showered down around me. More screams, and then I heard Lucy's voice, above the other noise. "You bastard!"

I opened my eyes and immediately wished I hadn't. My hands still gripped the ax handle.

In front of me stood Martha, her head split in two. Her face, in two parts, pulled backwards in a silent shriek, her mouth opened like a lunging shark. She and I were both splattered in the thick, viscous substance that filled my veins, and Martha's.

Martha was one of the Order's soldiers. She was the successful version of me. An older model, I knew in that moment during which time stood still. She had none of the enhancements I enjoyed. She couldn't see in the dark, couldn't hear. She was limited by her human abilities, while I was not.

But still, she continued her attack, her arms spread wide, her mouth in two parts ready to swallow me whole.

I screamed, and so did she. I swung the ax again. It hit her shoulder, embedding itself in flesh and sinew. I yanked back as she continued to drive at me, and I swung again.

An arm flew from her body, squirting fluids from the stump.

Her body was knocked backwards by the blow, and I hacked away at her as she fell. Finally, a blow struck true, and I decapitated the monster woman before me. She froze for a second, and then collapsed to the floor in a sticky, messy heap.

I fell to my knees beside her. The ax stood, embedded deep into her neck. I closed my eyes and folded in on myself.

And then came silence.

Or at least, mostly silence.

Someone was sobbing. Uncontrollable, choking sobs.

I was shocked when I realized it was me.

I wanted to open my eyes, but the sobs that shook my decrepit body made me terrified to move any other muscle for fear I'd dissolve into nonexistence.

And then suddenly there was pressure on my body, and there were arms around me, pulling me up. Someone slid their legs beneath my head and stroked my matted, stringy hair.

"Shh, baby," whispered my mother. She'd maneuvered so that my head rested in her lap. "It's okay, baby. You did what you needed to do. It's okay, my love. Stop crying now, baby. It's going to be okay. I love you. Mama's here."

"Jo! You're crying! You thought you couldn't cry." Lucy lay atop my back, holding me tight like she had all those drunken nights ago.

"No tears," I managed, in between sobs. "Less satisfying." I forced myself to calm, counting backwards from fifty like my mother taught me so many years before. Slowly the sobs faded. "I think I can sit up now," I said, and Lucy pulled me up. I opened my eyes.

My father and Eli stood together, against the wall. They held the flashlights, pointed down at us on the ground.

Beside me, Martha lay. Dead. A decapitated monster. I'd destroyed one of my own.

We could be destroyed. I could be destroyed. I *would* be destroyed.

I clenched my hand into a fist, trying to keep from screaming.

It didn't work, though, and I screamed out into the darkness beyond the flashlights. Then I tried to turn off my super-hearing so I wouldn't have to hear my own voice echo through miles of otherwise silent passageways. It didn't work. I heard myself scream again and again and again.

Adam, too, lay dead beside Martha, a knife handle sticking out of his neck.

"Who did that?" I asked when I could speak. I looked at the two men against the wall, but they shook their heads and pointed to Lucy.

She flushed, and looked down. "I thought for a second about feeling guilty, but instead I feel proud. He's a liar and a thief and a killer, and he can't hurt anyone anymore." The corner of her mouth turned up, just a little. "It's a shame. He really was gorgeous."

I lifted my head from my mother's lap. "How are you?" I asked, staring into her eyes.

Her face was flushed and filthy, and her hair had fallen around her face and shoulders. Makeup ran down her face in rivers of mascara and eyeliner. But she was my mother, and she held my broken hands in hers. Somehow, in her grief, she looked younger, and more beautiful, than I ever remembered. "I'm here," she said. "That's all that matters right now. I'm here, and you're here, and your father's here, and we're all alive." She tried to smile.

"I'm so sorry I got you into this. I wish you were back home, safe."

"Baby, there is nowhere else in this world I'd rather be right now than here with you."

"But I'm a monster." I looked from her face to my father's. "A killer. How can you guys ever love me again?"

She did smile, then. "From the minute you entered this world, you've been nothing but trouble. You wouldn't sleep as a baby, wouldn't eat as a toddler, wouldn't leave my side as a kid. Don't even get me started on high school. But I've loved you every minute of every day, and nothing will change that. Not even if you become a murdering monstrosity."

She leaned over and kissed my face.

She never even flinched.

Then she pulled me into a hug, and seconds later my father held us both in his arms. I felt safe and warm and hundreds of miles away from the tunnel in which we sat, lost and trapped.

But it didn't last.

Eli spoke, and he sounded wheezy and ill. "I hate to break this up," he said. "But do we know where Sondra is? She's not here, and she's not dead. And if I'm not mistaken, haven't you mentioned some others?

On their way?"

I pulled away from my family, wiping at my face out of habit instead of necessity. "How many guns are on the floor?" I said. "She had one. Adam had one. Tell me there are two guns on the ground."

But there weren't.

There was only one, still clutched in Adam's stiffening hand.

Wherever Sondra was, she was armed.

And now that we knew I *wasn't* the first monster-girl, we had no idea if Sondra was even human.

FLASHLIGHTS PROVIDED MEAGER light in the bowels of the mountain where we sat, battered and broken but together.

"Do we just leave them here?" Lucy asked, stepping over the dead bodies. She kicked Adam's as she passed it.

She was so strong, I envied her. Even though there was no physiological reason for it, I shook from head to toe. I kept picturing the ax slicing through Martha's arm, her skull. I couldn't believe I was a killer. I'd destroyed another life, such as it was, and I was horrified.

Add to that the fact that we still weren't out of danger. I needed to get my family to safety.

Plus, I had another problem.

No one else had noticed yet, but there was a small hole piercing my chest, right through the center. While no one was looking, I stuck my finger in and felt the hum of my heart pump, and also a hole right through its center. It already hummed a little slower, a little less consistently.

I didn't have much longer.

My father pulled the gun, a small one that looked like a track meet starter pistol, from Adam's dead hand. I stood beside him. My mother and Eli were unarmed, as was Lucy.

Lucy looked at us, then back down at the bodies. The ax was still imbedded in Martha's neck, and I made no move to remove it. Nor did she look willing to pull the knife from Adam's throat.

"Well," she said. "We need weapons. More than just one gun anyway. I'm going to hop back up there and see what I can find. Jo, care to give me a boost? Just watch my ankle, okay?" She smiled and winked.

"Why not?" I stepped away from my father's side and tossed her up through the trapdoor. Without the chaos around me, I heard more of the tendons popping and bones creaking than I'd heard earlier, but it was still surprisingly easy.

She turned on the light, and everyone jumped. The additional illumination settled on the pools of blood and embalming solution surrounding the dead, and I shuddered. My mother put her arm around me, but I could feel her trembling, too.

Eli stood below the trapdoor. He was stiff, partly bent at the waist, but he craned his neck upward to look into the vault. "Maybe grab some of that food we saw. It's been a while, we could probably all use a snack." He glanced at me, and then looked down. "I mean, most of us. Sorry, Jo."

"No problem."

"You sure?" Lucy called. "Didn't Mr. Hall say it looked old?"

My father nodded. "Yeah, that stuff looks like it's been up there since I was a kid. I think you can wait."

"But look at this!" Lucy appeared at the hole in the ceiling. She dropped down a rope, a shovel, and a baseball bat. It was an old one, wooden, and I picked it up. It felt solid in my hands, like it belonged there.

Eli picked up the shovel, and my mother the rope, although she looked at me and whispered, "I have no idea what she expects me to do with a rope!"

When Lucy dropped back down, she held a garden hoe. "I'm not sure where they were planning on putting the garden, but they were prepared. There are seeds up there, and all kinds of other gardening things. I guess they thought they'd celebrate the end of the world by growing a victory garden?"

"Well, if nothing else, I feel pretty invincible with my shovel," said Eli, but with the way he winced as he spoke, he looked anything but invincible.

"We need to get you to a hospital," my mother said to him.

I tried not to be sad about the fact that even she knew a hospital couldn't help me.

My father came up behind me and draped his jacket over my shoulders. It came halfway down my thighs, and I buttoned it up to make him happy.

We headed back the way we'd come. It was much easier for the group now that we had some light, but the twists and turns were still difficult to navigate, and the floor was less than smooth. We had to move slowly, carefully, and by the time we reached the room in which I'd awoken, I was running low on battery. There was no sign of Sondra Lewis. She'd disappeared completely into the darkness.

I sat down on the table and my mother plugged me in. I felt better as soon as the electricity flowed in, but the flow was no longer steady. It came in fits and spurts, like I was short-circuiting somewhere. I knew it was my heart pump, not doing its job.

I could tell that, even plugged in, I didn't have much longer.

But there was no reason to tell anyone else that. Not then.

I looked at Eli. "You need to get to the hospital as soon as we're out of here."

"No." His voice was flat.

"Yes," I said, glaring at him. "You're hurt. You need some help."

"If I go to the hospital, they're going to ask what happened. If I tell them what happened, they'll come for you. If they come for you, you'll die. And I'm not ready to say goodbye, after all we've been through. I love you."

My mother walked to him and put her arm around him. Her eyes were again filled with tears. "I'm not ready, either. I'll never be ready. But Jo's right. You need to go."

My father nodded. "We can tell them you were in a fight. We can stall long enough to give Jo a chance."

"A chance at what? I don't know what chance you all think I have." My voice, though much repaired and more like the old me, was still harsh.

"A chance to stick around a little longer," said Lucy. "A chance to be with us some more."

I nodded. "Let's get out of here first. Get me back to the dorm. Then I want you all to go with Eli to the hospital, and then to the police. I think I need some time by myself."

"I understand," my mother said. "But I'm not leaving your side. I hope you realize that."

"I do."

Eli grew angry. "Don't I get a say? Don't I get to choose when I say goodbye?"

"Eli, I love you. I'm sorry things worked out this way, I really am. But I'll be around for a while yet. There's no way to tell when my battery will run out for good. I need to know you're safe before I go."

RIGHT BEFORE WE WERE ABOUT to leave the lab to find the rest of the way out, Lucy pressed something into my hands. It was a sheath of papers, spiral bound, covered in a thin, transparent layer of plastic.

On the cover: The Order of the Adversaries It was their manifesto.

"This'll be great for the cops," I said, and everyone nodded.

And so we left. The way out was simple. A few sterile, fluorescent-lit hallways, and suddenly we were at a door that opened onto a campus parking lot. It was a back entrance to the campus police station. Parked near the entrance were three large, gray vans, like the one that filled me with such dread. These were newer, cleaner, still sparkly, even in the snow, but they were the same. And we were only minutes from my dorm. Something about that sight, the vans parked at the police station, terrified me.

But at least it was quiet. No one was nearby, as it was dark and, once again, snowing. Streetlights glowed faintly in the distance, but we were protected by darkness.

Adam's cruiser sat right next to the door.

"Who's driving?" Lucy said, and she opened the door.

"Not me. But I can ride in the trunk."

"Don't be ridiculous."

In the end my father drove, with Eli beside him in the front seat, directing him to Calvin Hall. Lucy, my mother, and I sat in the back seat, squeezed together like little girls out for a fun afternoon outing.

"Jo," Lucy said, and I wondered what was coming.

"Yes?"

"No offense, but you really stink."

"I love you, too," I said.

When we got to the dorm, Lucy ran ahead to clear the way for us, but it was conveniently mid-term week, so most people, in my dorm at least, were inside studying. We snuck in easily through the side door and headed up to my room.

I settled immediately onto my desk chair and plugged myself into the wall socket. I could barely feel the current anymore.

No need to tell them that.

"Okay, you guys. I'm safe. Dad, you'll take Eli to the hospital now?"

"Yes, baby. Sit tight. We'll be back soon. I'll see you soon, Champ." He looked like he was about to kiss me, then reconsidered. I didn't blame him in the least.

Lucy looked at me, and I could tell. She knew. "Eli, I'm gonna stay here with the girls, okay? I'll get my ankle checked tomorrow," she said, taking his hand for just a second. He nodded. He had no idea.

But he walked to me anyway, every step looking more and more painful. "You'll be okay?" he said, and he rested his hand on my cheek for a moment.

I smiled. "Of course. You go get yourself checked out. I don't like the sound you're making while you're breathing."

He winced. "Yeah, I don't feel so great. You'll still be here when I get back?"

I nodded. "Yes. And when you get back, we can talk about that German guy some more. Remember him? When you think about it, all this, it's obviously his fault."

"It's always the Germans' fault, right?" Tears flooded Eli's eyes and he leaned so close to me our foreheads touched. We hadn't been that close in days, not since I left his apartment in the middle of the night. He slid one hand around my waist, then another up to the back of my head, squeezing me tight. "I'll never forget you, Jo."

"I know," I said. "I'll never forget you either. Now go. Go get well. And maybe someday you'll find a nice German girl."

I pushed him away so I didn't have to see the tears spill down his cheeks. Lucy slid an arm around his waist and let him lean against her as she walked him to the door.

Then I turned to my father. "Come back soon," I whispered.

"I will," he said. "This isn't goodbye."

But it was.

Dear Mom,

It's been a few hours since Dad and Eli left. You and Lucy are both sleeping. I'm watching you, listening to you sleep. It makes me feel like we're back home, like this has all been just a bad dream.

But I know that's not true.

The Order of the Adversaries manifesto sits on my desk, staring at me, daring me to open it and read more. I can't finish it, not now, and I don't want to.

I'll leave it here, though, for Lucy. For Eli. Because I've read enough. I know they're not done with the battle yet. I thought about burning it while you slept, like maybe that would erase the Order, erase all that's happened so far. But I can't think that way anymore. I have to think about your safety. Yours, and Dad's, and Lucy's, and Eli's.

Please, tell Lucy and Eli, as soon as you can: they can't go to the cops. Open the manifesto. You'll see. Adam really was a cop. His twin brother, too. It's right there, on the top. Their information. And there are others as well. It's all part of their plan. Some of the names are code names, though, so I don't know how to tell you whom you can trust. I can only tell you not to trust anyone.

Because I believe this, and only this: they're still going to come for you. All of you. You're not safe.

So you have to take care of each other.

Especially you. I know you. You'll try to take care of everyone, the way you always took care of me. And you need to do that now. But you also need to remember to let them take care of you. You can't do this on your own.

But Mom, this is the most important thing. You have to tell Lucy and Eli: they have to stop the Order. They have to wipe them out or else you'll never be safe. They want to destroy everything.

I'm listening to you snore. It's all I hear right now, even with my bionic hearing. I wish I could lie next to you on my bed, curl up in your arms like I did when I was small, and forget all my troubles.

I love you and Daddy so much. You've been amazing parents, given me more than any girl could ever possibly deserve.

I wish I could lie down with you. I think it's almost time.

Because I'm so tired.

I can feel my brain dying. It's getting fuzzier. My battery is dying. My heart pump is ruptured, which means my heart is officially broken.

I'm going to unplug myself now. I'm going to stand up and walk to you and kiss you goodbye, Mama. Please kiss Daddy for me, too. Thank you for giving me everything I ever wanted, and for being here until the end. If I never seemed to appreciate it, please know: I do. I did.

And please, when you wake up, don't plug me back in. Don't wake me back up.

I'm so tired.

And I'm finally ready to sleep.

I love you.

Love, your Jo

EULOGY

Dear Jo,

You're dead now. I have to keep repeating that to myself, over and over and over. Otherwise I forget, even for a second, and then I have to remember again. You're dead now. The memory hits harder and harder each time.

Jolene. You were my best friend, and I loved you. You never knew how beautiful you were, how amazing your life was going to be. You never once realized how much we all loved you. And we did. Oh my God, Jo, we loved you so much. So I'm telling you that now, even though you're dead and I know you'll never, ever read this email.

Or maybe you will. I don't know. Maybe it's time I find some religion. God knows I'm going to need all the help I can get, if I want to succeed at the task you gave me.

Stop the Order, you said. Take care of each other.

Oh, Jo. I'm going to try. Please know how hard I'm going to try.

And I'm going to miss your face, every day. Miss your laugh, your cry. Hell, I'm even going to miss your smell, at the end, if you can believe that. It was my final tie to you—I smelled it for days after they took you away. If I focus real hard, I can smell it still. It's in my clothes, I think. Or my nostrils, etched in there like the incision was etched across your stomach.

But I loved you. And I'm going to try so hard to be brave. And to take care of Eli. But he's yours, still, Jo. He loves you. I hear him cry sometimes, even though he doesn't want me to. He loved you so much, and his heart is broken, just like mine. Maybe together we can heal. Who knows.

But in the meantime, I just want you to know. I love you. I'll never forget.
Love, Lucy

LucyGoosie: #SmythvilleStudentLife @EliPete21 Services celebrating the life of Jolene Hall today at the Greene-Locke Theater. 12 pm

IT WAS HARD to keep from crying as I stood in front of the huge crowd of people, all gathered to mourn the death of my best friend, who'd been buried days before in a small, private ceremony in Colorado. Her parents flew Eli and me out there for the occasion; they knew how much we both needed to say goodbye in person, and that Eli couldn't have afforded a ticket on his own. Not with his student loans. They threw in my ticket for good measure.

At Jo's funeral, Eli held my hand. Or I held his. We held onto each other for dear life, but now I was alone, with no one to hold. This would be the last goodbye.

We were in Smytheville College's huge theater, but all the seats were packed. It was early March, and the snow on the ground was just beginning to melt with the promise of spring. Most of the campus had turned out to mourn their fellow student. We weren't used to losing one of our own.

It hadn't been easy to even reach this point, since Jo's death was nothing short of mysterious to anyone except for the small handful of us who knew what had happened. Luckily, Jo's father had enough contacts in high enough places that he was able to reach an agreement to keep investigators from nosing around too much.

Her poor father. He was a mess, even as he worked hard to keep Eli and me safe.

Mrs. Hall seemed to be a bit calmer and accepting about the whole thing. She'd been asleep on the bed when Jo unplugged. She found Jo lying peacefully on the floor beside her when she awoke after that terrible night. Jo was already dead, then, or at least her battery had run out. Mrs. Hall came and got me, and we sat with Jo until Mr. Hall returned, alone. Eli had a punctured lung, and was still in the hospital when Jo died. I'd gone to him as soon as I could, to tell him the news myself.

In the dorm, Mr. Hall wanted to plug Jo back in, to wake her back up to say goodbye once more. He held her lifeless body in his lap like a baby, stroking her matted hair, caressing her broken fingers. He kissed her again and again, like a prince trying to awaken the sleeping princess.

But Mrs. Hall stood firm.

Jo didn't want to wake back up.

She'd been through enough. I was there with them that night, and this day, they were there in the amphitheater with me. They sat just a couple feet away from me while I stood in front of the packed house. Mrs. Hall's eyes were red but calm. Mr. Hall had obviously taken a truckload of Xanax to get through the service; his eyes were vacant, dead.

Dead like Jo.

Eli sat beside them, still hunched from the pain of his broken ribs. When I faltered before starting my speech, he gave me a thumbs-up. *You can do this*, his smile said. *You're going to be great.*

I wasn't so sure, but since Mrs. Hall had asked me to speak a few days earlier, it seemed like the right thing to do was to honor my best friend as best as I could. It was the least I could do, really. The very least.

Jo charged us with saving the world, or at least each other. The Order's Manifesto sat on my desk now, instead of Jo's. I was going to read it that night. She thought I could do it, just like Mrs. Hall thought I could speak on her daughter's behalf. I wasn't sure about that one, either, but I knew one thing: I didn't want to end up like Jo.

I tried to speak again, for the crowd of shocked and crying students were looking to me to make sense out of the death of our classmate.

Of course I *could* make sense of it, to a point, but I couldn't exactly tell them that.

So I stayed generic.

We're here today to honor my best friend, Jolene Hall. We met a long time ago now, Jo and me. It was late August. We shared a bathroom. I didn't know that first day that I'd met the best friend I'd ever have, but I had.

I faltered, and this time, I looked out into the crowd. I smelled something. Something familiar. A mix of chemicals, and decay. It was faint, just a waft across the tip of my nose that made me turn my head and stare.

That smell could only come from one thing. I stared at the crowd as I spoke from memory, rather than the cheat-sheet I'd placed on the podium in front of me.

Finally, I saw her in the last row, last seat next to the aisle.

She wore a large black hat, the kind which you only see at British royal weddings, and dark, round sunglasses.

It was her. The false literature professor, the recruiter for the Order of the Adversaries.

Sondra Lewis.

Beside her sat a beautiful blonde girl. She sat ramrod-straight with the posture of a prima ballerina, almost as though she *couldn't* slouch. As if something held her in place. Her face was placid, calm. She was more still than anyone in the room. It was from her that the smell emanated, and I had to pause my speech to swallow back the bile that rose automatically in my throat.

She was one of them. She was the girl who'd been circled on the wall. A soldier for the Order.

Beside her sat Adam Strong. When I saw him, I almost fell over, and had to catch myself on the podium to regain my balance. Eli hopped to his feet, as best as a battered boy could hop, but I stilled him with a quick nod and a warning glance.

And all the while I kept talking about Jo. Her smile, her sense of humor, the joy she brought to those who knew her.

But no, I reminded myself. *Adam's dead. I killed him.*

No matter how many times I repeated that to myself though, no matter how many times I closed and reopened my eyes as I stood in front of the student body of Smytheville College, Adam Strong still sat there in the crowd. He mocked me by being alive.

Oh, hell, no, I thought. *Wrap it up.*

I stumbled on through more generics. I should have done better; I could have shared a million memories with that crowd, brought them to laughter and to tears. It would have been a defining moment for Jo, and for me. But I had only one thought. *We have to stop them.*

As soon as I finished speaking, the room burst into a standing ovation of applause. It startled me. *Did I really say anything that impressive?* Then I remembered they were clapping for Jo, not me.

I stared out at Sondra, Adam, and the girl. Eli joined me as soon as I let him. He smelled it, too. The rotten chemical smell. "There she is," I whispered.

Sondra saw us stare. She took off her glasses. Her eyes were red. She'd clearly been crying. She waved, and then turned to head out the nearest door, pulling the blonde along beside her. Adam trailed behind, stopping to look me up and down with a dirty-old-man stare.

I picked up my cane, an artifact of my tour through Primrose Path, and limped after them.

"That was a beautiful speech, Lucy," someone said, grabbing my arm as I tried to walk. It was the Dean of Students. "Very touching."

"Oh, thanks," I said, trying to pull away. "I really did love her."

"You conveyed that so well, dear," she said.

"And if you'll excuse…" *She called me dear, like Sondra did. Is she one of them?* I tried to pull away but she kept on talking to me, blathering on and on about touching and feelings and did I need to talk to a therapist.

Finally, Eli came to the rescue. He removed the dean's hand from my arm, wincing when her elbows brushed his ribs, almost like she knew right where it would hurt the most. "Lucy, I need you." Then he pulled me through the crowd slowly, deliberately.

Others tried to stop us but he kept on pulling. Soon we reached the doors to the lobby, and then the doors to outside.

"She's gone," he said, deflated.

"I knew she would be," I said.

"Are you ready to get out of here?"

We headed back to my room, clutching each other for support.

We didn't even say goodbye to Mr. and Mrs. Hall, but I knew they'd understand. I knew Mrs. Hall had seen what we'd seen, smelled what we smelled, because I'd seen her lips form two words.

That bitch.

There was work to be done, and Eli and I were up to the task. Because with the Order around, none of us was safe from the fate that claimed the life of Jolene Hall.

THE END

ACKNOWLEDGEMENTS

It's always funny to write acknowledgements for a book, especially one that's been in the works so long as HEARTLESS. When I wrote the original draft (over four years ago, now), I was a different person, living a different life. I'd been focusing on zombies, up till then. All I knew was writing my zombies.

So the first thank you goes to Charles, my husband, and Jonathan, my brother. This book is dedicated to them because they told me I had something here. Conceptually, at first, and then in practice as well. They both loved my Jolene, and wouldn't let me let her go. Months would pass, and one or the other would say, "Hey, Leah, what are you doing with that Jo-book these days?" They wouldn't let Jo die, and so neither could I. Thus you're holding this book in your hands.

Thank you, of course, to the rest of my family as well! Zoe, Daniel, Mom and Dad – without your support, writing would be impossible. Your words of encouragement and enthusiasm mean the world to me.

To Jason Pinter at Polis Books – thank you so much for giving my Jolene a second chance. For resurrecting her, so to speak. I will work SO HARD to make this worth your while.

To Rob Hart, for your loyal friendship and kindness in this writing world. I would not be right here, right now, without it.

To my LitReactor family – Renee, Bree, Dennis, Kirk, Brandon, and Emma: you guys may not know it, but it was in Minneapolis last year that I got up the courage to submit to Polis, and it was mainly hanging out with y'all that gave me that courage. Thank you!

To Meredith: thank you again for your editing prowess. This book would be a different beast if you hadn't left your mark on it.

To my home-friends – you know who you are, ladies and gents: you make my life easier by being the people I can count on to pick up my child from school on those days when I just need one more hour of writing, or you've become my family during long hours on the soccer field. Without you, my life would be incredibly dull! Thanks for spending time with me! I tell people I love them a lot, and I mean it a lot.

To all of you – readers, friends, family – I love you. I mean it.

ABOUT THE AUTHOR

Leah Rhyne is a Jersey girl who's lived in the South so long she's lost her accent...but never her attitude. After spending most of her childhood watching movies like *Star Wars*, *Alien(s)*, and *A Nightmare On Elm Street*, and reading books like Stephen King's *The Shining* or *It*, Leah now spends her days writing tales of horror and science fiction.

Her "Undead America" zombie trilogy was released via MuseItUp Publishing and her short fiction has appeared in such publications as *Abyss & Apex Magazine* and *Revolt Daily*. She writes for LitReactor.com, and for herself at www.leahrhyne.com. Leah lives with her husband, daughter, and a small menagerie of pets. In her barely-there spare time, she loves running and yoga. Follow her on Twitter at @leah_beth.